theHILL

a Boss Corbu novel

P E ELLENBOGEN

the HILL
a Boss Corbu Novel
Copyright © 2017 by P E ELLENBOGEN

ISBN 13: 9781545582862
ISBN 10: 1545582866

PRINTED IN THE UNITED STATES OF AMERICA

Ear bugs: *'Amazing Grace'* Old English hymn; John Newton (1725-1807)

'Dixie,' Daniel Decatur Emmett circa 1860

'Maria' from Westside Story, Leonard Bernstein and Stephen Sondheim

'Everybody's Talkin' At Me,' Harry Nillson

Dedication

Woodrow Wilson High School Class of 1952

A R Myers AIA

"Architecture is the story of how we see ourselves. It is the architect's job to service everyday life."   Thom Mayne

"Architecture is not a profession for the faint-hearted, the weak-willed or the short-lived."   Martin Filler

"A building has integrity just like a man. And just as seldom."
          Ayn Rand

"Prose is architecture, not interior decoration ….."
          Ernest Hemingway

"Form follows profit is the aesthetic principal of our times."
          Richard Rogers

"I see music as fluid architecture."   Joni Mitchell

"A doctor can bury his mistakes but an architect can only advise his clients to plant vines."   Frank Lloyd Wright

1

The access road to the site was a mess. I was two days late for the monthly inspection visit. The client was over thirty days late with his previous month's payment. He was always late. I was retaliating by not approving this next draw on schedule. He was surviving day to day living the good life; I was for the most part surviving. He always had an excuse, and when the check did arrive it was written on a California bank, and took five days to clear. My payroll account was getting thin. The environmental controls for the site were in disarray. The sagging silt screens were useless, lying on the ground covered with sweet-potato-like puke - the sediment pond had caved in and the storm water was running into the drains of the main road. I was sure the city was not happy. How could they miss it - the blacktop was covered with debris one hundred yards or more in both directions. Early afternoon rush-hour traffic was picking its way over the uncertain surface - Friday afternoon was optional in many businesses in town, allowing a head start to the beach. I was not happy - the building inspectors liked to hand out daily fines to everyone listed on the building permit. Did I mention that it was raining - again - five days straight. My twenty- plus-year -old car was not designed for off-road use? The tires could have been in better shape. A thousand dollars for a set of tires was ridiculous. The car slipped sideways threatening to go into the endless field of mud. Upon my last visit this same field held hundreds, maybe thousands of pieces of reinforcing steel, rusting in place, far in excess of what was needed to finish the job. I was sure they were still there under the mud even though the concrete work was nearing completion. Early in my career, my experience with multi-story buildings was with structural steel - it was easy to view and inspect the bones of the building before the structure was covered up. With concrete, forms were set, re-bars laid out and concrete slushed into place - there were too many chances for mistakes. Behind me, an ambulance, red lights flashing and a constant siren was asking for the road. I pulled into the no-parking zone closest to the construction trailer. There was a concrete truck idling next to the soon-to-be completed apartment building, its seven-yard chamber rotating, no operator in sight. Dozens of workers in yellow slickers and company hardhats were idling about. The Linden crane, now set well above the roof level, was not moving. The door to the contractor's trailer was wide open. Something was amiss .a few workers gave up shelter to meet the slipping and sliding ambulance - the rest remaining where they were, hands gesturing toward the top of the structure - more precise direction as to where the medical assistance was needed was being provided at the driver's side door of the ambulance. The rain continued to fall. The EMTs headed towards the unfinished exit stairs. The combination of apparently cumulative trips to McDonalds and the burdensome equipment necessary for any eventuality was not a harbinger for speedy first aid - they did not look happy at the prospect of a twelve story climb. It was probably not a good time for me to be out and about. I needed to look at the paperwork for the certificate of payment that was supposed to waiting on the super's desk. His pickup was here so I assumed he would get to his home base and hence to me eventually. I locked the car leaving hardhat and boots in the trunk. The trailer interior was sticky hot, the window shaker AC unit vibrating, as if in its death throes. Dried mud was inches deep on the floor. I thought about using the toilet but rejected that idea sight unseen. I left the entrance door open and sought out Jose's swivel desk chair, a brand new one since my last visit, this one visibly marked, 'Property of the US Government.' I could not tell if this label was a statement dealing with Jose's immigration status or whether the chair had left its previous premises in a hurry, so to speak - the seat was refuge nonetheless. The chair's casters were difficult to navigate due to the condition of the floor but I was soon ensconced at Jose's desk, the payment schedules, in triplicate, arrayed on top of multiple copies of shop drawings that I would need to take away. The chair was very comfortable - Jose and I were about of the same size and weight - I was used to working standing up. In a few seconds, I fell into a stupor.

Dad's new car was a red and black DeSoto, huge brake light ensconced tail fins projecting from its rear, the engine compartment over-sized to emphasize the length and luxury of the vehicle - automatic transmission - vinyl seats. Air conditioning would be a thing in Detroit's future. Appalachia's climate at the three thousand foot elevation made little demand for artificial handling of heat and humidity.

I returned home every summer from college to work for my Dad. I got paid and since I lived at home most of the money went toward school expenses. I had done some of the same work while off from high school. College was a very highly regarded small state-funded liberal arts school in Virginia - several of my high school classmates went to VPI or WVU, or into the mines or into the Army. The Army awaited me if I screwed up at school and even later once I graduated. Dad paid the tuition.

Dad had morphed into a builder. The end of the Second World War signaled the return to addressing the housing shortage. People needed jobs. Industry was returning to peacetime status. Priorities were shifting to the civilian population. The government wanted to help - there was a lot of confusion.

The thought of confusion brought me to consciousness or maybe it was Jose slamming the door while cursing in

Spanish at someone outside. He did not demand his chair as he usually did. He sat down on a case of plumbing supplies, head in his hands, cursing in Spanish to himself. This had to do with the ambulance and the idle workers I was sure.

"*Que paso, Jose?,*" I offered, hoping to break the ice. "Your accent is lousy as usual." Jose's English was quite good. "I don't know where to start."

Jose did not differ significantly from most of the Hispanic workers swarming the site: squat, bow-legged, barrel-chested, olive complexioned, full head of slicked back hair, some gray at the sideburns, Viva Zapata mustache - he was older then his crew members, and his sharp piercing eyes that betrayed and intellect above and beyond that of his colleagues.

"Let's start with the ambulance. That is out of the ordinary for a Friday afternoon."

"I should call my mother-in-law." Jose was looking for the phone which was probably under the pile of paperwork.

"The ambulance?"

I was not at home when the ambulance took my father to the hospital. The crippling nature of a recent mini-stroke had caused him to fall and hit his head.

"The ambulance?" The phone's battery had lapsed but Jose did not seem upset.

"We were pouring the last of the roof slab and the cable gear on the bucket snapped." He drew a deep breath. "The bucket came down right on Miguel." I wanted to say ouch. "It was as bad as anything I saw in Iraq." Ouch was definitely not an appropriate response to an ex-Marine. "Miguel is - was family. I got him this job."

I wanted to ask about the uncovered lately poured concrete but I would leave that up to the structural engineer at a later date. "You called the police?"

"They were busy, but they sent the ambulance."

"Someone has to investigate - make a report." I thought of my name on the building permit once more.

The wail of a siren broke the impasse. The police had arrived. Jose went out to meet them. I tested the new chair once more.

My Dad died in the hospital. A very impersonal intensive care doc informed me, "The patient has passed." I peeked into the room where personnel were removing tubes and wires. I had never seen a dead person before, never even been to a funeral. The glimpse was enough to rush me out to the UMW Hospital parking lot.

"You want to go up?" Jose had opened the door halfway. I could see two state troopers immediately behind him. My blank face gave him his answer. I don't know how much time passed.

That day in the new DeSoto, Dad and I talked as we usually did of the plans for the day ahead. At the Eatwell Cafe we had our usual breakfast among the same folks who routinely started their day at this early hour. Hal Rudin was our usual table-mate. He ran an auto supply store in town - he ate the same thing every morning, so routinely that the short order cook called it the Hal Rudin Special. I think it was two pieces of grilled bread, each hollowed out at the center with a sunny side egg fried in the middle. I was never able to quite replicate it at home. Who knows what was on the grille when Hal's order was being prepared

The thought of food brought me back to the real world. The rain had stopped and the temperature had dropped. There was actually a chill in the air. There was no sign of Jose or the or the ambulance people.

The construction workers were still milling about, trying to keep dry, eating remainders out of lunch buckets, - chain smoking - they had probably been ordered to stay put - or else. I surveyed Jose's food resources. The refrigerator held nothing but super caffeinated drinks. There was nothing in my car. I took two aspirins and started looking at the paperwork.

As usual, the requests for various payments were exaggerated obscenely over what could possibly be due. I was allowed to hold back ten percent but that rule only applied after correcting the various categories to a percentage of completion in the real world. The banks were eager to get the money out on the street to collect interest, the owners and the contractor wanted money to use as capital on other projects. Then, there were the boat payments. I could participate and get more than I deserved. I would probably be screwed at the end of the job anyway. I just wanted to pay my people - I didn't have a boat. I could never figure what made me play it straight - no one appreciated it.

The shop drawings were garbage. Unfortunately, my stamp with the word, "REJECT" on it was back at the office. I rolled the drawings up and thought about leaving but leaned back in the chair once more.

Morals and ethics. I think about these words quite often. My parents never offered me any rules to live by. We were not religious. My family had been unsuccessfully displaced to the segregated South - I never heard from my folks any disparaging remarks about the Negroes in the town. Some worked for my Dad - we built houses in the ghettoized parts of town,

It all seemed to boil down to trust. When I was growing up there was for me no codification as to morals or ethics. Yes - there were rules and laws ....

A commotion outside brought me back to reality. Some of the workers had been enlisted to bring a covered stretcher to the ground. The EMTs and police were exchanging information. The rear door of the ambulance slammed shut and the vehicle wailed its way back to the main road. The police had probably interviewed those they wished to speak to as they departed immediately thereafter. I was relieved - no one would know I was there. Jose waved everyone out of the parking area. I stood next to the door to make sure that he did not lock up leaving me inside.

"*Que esta pasando?*"

"Get out of my chair."

Things seemed to be a little better. "I'm ready to go. I'll take the shop drawings with me."

He glanced at the Payment Certificates. "The boss is not going to be happy."

"Have you called him yet?"

"He's in Maine."

"They have telephones there. Reception is spotty but ..."

"I'll see you next month."

That was an exit line if I ever heard one. He had the newly charged telephone in his hand and was punching in numbers as I nodded goodbye.

It was raining again. The road out was a disaster. My hands were shaking. I could not decide whether I was hot or cold. Some guy I didn't know woke up this morning brushed his teeth, kissed his wife goodbye and a few hours later he was dead. I could not decide which way to drive. Once I got off the site, I parked at an Exxon station, out of the way, and watched the rain on the windshield until late dusk.

That oddly hot day in the new DeSoto, windows wide open to catch the breeze, the AM radio giving out the latest local news and the weather report, crop commodity prices and the like, I realized that I had no idea who I was. I was responding to what the people around me perceived as the right thing. I needed an epiphany.

***

The office was totally dark. The cleaners had come and gone. The refrigerator offered little inspiration - dead carrots and other rabbit food - why was everyone on a diet? My desk was littered with pink message slips and the day's mail. My secretary's to-do list for Monday included the usual happy face. It always made me smile for a brief instant. I turned on the lights in the drafting room and walked from table to table. Good work was being done - if only spelling were taught in architecture school - which led to the second problem of innovative abbreviations that even I couldn't figure out. My lecture about misspelled wording leading to misinterpretation in the field and disrespect of the whole needed to be repeated. Then, there were the law suits.

The weekend loomed. The kids were at some faraway beach resort with their mother. I had stopped wearing a watch - the vintage IBM clock on the wall announced a long night ahead. I dropped the shop drawings on Chuan's desk with a note telling him to find a reason to, "Approve as Noted" - I added a smiley face. He was very imaginative in these matters. I turned off all the lights and sat down at my desk, noting how similar my chair was to Jose's.

I had always felt like a fish out of water. I was a voracious reader. The encyclopedia was just as interesting as a novel no matter what the subject. I had some friends who introduced me to the Boy Scouts; the building of stuff like Floyd's doghouse and listening to the radio late at night from faraway cities where I'd never been. From all my reading, the proper use of language and correct spelling intrigued me. I hated diagraming sentences or even separating out adjectives and ad-verbs - it either felt right or it didn't - that instinct slopped over into my dealings with people.

I reached for the phone in the hope of finding a friendly

voice at the other end, hopefully not sitting in the dark, hopefully ready to join in some activity - I was open.

"Dodie - made the big sale yet?" Dodie was a realtor, desperate to make a pile of money in a hurry, always involved in at least one big deal that was going to put her over the top. We met at a zoning meeting on the Hill; afterwards I invited her for a drink, followed by dinner, followed by a night at her apartment. We had kept in touch.

"No time to talk - have to meet a client," out of breath as usual.

No need to appear needy. Where was the nearest restaurant? Chinese sounded good. Leftovers would make breakfast. My favorite place had beer.

2

Monday morning. Lots of chatter. Everyone looked reasonably well rested - no absences. Chuan gave me a thumbs up which I assumed meant the shop drawings would be taken care of. I dug into the mail and the phone calls of importance.

"Coffee, Boss?" It was a standing joke like the smiley face. I had told her, when she was first hired on Father Gomez's recommendation, at the review of her job description, it was demeaning for staff to fetch me coffee.

She placed the cup on the corner most distant from all the paperwork, "That job superintendent, Jose, wants to talk to you."

"Where is he?"

"He was in the lobby earlier. He gave me this number. It's not one I recognize: - maybe it's home."

Jose deserved a return phone call. Miguel being family, maybe he had to tend to all the relatives. His weekend could not have been great. There had been no word from his boss. I wondered if things were back to normal at the project. A woman speaking Spanish answered my call, "Jose, por favor?" There was shouting in the background. The next voice on the line was not my Jose.

As with similar situations in the past I turned the phone over to Angelica, who was still standing by, *"Jose, el gran jefe, por favor?"*

Angelica represented the latest generation to come into the workforce. Her parents were pleased that she was blooming in the white collar ranks. Born in the USA, educated in a decent public high school, college material but no bucks for same, she personified the cell phone clinging matured teenager, pretty and petite, curious and wanting to learn.

"It's all in the wrists,'"Angelica professed as she handed me the phone.

I listened and I listened some more. I'm sure my mouth was agape. "Tampered? The crane - the investigation - what?" I was upset.

Jose answered, "The transfer gear, right near where it's hooked to the cable - cut almost all the way through."

"You can't mangle that kind of metal - you need mega tools in a shop that has the right equipment."

"That's what the people from OHSA said. They want the crane completely taken apart and sent somewhere to be looked at by experts. We can rent a new crane but it will take weeks to get back to normal." Jose was out of breath. I had never heard him talk so much. "First thing the boss is going to ask is, 'On who's dime?'"

"I'm staying out of this," and handed the phone back to Angelica. In the back of my mind, I knew this was wishful thinking. She raised her eyebrows making query as to whether she was needed further. My silence was her answer. No one was talking about the poor guy who had been killed.

There was work to be done. I had not done much in the way of drawing of late. There were meetings, many meetings - clients, consultants, building inspectors, construction job visits, potential new clients. Sometimes, I was just a bump on the log. I was on the road more then in the office. When I had a chance, I would sketch out some ideas at my desk - I missed being in the drafting room. My ideas were turned over to people who were good at disagreeing with me - in a kind way.

Mr. Peery taught mechanical drawing both in junior high and high school. He was also the shop teacher - he did the same at the local community college. His twin boys were in my class and we were good friends. The family had a workshop building on the property behind their home and I visited there, sometimes staying the night.

In drawing class, I was fascinated in see my drawings on tracing paper transferred into blue prints by exposing coated paper to the sun within a glass covered frame and then curling the potential print into a tube that exposed it to ammonia fumes. The results were white lines on a navy blue background, something I could take home and show to my parents.

It was soon time for lunch. The staff usually ate together in the conference room. Almost everyone brownbagged it - sometimes there was enough to share - I treated from time to time - we celebrated birthdays. Vendors offered to bring lunch in return for making a pitch for some building product - this was strictly voluntary as free time was given up for a free lunch. It was a well knit group. The conversation, for the most part, was anything but work. The day continued without interruption. The office was emptying out at the end of the work day. I usually enjoyed the quiet and privacy that time of day brought but did not want to deal with late-in-the-day visitors who sought company to wait out rush hour and I was at the door ready to follow the staff to the parking garage.

"Hold the line for Lawyer Kline," the very bossy androgynous voice instructed me after I picked up the phone on the tenth ring. I counted to ten. Lawyer Kline was probably now billing two clients at the same time. I hung up.

"Tried to get away?" A jovial used-car-salesman laugh followed up this greeting when I picked up the phone the second time. "Got a minute?"

"Who are you, exactly?" I knew his name and reputation but I wanted him to clarify who he thought he was at that instant - I was sure he was not going to ask me to do some work for him - we didn't travel in the same social circles. A voice, less jovial, responded,

"We met at that zoning hearing for that apartment building under construction on the Hill."

"Aha - what can I do for you?" I was still not sure of the purpose of the call. The billing minutes were ticking away - his, not mine.

We had now both pissed on the fire hydrant. "A client of mine is curious as to what you know about the accident on Friday."

"It's always good to hear from Cliff, it is Cliff isn't it?" that said, and not wishing to prolong the posturing, I moved on, "I was there on Friday, just after the accident, to pick up some paperwork. It was raining really hard and I never left the trailer. The super filled me in after the police and EMTs left."

"Something about a failed crane?"

"Jose told me that the crane bucket fell and killed a worker."

"What caused the bucket to fall."

"No idea."

"We hear there's some sort of investigation?" The papal "we" I thought.

"A young man died. I would hope things would be

looked at to make sure it didn't happen again." Let us say there was anger in my voice.

The small town where I grew up was a County Seat and it was there that I first became aware of lawyers. An important looking courthouse with jail formed the nucleus of the commercial district - local lawyer's offices clustered close by. Due to the influence of our home town United States Senator, and the largesse of Congress there was a complex of Federal functions and another courthouse as well. Lawyers came and went. The out-of-towners stood out like Martians. Not surprisingly, no one from my high school graduation class became a lawyer.

life.
      "A terrible accident." No acknowledgement of loss of

      "Say hello to Cliff." I hung up the phone still wondering why the lawyer had really called and on whose behalf?

***

      I lived in a small complex of townhouses that included the amenity of a swimming pool. The style of the units was what the realtors called traditional, analogous to the stuff my own office cranked out. I would have preferred something more contemporary, lots of glass, big open spaces but the market was somewhere else or so the real estate people said. My unit held the requisite kitchen and bedroom - I might as well have lived in a hotel room considering how much I used living-dining area.

      I took a sandwich and a beer to a table outside the fenced-in pool and watched a few fathers and kids paddle around. The sun would set over the few sparse trees at the property line in about an hour. No pool parties were scheduled so the area would remain quiet. I tried to read the newspaper. The comics and the obituaries were my favorite sections. I doodled in the blank spaces of the various ads for stuff I didn't need.

      "Doodle, doodle, doodle," Marcie chanted as she took

away my pen with an exaggerated flourish that provided great exposure of her cleavage.

"Marcie, where you been?"

"You want the long or the short story?"

"Your choice."

She took a long sip of what looked like water but was probably straight vodka, "I'm out of work again."

Marcie had been employed in just about every facet of the construction business. She understood how everything worked and was a prodigious employee. She generally got fired when someone's wife showed up at the office unexpectedly for whatever reason and soon instrumented a coup with an 'or else' ultimatum. The next job usually came easily - not with me, however. "I'm not hiring."

"You know everybody."

"Type up a letter of recommendation and sign my name."

We gossiped about who was doing what and to whom. The sun retreated in a splashy display of reds and yellows. Marcie sighed, "Come by if you want."

"Give me an hour."

***

Telephone calls to the beach yielded an answering machine that probably came with the condo. I did not want to leave a message nor did I want to use the kids' telephones and embarrass them with their friends. I left a comical text message for each.

Marcie had candles and incense aglow. As I came through the door, she flitted about doing her Isadora Duncan thing, flimsy gauzy gown and all, dramatically snuffing out the candles one by one. There were no further preliminaries - we went directly to the shower and bedroom.

I thought of the, 'first time,' as most people do - a fumbling schoolboy wanting to get it out of the way - no romance involved - front seat of my car with the scratchy upholstery - needed some assistance and gladly given - she had been there before.

3

Cliff awakened without prompting at his usual time. He removed himself from the sleeping bag, and sat up on the edge of the army surplus cot, staring across the otherwise unfurnished room, listening to his own thoughts.

No natural light penetrated from the world outside. A dim glow gave direction to the bathroom beyond. Blocking the room's windows were packing cases such as those used by moving companies which held his few possessions. It was as always.

He padded unclothed and barefoot to the bathroom. After a two minute shower he dressed in his usual pressed jeans and blue Brooks Brothers oxford shirt, loafers with no socks and prepared to leave. He wore no watch and carried no wallet or keys . There was no need to turn on any lights during the time he prepared to go to work. It was as always.

The door out of the room was marked, 'Fire Door Only - Alarmed.' No alarm went off however and none went off at a similarly marked door at the end of a narrow shabby corridor, lighted with sparse bare bulbed light fixtures. He passed through a storage room containing maintenance supplies and exited through this room's entrance door into the building's ground level elevator lobby. He nodded to the security person seated at an elevated desk and entered one of a bank of elevators full of chattering office workers. He went through an unmarked corridor door on the 25th floor using his palm print to gain entrance. He was now in his private domain.

He was aware that his 'posse' was gathered near at hand, in the coffee room and lounge. It was seven am by the vintage IBM clock on the wall. It was as always.

At the orphanage, he had not been Cliff; he had not been anybody. The keepers had caused a social security number to be issued for him for record keeping purposes. His birth date was a guess. Bo was as close as he came to a name. There were others just like him and it was easy to be lost in the crowd. When he could remember how things were, it was schooling, working in the kitchen and garden and keeping the dormitory neat and clean. There were field trips to the beach, to the library, to a ball game - rare enough but sufficient for him to realize there was more to the world than the cyclone fenced orphanage. He liked his privacy most of all. There were plenty of places to hide from the others and he did so.

He opened the door to the general office area and the 'boys' entered quickly with half-finished coffee. The secretary brought Cliff a tray bearing the products making up his special diet. She distributed the day's agenda and took her place, pad in hand at the rear of the room.

None of these people meant anything to him - HR had done the hiring based on who and what he felt he needed in specialized fields. Socially, they were oddball misfits like himself - no MBA's - just earnest people needed to get the job done. He had tried to avoid hiring minorities but soon realized this was an unnecessary criterion. All were well paid. Each carried Cliff's authority; Cliff rarely had to step in. If he needed to leave the office, one of them acted as his driver and carried the company credit card. If he needed cash he asked for some from the accounting department. He was not sure if he had a bank account. The daily meetings were strictly business. There was no chitchat concerning wife-and-kids and sports results and the like.

The matter of the accident concerning the failed crane was brought to his attention. One of the staff suggested it could have been sabotage, the motive unknown. He had heard about the accident but sabotage was something new. Cliff was incredulous. "Who said that - find out more?" He did not need any more lawsuits. The banks did not like lawsuits.

Otherwise, things were going smoothly. He spoke briefly to Lawyer Kline. Once he hung up, he drew his attention to the future.

He had a goal.

4

I left Marcie early in the am - reluctantly, but I knew there would be a return invitation. I made no mention of the job search - I knew she was self-motivated on a number of levels. Back at my place, there were text messages from the kids, quirky as usual. I had showered with Marcie before heading to my place to change into fresh clothes. So far the day looked good.

Angelica's to-do list included the prospective payroll needs. Our workweek ended on Wednesday - checks were issued on Friday. That account looked a little thin. We were owed a bunch of money but that's not the same as having it in the bank. It was time to make some phone calls. I reviewed the accounts receivable list and made a goal amount - Angelica would get on her motorcycle and go from office to office to collect the promised checks and thence directly to our bank.

"Steve, how's the missus, the kids doing well in school?" There was a pause and I went further, "Fifteen thousand would do for now - Angelica will be by." This was the same routine that was repeated every month. Steve was not married nor did he have kids. I kept going down the list trying to ensure that Angelica on the motorcycle was not a wasted venture.

"Okay, Angelica here's the list." She already had her leathers and helmet on, "Do not answer the phone while you're changing gears, or ...." She was already out the door. I would go down the secondary list tomorrow. I didn't want anybody to think we had gone out of business.

I ventured into the drafting room. Standing by Murphy's desk and looking over his shoulder, I waited for him to acknowledge my presence. His earphones were vibrating. He mouthed, "Study course for the exam." I was sure that was not true. His latest version of the attire of the well-dressed architect was questionable. I scrawled on his board, "See me," and moved on.

We had bought our first computer with accompanying software and put an intern to work on a simple project to test out the process. The technology was touted as the wave of the future. I was not so sure. The drawings looked clumsy and sloppy. On the other hand, the dimensions always added up. The intern was enthusiastic - this was what he learned in school - he had never drawn in any other way. He was glad to have a job and was giving it his best. Some of his fellow workers looked over his shoulder from time to time showing interest. I would wait and see - pencil and paper cost basically nothing - labor was the most expensive outlay.

***

"How much without the soft drink?"

"One dollar fifty." This was the same as the cost with the soft drink here at Costco. I knew this but always asked anyway. It was my way of being friendly to someone having to serve the public in such a limiting job. Angelica had a list of supplies for the office that she handed me when she learned I was going shopping to stock up my own larder. I enjoyed walking around the store considering all the stuff I didn't need.

The pizza looked good as well but my conscience told me to resist.

"That's it."

The food handler looked both ways, as he placed my foil wrapped dinner and accompanying paper cup in my hands with the change, "Aren't you Jose's boss?"

"Jose?" I was confused.

"It's my break," as he motioned with his head towards the outside. I pushed the cart in the direction of my car with him following. He helped me put the goods in the trunk, I saw him eyeing my vintage Toyota. "Jose, the big boss for that new building on the Hill," he added at last, clarifying in his mind which Jose he was making reference to. I waited for the pitch for a relative who did bodywork on cars on the side.

"I think I know who you're talking about but I'm not his boss."

"You were in the store one time - Miguel pointed you out to me."

"Miguel, the worker who was killed recently?"

"He's my wife's cousin on her mother's side - was."

I hesitated for more. "I'm sorry for you and your family." I was sure I had never met Miguel, but it seemed the appropriate thing to say - it was insincere small talk but necessary.

"Jose respects you." I nodded still waiting for the pitch involving my Toyota. "Jose is scared." I sensed that my Toyota was safe until its next State inspection, "He's afraid to talk to anybody."

Now, I was looking around. "You could run into him here tomorrow - about this time of day?" he suggested over his shoulder, heading back towards the store, "And, I'll have my cousin look at the Toyota at the same time - he can work wonders."

***

Angelica was staring into space when I returned.

I always wished I could have gone to college, knew more stuff so I could get a better job, meet a cool guy, have a family of my own. Some of my friends got knocked up in high school, dropped out, kept the kids - sometimes - no boyfriend or husband in sight. They worked at the 7/11 and Grandma was day care. For them, there was no husband material around, just guys who wanted the same old thing which is how everything went downhill in the first place. Sharing a joint from time to time was as close to excitement as things got - I wanted more then that.

I awakened Angelica from her reverie and asked her to find Murphy and send him down to the coffee shop off the lobby.

***

"You speak some Spanish, right?" Murphy looked confused. "It is time you got some field experience." Murphy looked lost without his headphones. "You know what a clerk-of-the works is, right?"

"Are you firing me, Boss?"

"No. just giving you an opportunity for some new experience - you want to get ready for the exam - right - I'll work with you."

Murphy looked dubious.

"Work with Angelica to improve your Spanish, I'll fill you in as the week goes by. Buy yourself some construction boots, find a hardhat that fits you in the supply closet - this is a great opportunity."

We headed upstairs together. I had decided to say nothing about the content issuing from his earphones or the dress code for now.

***

Angelica handed me the summary of our accounts receivables - things looked good enough to meet our current obligations - there might even be something for me this time around. I took money out of the business on a sporadic basis. The CPA who did our taxes was perpetually confused as well as amused. Getting through another month was like a breath of fresh air. I spent some time forecasting the future trying to bring credibility to the various proposals out there that might be turned into actual projects. I made a few 'social' phone calls to test the waters, grading all of the proposals on a scale of one to ten.

***

Then, there was the reality of a changing marketplace. The city was growing, a magnet for new businesses doing business with the government. Real estate developers from out of town were exploring the opportunities to build new office space and housing. With them came their own architects and contractors. A few of my compatriots had sold out and moved to Florida. Some of the new firms featured the 'starchitects' that you read about in the glossy magazines; there were some of international stature. The poaching of others' key employees had started - the new entities were much better capitalized. Salaries were going up. We locals were less attractive - we were getting old and complacent and there wasn't much we could do about that.

I admired much of the new work I saw going up - new materials - not the same old dreary facades of red brick and punched in windows - attention paid to the environment.

Angelica and Murphy were in the conference room, laughter emanating from them both - I assumed it had to do with Spanish.

I fiddled at my desk past quitting time waiting for rush hour traffic to clear.

5

The shopping center was crowded despite it being the supper hour. In the Costco parking area, passerby's would observe three Hispanics and a gringo circling a vintage Toyota, raising and closing its hood, opening the trunk, and kicking the tires and, with all this actively, engaged in conversation. Luis, the food worker was the first to depart followed by the bodywork repair person, whose name I did not catch, leaving Jose and myself. We propped the hood open for effect.

I looked at Jose, shrugging my shoulders, waiting for him to speak. His face was drawn; there seemed to be a little more gray in his untrimmed mustache.

"Something funny is going on. On the Hill, I mean." I waited him out. "That crane bucket falling was no accident. I don't think it was meant to hurt Miguel - he was just in the wrong place at the wrong time." I waited still. "I don't know who to talk to without getting the blame put on me. There's been other stuff."

"For example?"

"Last week, three loads of concrete showed up, all with the wrong mix. You could see there was way too much water in the concrete even though the delivery ticket showed the right proportions. We sent it back. The supplier was really pissed."

"And?"

"A load of re-bars showed up that looked funny. The red tips at the ends gave it away. It was some understrength stuff from India. We sent it back too. The supplier says he got a fax okaying the change?"

"And?'

"A few times some of the guys got late night phone calls telling them not to come in the next day."

"What would be the motive, besides mischief or a

grudge or maybe union stuff? What makes you scared - I know what happened to Miguel - but why are you personally scared? Why don't you talk to your boss? Any one of those mistakes could have caused a lot of damage, people hurt, delays, extra costs - now, or in the future."

Jose nodded his head in agreement, "I think it's the boss. Maybe not the big boss - maybe one of the boss's crew."

"A name, maybe?"

"No clue."

"Uh-huh." Now I thought that having Murphy on the job was not a great idea. "What do you want me to do?"

"Help me figure out what's going on."

"I'll think about it." I didn't want to tell him I was already thinking about it. I put down the hood of the car squaring the sheet metal up with the adjoining body and testing the locking mechanism. I had tried not to look at the engine.

I took the long way towards the shopping center, through the parking lot crossing between aisles to look at cars, observing the makes and models as if I was going to make a choice to purchase. The variety was mind boggling. Most on hand seemed new and I could only imagine all the gadgetry and electronics and leather interiors. Perhaps it was time - I would have those annoying monthly payments just like everyone else. I started looking at colors - perhaps a yellow convertible.

There was no point in going home unfed. I stood in line at the snack bar observing my fellow Americans' choices. Luis was not working. I ate a chicken Caesar salad in the store's picnic tabled alcove; the hot dog I would save for a midnight snack.

***

By the time I got home, I was ready to go to sleep. The stack of books next to the bed, the collection of magazines, the newspapers from days past; all would have to wait.

Slumber did not come easily. Falling asleep was a lengthy process that took me through a parade of past events, mostly situations in which I was denigrated, one not related to the other necessarily, until I was asleep or so I thought. Then the dreams took over. The dreams were interrupted by trips to the bathroom or to the refrigerator. I was averse to taking any medication as it seemed to exaggerate the life-snubs parade and the nightmares left me sweaty and dry-mouthed at when I woke. Ask me what the dreams were about and I would say, "No idea."

The rough spots in my life were often repeated with no moral value added. Thoughts of revenge came to mind - some quite violent - I always wondered why the emotions were still stored in my brain at all. Could I actually hunt someone down and do them harm?

6

The Toyota struggled to start, an omen of the car's distaste for my consideration of a replacement the previous day. Despite my stocking of the larder, I would grab breakfast along the way to the office, the venue directed by whichever traffic jam selected the alternate route of the day. Breakfast was my favorite meal. There were some days I had a second breakfast and skipped the noontime meal altogether. I ate all the wrong things, at least according to my doctor. The owner of my favorite diner cured his own bacon and was generous with the portions served in the 'Meat Lovers Special.' The eggs came from his farm as well and were usually double yoked. His wife baked the bread. The coffee cup was always full - plenty of, 'half and half' to go with it. The newspaper was there without asking - I was a big tipper.

***

"Jose needs to talk to you," this from Angelica as she set a cup of coffee on the desk. "He sounded anxious."

I was still trying to make sense of Angelica's outfit which consisted of a masculine-like business suit jacket with wide lapels and chalky vertical stripes, and a barely visible skirt. "Where is he?"

"It sounded like he was calling from .... I don't know where - lots of noise - I could hardly hear him. Try his cell."

If there was that much noise, with my hearing, it was probably best I try the trailer. He answered on the first ring. He started speaking quite rapidly in Spanish. "English, *por favor.* What's going on?"

"There's a whole crew out here, techies with x-ray equipment, cameras, drills, you name it. They are examining the concrete all over the building."

"Who sent them?"

"There are two troopers with them. They handed me a warrant. They said it was an ongoing investigation."

"Investigation? What does the warrant say?"

"It mentions Miguel's name - the rest is a bunch of gobbledygook. They say it also covers the crane which is half taken apart."

"Call Allaine, the structural engineer - he might be interested."

"I did. He's in California looking at colleges with his daughter."

"How about the boss? Is he still in Maine?"

"I left word as to what's going on with his secretary - so far no one's called me back."Angelica was waving her phone back and forth just outside my immediate field of vision. She mouthed, "Lawyer Kline."

"Got to go, Jose. Semper fi."

I picked up the phone and found Lawyer Kline's assistant on the other end who told me to hold on. "What's with the outfit, Angelica? It looks very .... business-like?"

"Have an interview today - maybe some bucks for college - Father Gomez arranged it. He told me to .... 'dress conservatively.' I borrowed the ensemble from a friend who works at a bank."

***

Ensemble, I thought, just as Lawyer Kline got on the line. I had no doubt as to what would follow. "Got a call from Cliff."

"How's the weather in Maine?

"It's raining. Can you tell me what's going on at the Hill?"

"Talk to Jose." I feigned ignorance.

"I tried - I got a lot of Spanish out of which I understood, 'police' and 'warrant.'

Jose had his own way of stonewalling it seemed. "Time to get out of the office - get some fresh air - get some dust on the wingtips, show off the new Mercedes ...."

"I'll send one of my people who speaks Spanish."

The line went dead. Angelica looked at me curiously, "Anything for me to do?"

"What time are you and the ensemble going to be out of the office, Angelica?"

"One o'clock; I'll be gone about an hour."

"You plan to use your motorcycle wearing that skirt - you better take my car.?"

Angelica just smiled.

No mail as yet. It would be the time to see what everyone else in the office was up to. We actually had some interesting jobs. The Hill was big and offered prospects that could lead to bigger still; and would be profitable; it just wasn't something that stirred the imagination. This new intrigue made the Hill interesting - it wasn't architecture - nothing like what had happened in the last week was taught in school, not even in my, 'prehistoric,' school that my younger employees envisioned as the, 'good old days.'

Architecture School was an experience for which I was ill prepared. There were some very bright guys in my class - no women at all - no women in the engineering programs in adjoining buildings that I ever saw - the guys all seemed quite confident and well prepared for the six year haul. There were a few vets, much older than myself, married, living in an enclave just outside the campus. The professors were a mixed bag, none of them actual practitioners - to them architecture was an academic endeavor.

Cynthia was working several projects at the same time, a series of coffee shops in various locations around town. More could happen. She had brought in the work and was taking care of every phase of its execution.

Because each site was complicated in its own right, we were on a, 'time and materials' basis and so far the client was paying up without being prompted.

"Do you actually drink coffee?" I asked her as I rifled through the mark-up sets of drawings on the side board. I wanted to be brought on board at her pace.

"Can't stand the smell when it's being roasted but after its brewed, it's okay with a lot of cream and sugar." Noting my pen making notations, she added, "We actually have one under construction."

"I was in there the other day. They were busy trying to get it open on time. No trouble with the building inspectors thus far."

"So I heard. The problems always seem to crop up at occupancy permit time. That's when Ricardo does his thing."

"Don't tell me." Bribery was something I didn't want to know about even if it was just lifetime free coffee. "And, watch your rear end."

There was a rumor circulating around the building department, the source being someone who knew someone who knew someone who knew someone, that Ricardo imported more than coffee from Columbia. I always listened to gossip, storing the stories to test against my own observations. Sometimes I had to give up some useless information just to show I was, 'one of the boys.'

OPM was the lifeblood of real estate development. Other People's Money always had a price. There were the banks and insurance companies and then there was what was loosely termed, 'private equity.' For the developer there was the profit to be gained after all the, 'investors' had been satisfied.

School left me little prepared for the real world. I graduated with honors - that and a dollar would get you on the Metro. A great many of my class had decided earlier on to take up other majors, or left school for one reason or another. Being left standing at the end did not prove much. I assumed my folks were proud but that somehow never came across. Jobs were in short supply. The Army awaited.

Robbie, our intern, was informally in charge of developing interiors for the management of our building. Our office was very familiar with the building standards - the management people were right in the building and they felt comfortable dropping in without an appointment. Development of special needs was paid for directly by the tenant. The income was quite lucrative. Robbie was a great salesman, eager to please. His work on the computer was truly entertaining. I thought he had the potential to eventually go out on his own. I tried not to be envious.

My own path to independence twisted and turned its way, over the early years, through various employers. There was no one for whom I had worked that I had any respect - no one I could call a mentor. I wondered if my people thought the same of me.

My patrons of years past were educated for the most part, but not necessarily educated in the needs of the building industry, an assemblage of personalities not readily responsible for building construction destined to last many decades.

Murphy had managed to incorporate his earphones, now disguised as noise protectors, into a company hardhat, one with our company logo on the front and a newly lettered, 'Murph' on the back - he wore the hardhat all day long - I did not attempt to talk to him. As to his future, I was uncertain.

Angelica was waving the phone at me. I had not finished the tour and reluctantly went back to my desk.

"When can you get started?" I was trying to pick up on the voice over the background chatter from a speakerphone.

"Again?"

The speakerphone clicked off. "I sent you back your proposal." I was working on the voice and looking through the newly arrived mail.Angelica was opening prospective envelopes for me. "What's happening up on the Hill?"

I hoped this was not all about the latest gossip. "Aha. Found it. There are so many it somehow worked its way to the bottom. We're still looking for the retainer check." Angelica smoothed out the rumpled proposal's envelope thinking that there was actually a check to be found.

"I'll talk to my bookkeeper."

"Saul, it's always good to hear from you." His voice, just a few seconds before, finally connected to a name in my hearing impaired brain. "How are the wife and kids?" He actually had a wife and kids; the wife was a society snob of the first order. We did not like each other. I scanned the returned proposal for annotations. "We'll need to meet to discuss the program in detail."

"I'll gather the boys and get back to you." It seemed everybody had a posse. "About the Hill?"

"I only know what I read in the papers." I wanted to keep the gossip mill clear.

Saul was a former college scholarship athlete who excelled in the three-meter dive. Small in stature, his style displayed fearlessness that gave him the edge with the judges in the complicated dives that gained the points to win a competition. He missed the Olympics due to an injury but then parlayed his skills to gain a scholarship to law school while acting as coach of the school's aquatic team. An alum with big bucks took a liking to Saul and took him, upon graduation, into his world class construction business. The alum had a daughter, the stereotype American princess, who saw the opportunity for the largesse to continue forever. It was a romance of time immemorial.

There were some additional signed proposals in the day's mail. I started thinking about a new car once more. It was time for lunch - it would be good to share the news with the staff. Layoffs, due to lack of business, were always on people's minds. Our chief designer only liked to design and when he was given other work to do, had a habit of dragging his feet. We needed work at every level of effort and key people needed to be retained in order for us all to remain viable.

Lunch was starting to be spread out in the conference room. We each eyed the whole and measured what could be equitably traded. Based on Angelica's recommendations, what had been stocked from the Costco run counted for me and was up for grabs. Angelica's outfit was a hit all around. There was lots of talk of college experiences. I briefly mentioned that some new work was coming in and nodded towards Benito to make sure he understood he would be getting back to what he did best.

Benito, as with many designers, was temperamental. He did not think of himself as such but in the scheme of things he was hard to deal with. Design was not my strong subject in school. Myself and my classmates spent many hours, day and night, on design work, but hard work is not the same as talent. In recent times, I saw the work of others in my travels and admired as well as rejected the originality of the latest trends, Benito had his own style and often times there was conflict between what he envisioned and what I liked as well as what I thought the client would accept.

***

The hours slipped by. Angelica did not return. Late in the day there was a phone call, "Sorry Boss - I ran into some guys from my neighborhood .... "

"Angelica," I was upset, "we will talk in the morning."

The staff was filtering out; I went to the office next door to ours, that of Donovan, a landscape architect and friend, helped myself to a beer from his refrigerator, nodded to his secretary, Judy, who was on the phone, and I went back to my domain, turned off the lights and spaced out.

Judy, knocked and came in soon after with a beer in hand. In past conversations she had related to me and her boss that she had a daughter in the military, overseas, and had been in a state of loneliness ever since her household had been reduced to one. She had downsized to one of the rental apartment buildings around the corner. Now, she talked some more and I listened. She replenished our beers several times. I offered to take her to dinner; she demurred, "I'm going home, I'll order pizza in - stop by if you like?"

7

Traffic was light - early commuters and delivery vehicles of all sizes and shapes filled all the lanes, ignoring the speed limit, based on their own sense of urgency. It was going to be a hot day - this according to the 24-hour radio station, the only station that the Toyota could pick up - I needed a new vandal-proof antenna. The latest model cars came with all sorts of electronic equipment. The roster of 'past diners enjoyed,' flashed through my mind - in the new model cars you only had to say, "Find me the closest diner" - what was that Clint Eastwood movie where he stole the Soviet jet fighter that was piloted via a special helmet by merely thinking, in Russian, of what he wanted the plane to do? Perhaps I would wait for that feature to be adapted into my future car? A new antenna would do for now - maybe a set of tires.

I had started out planning to head home and soon realized that it would serve no purpose - I could change my shirt at the office. Maybe I could get an early start while it was still quiet.

***

Angelica had beat me to the office. She brought me coffee and shyly sat down in the desk's guest chair. I waited her out, "The interview went very well - I became really excited about college once again - I am going to study engineering in an accelerated program - lots of hands-on stuff," I nodded approvingly, "The Church has come up with a sponsor - I know you're upset with me and I'm sorry but I met these guys at the parish who used to work on the Hill. They told me some stuff that you might be interested in? I was so excited about it all - I took the bike on a really fast ride to the Bay." She took a breath.

"Okay, first things first. I'm very happy for you. When will college begin?"

"There's a lot of paperwork to be completed, tests to take - it could be a while."

"Keep me in the loop - that's assuming you plan to keep working here?"

"Are you firing me Boss?" she had been spending too much time with Murphy, "I like working here."

"No. Tell me about your conversations with the construction workers."

"They have been laid off waiting for a new crane to be put in place. They say Jose is a good boss, but ...."

I put up my hand up to stop her and greet the staff as they struggled in, coffee and breakfast in hand. "Go on."

"There's funny stuff going on - they are concerned about their safety." The phones were ringing. Benito was looking at me for direction. To Angelica, I said, "I'll catch up with you later. You owed me an earlier phone call yesterday." The Hill situation was otherwise quiet and that was fine with me.

Angelica headed for the phones.

I picked up a file and walked Benito back to his alcove. Benito had started out with a work station just as everyone else used but when the space next to him became vacant, he expanded. I expected to see a LazyBoy recliner in place any day now. The file contained the information he would need to get started on Saul's new project. "Here's our proposal - the scope of work in there is all I know at this time. The property is as you see in the site plan. We need some topo. I took some pictures of the neighborhood. There's no budget as yet but keep it in the real world. You need to check the zoning; also the building code - it's a tricky area as far as shopping centers are concerned. Absolutely no fast food allowed. There's a creek nearby that floods once and a while. There's an old building at the southwest corner - could have been a church at one time - find out if we can tear it down or maybe move it, or maybe incorporate it. Find out about water and sewer and power. Parking could be a problem. Any questions?"

Angelica was giving the phone hand signal, "I'll set up a meeting with the client early next week." I liked to keep Benito busy.

"Who is it?

"Allaine - from California."

"Shalom, compadre - how goes the college search?"

"A nightmare since you ask."

"Why California? Lot's of good schools around here."

"She wants to be as far away from her mother as possible - a feeling I am entirely in sympathy with."

"How is the divorce going by the way?

"Not well - I may have to bunk in with you. Getting down to business, I only have a few minutes before the latest tour is over. I had a call from a Lawyer Kline."

"Bring me up to date."

"You first."

"I get all my information from Jose. I haven't spoken to him today." I was sure Allaine knew much more then he was saying, "Tell me what Lawyer Kline wanted."

"The gonif knows somebody in the safety office at the building department. There's a preliminary report floating around but Lawyer Kline does not have the foggiest as to what it means. I didn't offer much help - who does he work for anyway? I told him concrete is tricky stuff."

"As well it is. Which school looks good so far?"

"According to my daughter, Stanford has the coolest food court. She doesn't have a snowball's chance of getting in there. On to the state of Washington, keep in touch."

***

If I was lucky that was all the time I would need to expend on the subject for the day - I did need to learn from

Angelica what she had earlier wanted to relate; that could happen later. I looked around the open office - no one was trying to catch my eye. The mail was waiting.

Just before lunch, a gaggle of pin-stripe clad personages who could only be lawyers came into the office accompanied by Robbie and a fellow I recognized as being from the building management office; and took over the conference room. Angelica distributed bottles of water while Robbie gathered some drawings from his desk. Angelica advised me that the visitors were a committee representing a new law firm that was considering leasing a whole floor in our building.

I introduced myself to the committee, "I'm going to, 'look in' - second pair of hands you know ...," and took a seat behind Robbie. It was clear that the committee had not gathered together before, there was no clear leader, and certainly no philosophy as to how they would work together. Each had worked in established offices where the physical facility was already in place; they were given a desk, the chair still warm, and told to, "Get those billable hours." I had to intercede without hurting Robbie's feelings or destroying his enthusiasm to learn.

"We need a little more information before we get started on your new venture. Let me just free associate for a moment," I sensed acknowledgment, "This will be both quantitative and qualitative, so to speak," the management guy looked perplexed, "First of all, how many of you are there and do you think you might expand? Lawyers, lesser lawyers, secretaries, bookkeepers, librarians; small conference rooms, large conference rooms, dining facilities, and so forth? Do you like cubicles, open offices, prestige offices? There will be more concerns after some initial decisions. Think about past offices you liked working in. Alternate schemes are not a good idea un-less you absolutely insist." There was silence.

"Tell you what. It's almost lunch time. Stay right where

you are. We'll order in lunch - my treat - stay as long as you want." There was gentle nodding of agreement, "Angelica will take your lunch orders." The yellow legal pads came out. I signaled Robbie to leave. I walked the management guy out, 'Not to worry - this will take time. Time is money - right?' I wanted to make sure he understood I would be billing him for same.

There were some additional proposals that needed my attention. Not all would involve Benito. Angelica placed a lunch on my desk and tiptoed away. I ate with my left hand and doodled some ideas with my right. It felt good to be an architect for a while.

***

Space planning, interiors, whatever you wanted to call it was a big industry eclipsing architecture as far as fees were concerned. Nothing resembling what was now being done was taught in school in my time. The Bauhaus folks who had trained my teachers disparaged decoration. Today, anyone could call themselves a designer and many did. The charlatans were everywhere. Architecture disappeared under the guise of decoration for decoration's sake. It was disheartening. To test the waters, my office had put on a woman who had some training and experience. The shelves and bookcases were full of samples. Manufacturers' reps were in constant procession with new stuff, weeding out the old in the process. Some brought gossip or lunch or both. I suffered the irritation. We were covering her salary for the time being. My philosophy was still in tune with Mies: "Less is more."

The meeting in the conference room broke up. Robbie shook hands with each of the participants, gave each his business card. As the door closed, Robbie shrugged his shoulders in my direction and went back to work.

***

The afternoon flew by. I shooed Angelica away several

times. Finally I told her, "Ask your friends from the parish to meet me at Costco tomorrow evening - in the parking lot. Tell them what my car looks like."

8

Pablo, Junior and Pablo, Senior. found me. I had put a, "FOR SALE" sign at the car's windshield and had almost sent them on their way as I already had several prospective purchasers, but they determined I was the one they were looking for. In appearance, each was the replica of the other, brothers rather than father and son. They asked me to open the hood. We actually looked at the engine for a few minutes as I told them the history of the car.

Pablo Senior spoke, "Angelica says you are *loco* but *confiable.*" I waited, "We need to work. The pay is good. Yes, it can be dangerous but we don't do anything *estupido.*" Junior nodded in agreement.

I waited, but there was no more. "Besides being thrown out of work because of the accident with the crane, what else is bothering you?"

They looked at each other. Junior spoke up for the first time, "There have been *errores*, miscues you may call them, *mas de lo normal,* far more than on other jobs." Pablo Senior nodded.

"For example?"

"Shoring removed too soon. Not enough concrete delivered and we had to create new reinforcing on the fly, too many workers; not enough workers. Lot's of stuff like that. The crane could have been part of it, I don't know.

There's lot of things we don't see but we hear about. It's got to be costing someone mucho money; dangerous too."

Follow the money they say, "Do you know who owns the project?"

They shook their heads. "*A quien le importa?* Who cares?"

I assumed that was probably true of all their fellow workers. Maybe? "You like the food here?"

We shared two different kinds of pizzas. I ordered several more for them to take home. There was no more talk of the Hill. Junior added in parting, "Let me know when you want to get rid of the *cacharro.*"

***

It was dark when I got home. The pool was closed. An unusually bright moon outshone the street lights. The air was still too humid to consider sitting outside. There had apparently been a power failure during the day shutting down all the electronics of the house including the AC thermostat. There was no point in opening the windows. I took a lukewarm shower and waited out cooler air. Opening the window shades allowed me to follow the circuit of the moon from east to west and away from the morning horizon. Phone calls to the kids went to voice mail. I thought about the day, trying to put into perspective what had been accomplished - I had no idea when I fell asleep.

***

I was on a solo trip to Greece, driving along the coast, visiting the islands by ferry; wandering, no objective in mind, checking off the sites from the guide-book, thousands of years of history, ruins exhibiting amazing building skills, stopping at hole-in-the-wall tavernas and markets to take in the local foods, sleeping where the guidebooks advertised two stars or less. One night, I was at a beach, my gear tucked into a nearby hotel, and there adjacent I spotted a dimly lit fish market that appeared to cook to order. The locals, all men, were sipping Ouzo and playing backgammon and seemed ready, except for the clicking of the tiles, to noiselessly wile away the night. It was a late dusk.

Cooking was being done on a charcoal fired grille. I ordered a whole fish, cucumbers and tomatoes and a bottle of local white. Facing out towards the darkened sea, the skyline brightened ever so gradually, a rounded white object took over the horizon; the calmed sea mirrored the light in all directions; at full bloom it was the largest moon I had ever seen. No sci-fi, three-D film could have crafted such a spectacle. I was in awe - "There must be a God," I thought. I flash back to that moment every time the sky offers an exceptional moon-rise.

***

In the morning I took note of a business card stuck in the door knocker. I didn't remember seeing it when I arrived home. "Rosanna Torres, Private Investigator," it read with a phone number; on the reverse, "Please call me"

***

Nothing interrupts breakfast. I called the phone number while awaiting the 'Meat Lover's Special,' and told the woman answering where I was. Twenty minutes later a very well put together lovely strolled down the diner aisle and slid into my booth, letting two knockout legs stretch out with languor into the passage.

"Nice gams there, sweetheart."

"You've been reading too much Dashiell Hammett."

A well read private investigator was always the best kind, I thought.

"I'm working on my PI jargon."

"Just be yourself." She had a nice smile.

"I will remind you that I like yes-no questions. I don't like to improvise. What can I do for you?"

She signaled the waitress away, "Don't you want to know why I want to talk to you?"

"No." There was no sign of a recording device; she exhibited no note-book and pen.

"Do you know a fellow, no last name, called Cliff - a real estate developer?"

"Yes."

"What can you tell me about him?"

"Yes or no, please?" I smiled politely.

She helped herself to a piece of bacon. "Okay - you are working with him or his company on the Hill?"

"Rule number two is no 'and-or' questions." I moved the bacon closer to me.

"With him?"

"No."

"With his company?"

"Yes - I can get you your own order of bacon if you like?"

"No, thank you." She singled the waitress, "Some tea please." Perhaps she was going to give up but probably not, "Do you know anything about accidents at the Hill?"

"Rule number ten covers non-specific questions in the plural." She was getting pissed - or so I hoped. "Also, rule number seven is - avoid hearsay."

"Have you talked to anyone about the crane failure that happened on the Hill last week?'

"Yes'"

I could see the word, 'who' being formed between her exquisite ruby painted lips but it never got to the surface. "A man was killed you know?"

"Yes."

The tea arrived. She took time to search her designer handbag for what appeared to be a notebook. The tea was sipped. Thought lines appeared on her forehead. "The building and the accident is being looked at by a number of agencies."

"Okay. I tend to say okay when there is no real question. Some people think I am hard of hearing - which I am - so that's why I say okay." By this time I'm sure she thought I was a complete idiot which was the effect I was going for.

There was some more tea sipping. She moved to leave. "Thank you for your time."

"Sam Spade wouldn't have given up so easily," I spoke this loud enough, to reach her retreating ears.

Chico, the diner owner and sometime cook, arrived to personally take away her cup and clean that portion of the table.

"Good looking woman - someone you know?"

I gave a knowing wink.

***

At the office, Robbie caught me immediately, "One of the lawyers, the tough-looking lady, is coming back to talk in a few minutes - can you be here?"

"Yes - try getting names from now on." The tough looking lady was maybe thirty and had been likely taught to present a stalwart demeanor in law school. Robbie probably thought I was the Ancient Mariner.

The drafting room was quiet.

I resorted to reading the latest copies of Commerce Business Daily. We had registered with the government, listing our professional qualifications, and now it was a matter of finding projects for which we could ask to be interviewed. There were always programs listed, many not necessarily in our purview, or with ridiculously unrealistic budgets or just not interesting. We were not minority owned or staffed by a majority of women which precluded us from much work that we were otherwise qualified.

There were no women or minorities in my graduating class; likewise during earlier work experience. Some Asians started cropping up, men though - women were in short supply - I was not sure where the government was going to fill its quota.

Ms. Benita Jones, the 'tough looking lady,' upon closer scrutiny met the minority description, or at least passed the, 'paper bag test,' as my friends who lived in our local 'ghetto' called it. There were some preliminaries. Her English pronunciation was perfect, a tinge of the South, probably North Carolina, maybe Tidewater Virginia. Robbie had introduced us.

"You gave us a lot to think about which is good - unfortunately there is still not consensus and that's not so good - I know I'm stating the obvious but that's where we are right now."

I was back to my yes or no problem. "That sounds like something you are going to have to settle among yourselves."

"That's true, but we need help."

"Yes, you do." Nothing like stating the obvious I thought, but at least it was a 'yes' answer, "There are people, firms too, who do this sort of thing. It is sort of like going to AA."

She laughed, which was hard to interpret. "Some of our senior members may have that AA experience already. What would you suggest?"

"I have no one to refer you to. Maybe one of your journals or magazines has ads for such services?"

"We want you involved. Our most senior partner told me to say to you, 'Cliff wants you on board,' end of quote."

I felt a chill. It was not the AC running amuck. Robbie was staring at me. It was obvious that Ms. Jones had no idea as to the portent of the message. I needed time. "The weekend is coming up - let's meet here bright and early Monday morning."

"I'll pass that on." She smiled, picked up her unopened briefcase and was gone.

Robbie just stood there; I didn't owe him any explanation, "Go see if Benito needs some help."

I wished to the gods of architecture, Vishmakarma, Vitruvius and Mies, whoever was available, there was someone to talk to. When in doubt, go to the beach - that always worked before. I worked with Angelica as to things that needed to be done before the weekend - nothing that important, but the list would replace my normal scrutiny. There would be a neat pile of notes on my desk on Monday morning. I went home, packed a bag and hit the road.

9

Over the bridge, through the tunnel, tracking familiar, winding single lane roads and soon the smell of the sea and then the sight of dunes and surf - it was as always, constant and reassuring.

When I was a kid, the family made trips to the Atlantic. It was a trek from Appalachia - we stayed at least a week before moving on. Some visits, it was at the Jersey shore where the New York City relatives escaped the heat, in beach shacks, ridiculously called cottages, suitable only for camping out, to gain fresh air free of humidity and urban pollutants but not necessarily free of frying food. Other times we visited these same relatives in the city where we spent most days at Coney Island. Both venues featured creosoted wood planked boardwalks with a variety of vendors of ethnic refreshments, as well as of souvenirs, and beach gear. There were exciting games of chance and rides leeward to the residential area, the beach all but obliterated from view. The adults yakked - I roamed the sand and surf, joined by newfound friends.

I looked around for, 'vacancy' signs and checked in at a place a few blocks from the sand. The area was familiar to me -

the boardwalk and its side streets would lead to watering holes and the like. I had no interest in bingo, auctions, bike-riding, deep-sea fishing, scuba-diving, or excursions to neighboring islands. A good sports bar with a wide screen TV and a view outside to the clusters of the strolling folks of all sizes and shapes was just about right. And, of course, there were the steamed crabs.

Sometimes I saw people I knew. But, that was not why I was here. This last meeting at the office had me confused and it had to be muddled through on my own.

My anonymity soon disappeared. A former neighbor, Beth, whose demeanor suggested she was looking for someone, spotted me, "We're looking for men to fill out a party at a friend's house tonight - come by - bring something drinkable. Give me your number - I'll text you the directions." She scouted the bar for other possible party prospects and then relaxed. We talked for a while - mostly gossip from the old neighborhood - I wondered what the new normal was in relationships.

The heat of the day was dissipating. The sun would set on the bay side - families were packing up tired sunburned children with all their paraphernalia necessary for a day at the beach - the lifeguards had left their posts, the old gents were out with the metal detectors hoping to strike gold before the sand cleaning machines came through, all of which made it a quiet time to stroll in the surf.

I had no new thoughts. The sun had given up and I did likewise. I grabbed a sandwich and beer and went back to the hotel to shower and dress for the group house party.

The party venue was within walking distance. I stopped by a package store and picked up several cartons of 'three buck chuck' - no sense in splurging on complete strangers. If some divorcee was looking for a new mate I would be disqualified on the basis of cheapness alone.

The address was one of the old time Victorians on the path above the dunes - no close neighbors which made the house good for parties. Lights were ablaze - the music went towards the sonic barrier as I took the wooden walk to the screened-in front porch. I spotted Beth and held up the wine - she mouthed, "kitchen," and gestured the proper direction. I helped myself to a plastic cup of much better stuff than I had brought. There was more silent direction which took me out to the rear yard complete with swimming pool. Someone owned a very expensive piece of real estate.

Of course, there was no one actually in the pool - bathing attire abounded nonetheless - skimpy on both men and women.

"See anything you like?"

The accent was South African. I knew this because of a former employee who worked with me for a year - he left the office at the end of the day with, *"Goeie naand"* with which I replied, or something close to that, as I turned toward the voice.

"Good evening. You've got to be kidding?" She was laughing.

"Is it close?" I was otherwise busy admiring a towering woman in a bikini made for someone half her size.

"My grandfather used to say that - how old was this person you learned it from?" She was still laughing.

"He was along in years - a very good draftsman nonetheless."

"Aha, you're the architect Beth was talking about. How do you like my place?"

"Let me say first, I apologize for the wine - the place deserves better." She looked at me puzzlingly, "Oh, you mean all that *draf* in the kitchen?"

Draf sounded like dreck - I assumed it meant the same thing, "Do you live here all summer?" I was changing the subject from the wine.

"Most," she gestured, "up in the tower. There's a cool breeze and a great view."

***

The view was great. In bed with Sonia, it was like climbing Mount Kilimanjaro, returning to base camp and back again.

"We *foked.*"

Another new word that sounded familiar I thought, "Yes we did."

***

In the early morning, Sonia, sans bikini, purged herself, swimming laps in the pool. A cleaning crew, mostly college age, tidied up the house and grounds - their efficiency suggesting they had done this before. I waved to Sonia and walked to my hotel to get some sleep. After a few hours' rest and breakfast I decided it was time to head home. I would hear out the lawyers right then and there on Monday morning.

***

The pool was active in my townhouse community. There was no reason to linger. I had had enough heat and humidity for now. I threw several days' newspapers on the couch, verified the AC was working and went to bed. Dreams of a new life with a gold mining heiress from South Africa, traveling the world into the sunset followed thereafter.

10

Ms. Jones returned alone. This time she opened her brief-case, and politely handed me a document, a revised AIA Contract with most of the standard clauses still intact. Robbie looked at his copy; he knew he was out of his depth but appreciated the courtesy nonetheless. The terms were essentially open ended. I crossed out the amount of the retainer and inked in a much larger amount and added my initials. Ms Jones smiled and initialed as well. She removed a prepared bank draft from her briefcase, then ripped it up. She then wrote a new payment from a pristine checkbook which she slid it across the table.

"It's nice to be able to deal directly with the person who writes the checks," I said, "Check Number One, I don't know whether to frame it or take it to the bank." I signed the contract. Ms. Jones was a great smiler. In response to her raised eyebrows, I advised her, "We can walk through the space together right now - Robbie will take notes." I called the management office and asked that someone bring us a key. To Angelica, who had hovered as usual, I said, "Bank," and handed her the check. Management's response was that the door was open.

***

There is nothing so depressing as viewing the wide open unoccupied floor of an office building, various wires dangling from the structure above, emergency lights providing the only interior illumination, the destruction, into debris, of the previous tenants' dreams, now being shoveled into rolling fifty-five gallon drums to be disposed of without thoughts of salvage or recycling. We were not alone. Several people were gathered in the shadows near the bank of elevators; remaining in place as the three of us went to the window line to take in the view.

"What are your thoughts? As you can see, you have a blank canvas."

Ms. Jones smiled coyly, "We are going to leave that up to you."

The group by the elevator broke up and one of the scrum separated from the gloom into the light and came toward us. Ms. Jones made motion to leave, touching Robbie at his elbow to signal him to go with her.

The reflection from the heat-resistant window glass showed me a man, neither tall nor short, average in build, dressed in a nondescript suit, dress shirt but no tie - his face said it all. I thought of those medieval age engravings that depicted Lucifer. His voice was measured and even - no detectable dialect or accent, "We meet at last."

Facing him, I could almost experience an aura of burning sulfur.

There was no effort to shake hands. "I am bringing together some legal minds to advise me in my work. I am glad you will be able to create an environment that will allow this to go forth."

"Cliff - is that right?," I asked, extending my hand as ordinary courtesy.

In acknowledgment, he shook my hand - not an overwhelming grip - no electricity "Anything you need, work with Ms. Jones - please?" The 'please' seemed an afterthought - it was appreciated, however. He returned to the several persons waiting at the elevators. The ding, signaling the arrival of a cab, was the only sound in the vacant space. The demolition workers appeared again as mysteriously as they had left. The space was even more creepy.

***

Robbie met me at the door to the office. "I have some information from Ms. Jones - number of people, organizational chart, job descriptions, and the like. What do you want me to do?"

"Study it. Make some bubble diagrams. Assign square footage to the various people. Have Angelica assign a job number. Get some help if you need it. Stay away from Benito. I'll get back to you this afternoon."

***

I thought about the meeting with Cliff. The Hill project was with a recently created development company which I had long suspected was controlled by Cliff - his business, not mine. I was not sure if I had really met 'Cliff.' Maybe there was some surrogate, like the Winston Churchill look-alike the Brits used to fool the Germans during World War II? How far could my paranoia go? Was the Hill somehow involved? Who did Lawyer Kline really work for? Was Lawyer Kline part of the new law firm? The payment check, just received, seemed real - I would wait and see.

Murph came by with a package of shop drawings. He gave me a thumbs-up which was difficult to interpret - his hard hat and ear phones had become a permanent part of his personality.

***

We had some new projects that needed to be staffed. We were working at full capacity - overtime was not fruitful - Temps were definitely out - new hires would mean competing in an expanding industry. We needed to be more efficient. I would call in some computer salesmen and listen to spiels. I retrieved the home phone numbers of some people who had worked for me in the past thinking they might want to return. One woman who had left on long term maternity leave was probably ready to get away from her child now entering the terrible twos'. It would probably be a little bit of everything.

I probably should have taken paternity leave myself at the time. I know many men do now and current law encourages this. Becoming a father was an out of conscious experience. I had little to none knowledge of my responsibilities - the grand-parents seemed to be happy - I would have to say I was ambivalent. There was the naming and the various rites of passage of officially creating a new person. I was okay with diaper changing and feedings and doctor visits. I was not so great at seeing physical similarities and behavioral traits that spoke of some ancestor, living or dead. And, did not care.

***

Benito brought me up to date on the shopping center preliminaries; he was ready to draw it up for the client meeting.

The solution showed a lot of imagination. Forthcoming battles with the building department were a certainty. I enjoyed the prospect of such differences of opinion and I made some mental notes for future reference. "Okay. Get it ready for Tuesday."

The office had an invitation to the grand opening of the first of the new chain of coffee shops. Cynthia had gone downtown to make sure there was actually a Certificate of Occupancy. I invited the staff to leave early if they wanted to partake.

I was tempted to call Jose on the Hill - just tempted.

Looking over Robbie's shoulder made me realize that I asked him to do too much. I looked around for someone with previous experience, Chuan was my go-to guy. I motioned him over, "One hour should do it." He showed some chagrin but I just ignored it.

At the end of the day, Chuan passed my desk, gave me a thumbs-up and offered me a container of some fried somethings. His Anglo live-in girlfriend was learning to cook native foods from Chuan's mother. Angelica interceded once he left, "I'll put those away for you Boss - the last ones I ate gave me cramps."

"Thanks. I'll get something to eat elsewhere." I hung around for a while, unfed, catching up with bulletins and code amendments and the like - necessary killing of time - then it was time to hit Costco.

11

In the parking lot, I spotted Jose who seemed to be loitering. When he saw me, we joined in the same course towards the store. I had a feeling this was not a coincidence. We stopped near a nest of shopping carts,

"We have a problem." I waited him out, and after looking around he told me, "There's a rumor that they're going to tear down the Hill."

"How did you know I'd be here?"

"Angelica says you're a regular. I took a chance."

"Tell me about the rumor."

"After all those inspections and tests, the info went to the Feds. The Feds agreed the building was a mess and beyond repair. The governor is going to take the heat off the local politicians and make the order."

"And, you know this, how?"

"The Latin Mafia is everywhere."

"Really?" I was dumfounded, but it was all believable. "When?"

"If you mean the demolition that could be way out there. The announcement could come any time. There's already a, 'stop work order' on the whole site."

"You want something to eat?"

***

"Do you always eat here?," Jose asked. We had settled in with our choices - my treat.

"Not always. I don't like to cook. Here, the food is fresh - a decent menu. There's no tipping. People are friendly - I'm never alone. The leftovers go home for the next meal."

"*Sin esposa;* You married?

"Not for a while."

"*Yo tampaco;* me neither."

"Kids?"

"Maybe - no one's after me at the moment."

"I have three - they're out on their own."

"Steady lady friend?"

"Friends - nothing steady."

"*Lo mismo*, same with me."

"I like to think it's the business."

"Iraq did me in."

His was the better answer. Living with: So-and-So has a new car; a new house, kids in the best schools and so forth is not the same as having your life in constant danger. What I did to make a living was extremely complicated, people's lives could be in jeopardy - there were many masters - it was a balancing act; day in, day out. There were many not so bright, lazy people that that had to be worked around. It was tiring. The rewards did not come often enough.

We left Costco, each ready to go in a separate direction.

"You like baseball?" Jose had paused to light a cigarette.

"Yes, I do. I enjoyed playing when I was a kid."

"Next week, a cousin will be in town, he has tickets to give away. I'll let you know."

***

Rush hour had long passed. I eased the Toyota into my parking spot - patted it's overheated hood and wished the car a good night's rest.

***

The announcement concerning the demolition of the Hill that was made at a press conference at the Capitol made the morning papers.

Upon my arrival at the office, it was difficult to open the door all the way due to the cluster of bodies just inside the entrance. The babble of voices I had heard as I approached the entry fell into complete silence.

"Good morning, Boss?, this from Murphy who was actually devoid of headgear and earphones.

"Anything wrong?"

"We going to be alright?"

It was unusual to have everyone in the same place at the same time."Yes. Give me some room to come inside and we'll talk about it." Angelica handed me a coffee, "I've lost buildings that I designed before." There was a sense of disbelief in the room, "Really."

I shepherded all of us into the drafting room, "There was the auto dealership that was burned down during the riots; and the just-completed small office building that was torn down to build an even larger structure. Listen - Frank Lloyd Wright had buildings torn down in his lifetime - it happens to the best of us." The group did not disperse. "We're not going out of business. Murph is back with us. We all have work to do."

To Murphy I said, "I need a debriefing." I decided for the time being not to be the lightning rod for everyones' economic concerns. "Let's have coffee downstairs." Murphy and I rode the elevator down in silence. A few of my fellow tenants gave me a thumbs up when we hit the lobby.

"You're not going to fire me are you, Boss?"

"No. Let's get that out of the way. The answer is no. Do you want coffee? We're down here for some privacy so you can tell me about your experiences at the Hill."

"No coffee. I actually learned a lot. I was terrified most of the time. The noise, and dust and always looking overhead was hard on me. Construction is really messy and dangerous."

I let Murphy get back his breath back, "Did you see any funny stuff going on?"

Funny stuff? In my very brief adult life I have not seen much of anything, funny or otherwise. I am an only child from a large family of seemingly infertile people. I was never out of someone's sight. It was determined early on I would be fashioned to be as close to pure American as possible. One of my uncles was an architect. I liked visiting his office and playing with all the special pencils and drawing instruments. When it came time for college, I was enrolled close to home and continued to live with my parents. School was pretty much the only time I was out of my family's supervision. I worked summers for my uncle while my classmates did Europe. I still live at home. My uncle found me my latest job so I could get better experience for my license. Studying Spanish with Angelica is fun but I'm sure that's not what Boss is talking about.

"Funny stuff?"

"People hanging around that looked like they didn't belong there; materials being carted away; workers not working .....?"

"The big crane was being taken apart. There was a temporary truck crane in use to do that. So, there were not that many workers on the job - no concrete came in - there were 'civilians' who, I was told, were, 'inspectors' - Jose was away one day because of a funeral - no one took his place. It was hard to tell who belonged. The inspectors took away pieces of concrete and boxes of stuff - the crane people took away parts of the crane - there was a lot of coming and going."

"Any idea about the, 'inspectors'?"

"They didn't sign in - I don't know who they were."

"No receipts for what was taken away?"

"I didn't see any."

"Okay, let's go back to work. See if you can give Benito a hand."

***

There were a few pertinent phone calls over the day - mostly of a nosy nature - not a peep from Lawyer Kline. I contemplated the lost revenue - it was not terrible - there were to be more buildings in the complex but I had learned a long time ago not to count on succeeding work. As to being involved in legal tangles that was another matter. I would need to read the report, more importantly, find out who wrote the report.

The office had been quiet all day - work was being done.

***

Over the next few days, the TV talk shows took over the discussion - the main theme being modern construction and how, "they don't build them like they used to." The newspapers did much the same. Lawsuits were filed - many lawsuits. As Jose said, "It's not going to happen soon." I sent a monthly bill to Cliff's company just as a matter of course.

***

It was time to make a presentation of our ideas for the shopping center that Benito had been working on. Saul would bring his minion so I had to add some firepower at the table. Of Saul's followers, the only one I had any respect for was the chief estimator. I added Robbie to bulk up our side of the table.

I managed to push the right buttons on the control device for the power point presentation and we began. The technique we used for presentations was by means of a series of illustrations, first displayed on the screen; the same artwork in hard copies pinned to the soft walls of the conference room for later viewing. Lights were greatly dimmed for the screen demonstration so the work on the wall could not be seen until later.

"We eschewed the usual strip mall and parking lot. We became nervous about what may be a historic building on the site and decided to save it, but in a special way. The neighborhood needs shopping choices of all kinds and that means diversity. Local businesses are important. We want it to be wide open and safe. Think of the building as a grand bazaar."

"It will be a simple structure, the roof will say it all. No decoration, lots of those new LED lights in various colors. polished concrete floors, prefabricated titanium panels for the exterior, a fabric roof. The tenants will construct their own facilities under the big tent. We would like to see use of discarded shipping containers. There will be tethered blimps to provide security cameras for the parking area and overall lighting for the site and space for advertising."

"The historic building, which was probably a church for free slaves, can be repaired and used as a small theatre, a community building or the like. With this scheme it will be out of the weather and much easier to maintain."

There were no immediate questions. The lights went on. Saul had not said anything and as a result none of his toadies went out on a limb. I offered, "Let's look at the boards on the wall; we're here to get your input so we can move ahead."

Benito offered. "Under the tent, you can do almost anything you want; you can build a conventional store if you choose, but much more simply be- cause you won't be exposed to the weather; utilities can be moved around in trenches below the floor; signage, lighting and the like can be set up in mini-blimps and moved around within the tent. A lot of these concepts have been tested in airports in the Middle East."

I added, "Much of this work can be done by experts; directly manufactured for this job - you will only be managers for most of the development. Components too large to be transported over the road can be delivered by blimp. It's a new world!"

The excitement I had expected did not occur.

Saul spoke for the first time, "We have to crunch the numbers."

That must have been a prearranged signal as the conference room quickly emptied. They left with some brochures we had made up so they had reference for further study. We numbered each brochure and marked the pages, 'Not for Construction."

We had learned that ideas traveled in a, 'New York minute.'

***

When the last of Saul's people were gone we listened to more silence.

Angelica came in to clear water bottles and the like, "It went well, right?"

"I have no idea." I went from board to board, "It's good work, maybe just not appreciated." That was my exit line.

***

A few hours later I had a call from Saul's cost estimator, "Tell me about these tents. First of all, could we get a permit? Are there any installations in this country? Who can I call that knows more?

"To USA installations of this size or planned permanency, the answer is no. The fabric is UL approved. The supporting structure would have to meet Code. It's a good idea to get some preliminary approval," not that you could trust anybody at the Building Department I thought. "I'll make some overseas calls."

Years ago, it was virtually unheard of to source materials or building systems from outside the Country; maybe some exotic marble but that's about it. Now, with cheaper labor in the third world, everything was up for grabs; whole assemblies could be fabricated and put on a 747, delivered cheaper than if made here at home.

12

Angelica handed me a small envelope, "Jose left this for you." The flap was not sealed. A ticket for tonight's much anticipated ball game was mine.

Angelica winked, "It's supposed to be a good one."

My favorite bar ran a bus to the games; I called and made a reservation. Ballpark food was the best next to Costco. Costco prices were much more reasonable; on the other hand it was a free ticket to the ball game.

I liked to get to the park early enough to watch the warm-ups. I would never miss the etiquette of the National

Anthem. My bus-mates were of the same mind. Standing above the section where my seat was located, I watched the TV monitor and the field simultaneously. I sang the Star Spangled Banner, lustily - I always became wet-eyed - I don't know why.

My grandparents came to the United States from European countries no longer in existence. I am sure it was emotionally difficult for them to leave home but their very lives were threatened. With barely a foothold here, they, 'went forth and multiplied.' A century-plus later, there is no trace of these ancestors. Europe has gone through two major wars and God knows how many other conflicts. Without the prudent exodus of these four people, I would not be standing here. Not even the futurists of their time could imagine the USA of this century. Like those early immigrants, there is no place I would rather live than home.

***

I gave an usher my ticket and soon spotted Jose and friends. I abstained from the perfunctory seat wiping by the usher, tipped and thanked the fellow, and worked my way into the row. The first batter was about to enter the box so I cut off the introductions for the time being. Jose told me everyone's names. I signaled the beer vendor and bought for all. I got into the moment.

Between innings, seats were exchanged back and forth until I was sitting between Jose and an attractive buxom woman of an uncertain age whose name I remembered as Maria.

"Maria is a cousin of mine. Our families go back to living on the same block in Havana."

"Cuba. I didn't realize that's where you're from?"

"You think all us Spanish-speakers come from Mexico?"

"Or, Puerto Rico, Guatemala, Honduras, El Salvador, South America.... Some of our local ball players are Commies as well; or at least they're here with the permission of the government."

"Best we stick with baseball." Jose had served in the US Marines - he was in the USA, safe and sound - I was certain he had family back in Cuba - the political system beyond their purview. He and Maria had heard it all before, I was sure.

"Pleased to meet you Maria; is it you I have to thank for the ticket?"

Maria smiled demurely, "It was our cousin," she pointed, motioning towards the overly lighted greensward below, "the right-fielder. He has a three year contract; he's a new capitalist."

"How about you, Maria - are you a capitalist?"

Maria glanced at Jose and he excused himself just at the seventh inning stretch began, "Jose tells me you're a capitalist."

"Some months that's true - it depends on the accounts receivable." Maria had not really answered my question, "So?"

"I travel back and forth."

"Between Capitalism and Communism or here and Havana?"

"Both."

"Uh-huh." This appeared to be a word game fueled by beer and the energized stadium still hot from the summer sun.

"I work for a non-profit."

"Uh-huh?" So, if I were to call you; would that be here in town?"

This gringo is toying with me. Jose said he was clever; that P I Torres never even got to 'first base.' The 'arquitecto' is checking out my 'tetas' waiting for me to give out my phone number. Perhaps it is time for plan B.

"I live in that high-rise," motioning beyond the scoreboard, "Come by for a drink."

"Some other time - I have to meet my bus-mates."

Jose returned with chili dogs and beer.

We won in the ninth, our pinch hitter scoring from second on a ground ball through the third baseman. The right fielder did not get the ball to home plate in time. I shook my head towards Jose and Maria, "Three year contract?"

I shook everyone's hand, and air-kissed the ladies; direct contact for Maria.

***

It seemed to take forever for the bus to get through traffic. It had been a long day. I left the car in the garage and had a taxi take me to the townhouse gate.

"I've just met a girl named Maria, and suddenly that name will never be the same to me.

***Maria!* "**

"I've just kissed a girl named Maria, and suddenly I've found how wonderful a sound can be! Maria!"

"Say it loud and there's music playing, say it soft and it's almost like praying. Maria!"

"Maria! Maria! Maria!"

Leonard Bernstein would be proud. Luckily, for my neighbors, the air conditioners were laboring away.

***

I sought my car at the usual early morning time forgetting that the Toyota was elsewhere.

"Do you have a dog?" It was one of my neighbors who kept the same schedule as myself.

I looked around, "Dog, what are you talking about, Ralph?"

"When I got home from the game last night," he said with a straight face as he put his car in reverse, "I heard you calling, Maria."

"And suddenly that name will never be the same to me - Maria! - Maria! - Maria!," I sang. "No dog, Ralph. "

***

I remembered the chili hot dog at the game being my only dinner. Ralph dropped me off at the diner - I would call a taxi from there.

13

The day ahead looked routine. Benito and Robbie were working on concepts for the law office. Several coffee shops were in various stages of development. The interiors person was doing what she did - I made a mental note to check her billings. It was too soon to hear from Saul about the shopping center. I put Chuan on a world-wide search concerning big tents.

"Saul on the phone, Boss."

"Good morning - that was a fruitful meeting the other day - what's up?" Saul was not that humor-filled, nor a great one to stay on subject and he did not function well without his side-kicks. "Can you come over after lunch?" "Should I bring anything?" The line was dead. His attention span had been exhausted.

The mail revealed our selection by the Feds for a year-long contract worth at least three hundred thousand dollars in fees, possibly renewable for another year. A meeting was required. Good news I hoped.

The first of the lawsuits involving the Hill was served by a guy wearing clown garb and carrying balloons - bad news for sure.

I swore to myself that I would not get upset. I didn't do anything wrong. That lasted about thirty seconds. Okay, breathe deeply, find out who else has been sued, hopefully all with deeper pockets. Read the lawsuit later. Stay calm for the day. Breathe deeply.

"Anything wrong Boss? Is that an invitation to a party? Maybe I shouldn't have let him in?" Angelica was trying to figure out whether to smile or not.

"Not a problem."

***

I left the office early and camped outside Saul's inner sanctum. Saul had an annoying habit of convening meetings earlier than the appointed time given to outsiders. This was supposed to put people like myself on the defensive. I ate my takeout lunch and listened, openly, to the annoyance of the secretaries, to all the various conversations with and about, boyfriends, parents, collection agencies, and the like - I thought I had a complicated life.

Saul appeared with lackeys in tow. The secretaries went into secretary mode. He ignored my presence. The cost estimator paused long enough to say, "Be right with you."

I recognized everyone including Saul's father-in-law - his presence was unusual as he was, by reputation, at his country club every day at this time. The pin-stripe-suit clad fellow in the corner with a yellow pad on his knee had to be a lawyer - him I did not know. Saul saw me staring, "You know Lawyer Kline, of course." offering this by way of an introduction.

Kline acknowledged me with a nod. He was younger then I imagined, his gruff voice on the phone did not match his demeanor. He sat hunched forward so as to observe everyone in the room and was otherwise expressionless.

Saul cleared his throat, "We have been spending a great deal of time on the prospects of the former stadium property. A preliminary prospectus prepared by our architect has created excitement for the Grand Bazaar."

There was nodding of heads - nothing from the father-in-law or the lawyer. I assumed I was the 'architect.'

"At first we believed that we could handle it all - development and construction - but our pockets are not quite deep enough even with a friendly bank or insurance company participating. There is always risk."

All heads were nodding in agreement.

"So, we have approached some potential partners. They will form a consortium. We will have minor participation but otherwise we will be the contractors on a cost plus basis." Saul addressed me, "We want you to be the architect."

"Who would I work for?"

"For us."

"Define us?"

"The consortium."

"Who exactly are they?"

"Can't say right now - we're still adding sources."

"No."

"It's an important job - it will put you on the map."

"It's still, no." I made rise to leave and Lawyer Kline did the same.

***

We met in the secretary pool. He directed the ladies to take a break and they scooted with purses in hand.

"I understand your position."

"Uh-huh."

"Saul isn't easily excited but in the case of the Grand Bazaar, he really sees the future."

"Uh huh." This was not going anywhere, "Do you have a real first name - I'm guessing it's not Lawyer?"

Kline looked around, "It's Shalom - my Mother was very religious - people think it's Arabic, which it can be - I just try to avoid all the ethnic references. My brother Yitzhak is Dentist Kline."

"Really?"

"Look, I didn't want to coerce you but Cliff wants you

on board."

I was stunned - this guy who I met once, for a few seconds - him with pitchfork in hand, wanted me on board?

"Do me a favor, stay with us for the time being."

"For me, this is strictly business. I'm not part of any consortium. My office will give you its best. I'll send bills at the end of the month and expect them to be paid by the tenth. Shalom - I'm with you for now." Perhaps I was too curt; we shook hands - I freed the ladies from their enforced cigarette break on the way out of the building.

Perhaps, perhaps what .... Perhaps we could do it all. We could steal some key employees, maybe from out of town. We would need those computers - then we could send work to India or China; have drawings worked on as we slept, even on weekends. All of this would have to be overseen. Now, I was the only one I would trust. Perhaps...

***

Lunch had not satisfied me. On the walk back to the office I stopped for coffee and a Danish. I nodded to one of the people from Saul's office. Being on board was a problem. I surmised that Lawyer Kline would soon occupy one of the new offices we were now planning. We were all in too close a proximity to each other. It would be cross fertilization of the worst kind. Cliff would be pulling strings from afar.

***

"Angelica, please find Allaine."

"I'll try - have to go on an interview in a few minutes, Boss."

"Okay - do your best." The desk was covered with lots of notes; many with smiley faces.

"We have him at lunch in Oregon - I'm leaving."

"Shalom."
"Aleikhem Shalom."

"No, that's Lawyer Kline's real first name. How goes the college search?"

"Really? I think we found it - Reed College - it's where Steve Jobs went to school."

"One semester. How's the food court?

"No food court - they grow their own vegetables and eat them raw."

"When can I talk to you - in person?"

"Tomorrow morning - meet me at the airport - I'm on the redeye - Shalom, really?"

***

I had to go through the paperwork, unanswered phone calls and the like. The drafting room needed to be addressed. Benito and Robbie had three good solutions for the law office. I still didn't think it was workable to present more then one. "Pick out the one that you think works best, hide the others for now and schedule a meeting."

I accepted a sample pound of coffee from Cynthia, a gift from our client.

Chuan had a stack of data on tents and tent material. "Make a summary."

Murphy was at a meeting. His hardhat was now hanging above his board, gathering dust. The contract with the Feds could provide some needed security. The Grand Bazaar had many hurdles standing between it and fruition - I didn't even want to imagine what could go wrong.

14

The terminal was dominated by maintenance personnel. Only a few counters were open for outgoing flights. People like myself yearned for coffee but none was to be found. There were sleepy eyed drivers with names held out on iPads, there to pick up scheduled fares and people like me gathered at the gate.

Allaine led the pack out of the arrival door somehow looking chipper.

"Where's your daughter?"

"Visiting with a cousin in LaLa Land."

"What do you want to do?"

"I have a hotel reservation here at the airport. We'll go there and have breakfast and talk."

"Where is home now?"

"With a cousin in town, but it's temporary."

I drove to the hotel while Allaine dozed off. We ordered room service. Both of us stretched out on each of the huge twin beds until the food arrived. We turned off the TV news, ordered another pot of coffee and went into business mode. Allaine just listened, occasionally scribbling on one of those freebie memo pads that come with the room . "And, that's all I know."

Allaine raised his eyebrows and looked out the window at the sunrise. The coffee arrived.

"What are you really going to do?"

"In for the dime; in for the dollar."

"You don't sound that enthusiastic."

"I would be more so if I knew you were involved?"

"It sounds like interesting work."

"You should have a separate contract."

Allaine nodded in agreement. His brother-in-law was the city's premier, 'gorilla in the room', among the local law professionals.

"You tell Saul I'm on board - I'll go see him in a few days."

"What do you think?"

"It could be fun."

I reluctantly raised myself up and put both feet on the floor.

"Do you want a ride to the office?"

"Give me a few minutes to shower and change clothes."

I noted his smallish roll-on for the first time, "Do you always travel so light?"

"My daughter has most of my stuff. She pays people to schlep for her like her Mother - her car's here at the airport - it's all laundry anyway."

***

We set out in the start of rush-hour traffic. Allaine dozed. He awakened when I hit the brakes too hard while I cursed out the adjoining driver who was applying eyeliner while using the rear view mirror and had drifted into my lane.

Our conversation continued, "I will need to add some staff; any suggestions?"

"It's a tough market." Allaine pondered, 'Okay, hear me out. I'm going to tell you about the Tucker boys - there's a set of twins and an older brother - I met them down in North Carolina last year - their father was the contractor on that big shopping center. The sons graduated from Tech - they studied architecture and building construction. They have some co-op experience. The old man thinks they're going to join the business but I think they have other ideas."

"Such as?"

"Such as, getting away from home."

"They come as a matched set?"

"That's what they have in mind. I told them that was going to be tough."

"Uh-huh."

"Any one taking all three could get them cheap."

"Is that a recommendation?"

"They're basically nice kids."

"But?"

"Let's just say you would have to give them time off on Lee-Jackson Day."

"Chuan takes off on Tet."

"These guys don't know from Tet; or Martin Luther King Day for that matter."

"But you would still recommend them?"

"It's a new world out there - I think they know that - it will take some adjustment. I know you are not too fond of sons of the Confederacy - something about people like those folks thinking we have horns - what is that all about anyway?"

"Do the Tucker boys have names?"

"The twins are Jeb and Nate, the oldest is Jubal."

"Real names?"

"James Ewell Brown Tucker and Nathan Bedford Tucker; and Jubal Early Tucker - I swear to God."

I honked the horn three times for no reason, "Give them a call and see if they are interested."

"I wish I was in the land of Cotton; old times there are not forgotten; Look away - Look away; Look Away ..... '"

After his numerous catnaps, Allaine removed himself from the car quite gingerly, "Keep in touch," this to his rapidly receding back.

I have lost hours of sleep for worse reasons. Right now it was best to look at my workload and try to imagine the stress, personal and business-wise. Talking to Allaine had helped.

***

Angelica met me in the lobby. "There's one of those people - he looks like that clown person - only he's not in a costume - he just looks like a bum - sort of scary. Murphy has him cornered."

We stepped out on the sidewalk. "It's okay - he's probably a process server. They come in all sizes and shapes. Send him down here with Murphy. "You did the right thing."

Once in the office with summons in hand I went over my messages and to-do list.

Angelica hovered. "That call from Jubba, or something like that - he was hard to follow - he talked very slow and funny - he didn't leave a number"

Allaine had done his thing. I was sure he was working on his contract as there was a call from Lawyer Kline to be answered as well. There was no more then the usual whispering coming from the drafting room which meant we were all getting accustomed to the oddball intruders.

"Shalom, Shalom," I now had Lawyer Kline's private phone number and did not have to go through his obsequious assistant, "you called?"

"Allaine's lawyer called. They have a contract to present. He's going to work directly for the consortium - is that alright with you?"

This was a good start - everyone was being polite, "We make a good team.'"

***

I called a fellow that I had met at a conference who taught in the architecture department at Tech, "Do you know some recent grads - last name Tucker?"

"Are you looking at one of them as an intern?"

"All three."

"Oh boy; the old man is a big giver to the school. He thought they were going home. You never heard anything from me; okay?"

"My lips are sealed."

"Together they are a piece of work - very smart - hard working - good students," he hesitated, "they have some funny social ideas."

"For example?"

"This is the South, man - I'm Chinese and that seemed to bother them - enough said."

"Do you enjoy teaching?'

"It's the life - you'll never catch me in an office ever

again. I'm due for a sabbatical next year ...."

I hung up on him - I was sure he understood.

There was a pile of resumes to go through and then I would make up my mind.

***

By mid-afternoon, I could not stay awake. "Go home, boss." Angelica had me nailed.

I had read all the resumes and nothing sparked my desire to ask for an interview. "Okay; one more phone call."

I had no phone number for the Tucker boys - they now lived at home - I didn't know where in North Carolina they actually lived - I could find the family construction company, but that was not a good idea. I called the registrar's office at Tech and cajoled a home phone number from a reluctant privacy nut. I decided to ask for Jubal, the elder.

Mrs. Tucker, it seemed, was expecting my call. "Allaine spoke to my husband's secretary," she explained, "we have our little secrets." Secrets came out in four syllables, "He's in the garden, I'll get him." I was catching on to the language.

I explained to Jubal who I was and asked that he and his brothers get to my office on Friday if they were interested and gave him my phone number. All this intrigue left me even more exhausted.

I ran into Judy who was locking Donovan's office door. "The boss told me to go home," she offered.

"That's where I'm headed as well - want some company before dinner?" There was tired and there was tired.

15

The Tuckers showed up promptly on Friday morning. Angelica brought a pot of coffee to the conference room. The boys openly admired Angelica showing that they still had plenty of energy left from their all-night drive. They introduced themselves. The twins were fraternal, easily distinguishable one from the other - while there were clear physical resemblances among the trio - each had a distinct demeanor. "Her name is Angelica." The boys blushed at being so obvious. "Thanks for coming up here - I'll cover your expenses of the trip, of course. Show me some of your work."

There were three separate rolls of drawings, and cartons filled with models. They took turns explaining what I was looking at. I asked a few questions. It was decent work for recent grads. I gave them a brief synopsis of the work underway in the office. The Grand Bazaar presentation was still on display. "That's our latest project - it has barely started."

They looked at every aspect of the presentation, commenting to themselves in soft whispers, ignoring my presence. "I'll show you the rest of the office." I walked them around to let them get the feel of the working atmosphere - I made no introductions. Back in the conference room I asked, "Any questions?"

Jubal appeared to be the spokesman, 'What would we do here exactly?'

"Anything and everything - we operate as a studio and share the efforts. In time, you can have my job if you want it. We will be receiving new computer equipment in a few days; state of the art I'm told. That will help us all. Would you like to talk about salary or benefits? You are welcome to hang out here for a while and discuss it among yourselves."

"We know what our friends are making and expect you'll do the same."

"Maybe. Make yourself at home. Angelica will bring in some forms for you to fill out so we can do a background check, credit check and so forth."

"At this, they acted surprised. "Nobody knows us around here."

I just smiled.

***

On Monday morning, I was greeted by Angelica in our office building lobby. "More clowns, Angelica?"

"No clowns. You have the Tuckers and their mother and a very, *importente hombre,* waiting in the conference room."

In the elevator ride up, I went through ludicrous permutations of the unplanned meeting awaiting me. I glanced into the drafting room to check attendance. Computers and accompanying gear were being unpacked and made ready. I entered the conference room where all conversation instantly stopped, "Good morning. Needless to say I was not expecting you this morning - I have spoken to Mrs. Tucker ..."

Before I could go further, she offered her hand, "This is Judge Beauregard, an old family friend. We apologize for coming unannounced."

All heads nodded in agreement. "What can I do for you?" I noted that the three young men were neatly dressed in coat and tie. I was not going to assume anything though inner paranoia advised me that judges were usually lawyers.

Jubal spoke up, "We did not know how to exactly deal with those forms you asked us to fill out on Friday - we asked Angelica if we could take them home and she said yes."

"And, you brought them back today?"

The judge spoke up, "We did, but the boys asked me to help preempt any information that you would gather. You are perfectly in your right to check out future employees - I did the same thing when I was practicing law."

I thought back to, '*Gone with the Wind*;' and my first exposure to genteel Southern colloquy. I waited him out.

"Young men sometimes do foolish things in their lives that they live to regret." He waited for me to concur. "You will find evidence of ill-advised use of an automobile, illegal drinking and a trail of bad debts, and other inappropriate behavior." He paused, "All of which have been dealt with."

I directed my answer straightaway to the three young men, "You have to understand that if you ever hope to become licensed, how you interact with society is taken into account. What we do affects people's lives in many ways. I will still draw the reports and if I find anything that I find truly reprehensible, I will not employ you. Give me a week. In the meantime you could make inquiry as to places to live, and so on, so that you could hit the ground running."

"Mrs. Tucker, it was pleasure to meet you in person. Judge, thank you for being so forthright."

All stood. We shook hands. The future architects looked longingly into the drafting room where the new computer equipment was being tested.

Inappropriate behavior - was I being a hypocrite? I thought about my high school years, driving around late at night with my new friend Willy. Willy was a towering presence, a star basketball player who would go on to play at the University. He was a fellow night-owl who did not want to be home. We discovered each other at the drive-in one night after closing hours. He had been abandoned there by his buddies and I had arrived too late for my post-midnight snack. We drove this way and that, the sun creeping over the horizon at last. An early opening PigglyWiggly was available for sustenance. On later nights we just drove around. Neither of us smoked or drank - we howled at the moon and that was enough.

***

Angelica was staring at me. "They'll be back." I think she had taken a shine to Nate. I have no idea how the female of the species culls from the herd.

The computer people were winding up. There were papers to sign. I was uncertain as to how I was going to pay them but they offered financing at a friendly rate and that was sufficient for now.

"Who were those hillbillies that were in here a couple of times?" This from Murphy as the last of the computer people departed.

Cynthia chimed in, "Looked like a few Klanners to me."

"Now - now, children remember how you all thought Chuan was strange when he first came to work here."

"Who thought I was strange - who?"

"I have some things I have to do - now," averting the discussion temporarily, "we'll get together at lunch."

Angelica caught me on my way back to my desk. "What's a Klanner - what's a hillbilly?"

"We will all learn more at lunch."

It was time to make some lists. If the Tuckers came to work, we would be bursting at the seams. That was both good and bad. There was plenty of work but I knew that not all projects went to fruition. Income could stop mid-stream. We needed to work as a team and be flexible enough to turn on a dime. Perhaps we needed company t-shirts. I was having a melt-down.

"Saul on the phone, Boss."

"Company t-shirts - do you think that's a good idea?"

Saul knew my voice well enough by now to ignore the t-shirt question. "Can you make a meeting late this afternoon - things are falling into place very fast."

"What time?" The line was dead. I would have to call his secretary for the time as well as the subject of the meeting. I got the information, entering the time a half-hour earlier in my calendar. I had nothing new on the Grand Bazaar to offer - I hated going into meetings unprepared.

***

Lunch started a little earlier than usual. Angelica had raided the petty cash to provide for me. There was some dancing around before we got to the subjects that were on everyone's mind.

"We have a lot of potential work, more then all of us can handle. The computers will make us more efficient but ....."

"Who said I was strange?" Chuan interrupted, and was ignored.

"Okay, you want to talk about the Tuckers." I gave them all I knew and how I had found them. I discussed my lack of success in finding new people through conventional channels; not really all I knew, as the reports had not come back.

"They still look like Klanners to me and I don't like how they were looking at Angelica."

I hesitated between "I am the boss here," and "You can't tell a book by its cover." I thought back to Management 101 and punted. "They're not hired yet - who brought the Baklava?"

They all got the hint.

***

I walked the several blocks to Saul's office, stopped for coffee, drank it on the way and arrived just in time for the meeting. Saul had not caught on that I had caught on to his timing scheme. The same crew as before had gathered in Saul's office. There was no father-in-law or Lawyer Kline. Allaine entered, just as Saul cleared his throat to start, having been tricked by Saul's propensity for telling different people different starting times based on some advantage only Saul foresaw. There were introductions. Saul took a phone call. We were off and running.

Allaine looked at me and shrugged his shoulders.

"We want to get started," Saul was cradling the telephone between his shoulder and his ear. "The concept has to be fleshed out. We hope to attract future tenants with some glossy magazine articles - free publicity. We need enough information so that the civil engineers can plan for site development. We plan to get permits a piece at a time. Let's all get to work." He returned to the phone call.

***

"That was worthwhile."

"Did you get a contract?"

"My brother-in-law made an appointment with Lawyer Kline; so far no response.

"What do you have?"

"The same - nada."

Allaine and I walked slowly down the hall of his offices, towards the exit stairs, hoping to intercept Saul by himself - that proved futile. We convened on the exit stair landing - Allaine was disgusted and wanted to talk. "My stockbroker tells me that, Grand Bazaar Ltd, is floating high interest bonds with big commissions for people like himself. Some Mid-Eastern prince has supposedly put up big bucks, sight unseen."

"Uh-huh."

"We should look at the prospectus, right?"

"Uh-huh."

"I'll get on it."

"Uh-huh."

"You're worried?"

"Mostly about why two grown men who are sitting on the unswept cold concrete of a stairway. Why were you at the stockbroker?"

"Cashing in some stocks. My daughter is going to college in Hawaii - the West Coast was not far enough away."

"Want to look at my new computers?"

"I'll pass."

***

The rest of the afternoon went quickly.

Angelica paused before leaving for the day, "Are you a hillbilly?"

"'*I was lost but now I'm found,*' I was never a Klanner if that's what you're worried about."

Costco beckoned.

16

It was time to address the tasks at hand. I scanned the job list to set the way. As far as I could see, the Hill was definitely dead. I would have to spend time with various authorities and their lawyers - I would not get paid for the last several months' work - it was as dead as it could be. The other jobs in the office were viable. I did not count the Grand Bazaar, necessarily, as being one of them. There was no contract. Some unseen force was propelling Saul forward - he was up to his old tricks as far as making a commitment - when the money stopped that would finish our efforts. Cliff was lingering in the background.

I had to decide whether to engage the Tuckers - they would be perfect for the Grand Bazaar. Back to the real world.

"Robbie, where do we stand with the lawyers?"

"We're ready for the meeting."

"And?"

"Benito and I are uncertain as to which alternative to call number one."

"Okay, bring them all to the conference room and we'll do it together. In the meantime call Ms. Jones and see how and where she wants our presentation."

"Cynthia - you sick of coffee yet?"

"I'm still at my one cup a day - otherwise I can't sleep."

"Where do we stand?"

"There are five more sites to go. Some of them are very tricky as far as meeting Code. The client is happy - his business is good. Free wi-fi is like a magnet."

"Need any help?"

There was no answer to that. Her enmity towards the Tuckers had not diminished.

I was not sure what brought Cynthia to town. Her school credentials were dubious but the letters of recommendation, based on work effort for people I knew, were impeccable. Her life was the story of two mothers - one at birth in the rural South, another, really an 'Aunt' who offered some opportunity for health care and education and a much better chance to survive to adulthood. This second life, was geographically above the Mason-Dixon line. Dixie had left it's scars as had maternal abandonment.

Susan was on the phone and leafing through a stack of drawings. She hung up the phone disgusted at herself, "I can't keep it all straight."

She was in charge of new residences and high-end remodeling of residences and apartments, "Too many pieces of paper, Susan?"

"And forms and calculations and bids, all of that."

"Aha, I'm going to help you. You are going to scan all the paperwork and drawings you consider important into our new computer system."

"I don't know how to do that."

"Not to worry. Ask Angelica to arrange for a work station to be set up at the empty desk next to yours. Keep cool - help is on the way."

Genevieve was on the phone, obviously a personal call, and turned her back on me so as to protect her privacy. I started going through drawings on her desk at which she became very defensive and hung up the phone with a, "I'll call you later."

"Gini," she hated that nickname, "I need for you to bring me up to date on what's on your plate."

"I'm still getting set up here."

For weeks, sales people had trooped through the office bringing catalogs and samples and spending time socializing with Genevieve. It was now obvious she had not even looked at the work I had assigned her. She was looking at the phone as if it might rescue her. I took it off the hook. "Here's the story - I gave you a chance to work here because you parents begged me to do so - your job at the department store was going nowhere. Having someone with your training was something I had been thinking about for a while. So, here's the scoop, Gini - from now on, all these samples and catalogs will be dumped at the front door - Angelica will be authorized to shoot any vendor who tries to get past that point - fill out a time sheet every day and put it on my desk when you leave. Stay around for lunch and meet your associates. Any questions?"

Chuan was hard at work and I left him alone. I asked Angelica to track down Murphy.

I motioned to Robbie and Benito to meet me in the conference room. We spread out the drawings they chose to call Scheme Alpha and handed me the program that they had developed as to personnel and ancillary spaces.

"Well, it works - it could work for anybody."

We looked at schemes Beta and Gamma that were innovative in placing personnel in work groups in a variety of ways. "We know nothing about these people - they are all new to each other - this is chaos."

"Okay, no fixed partitions - space out some bathrooms around the core - use scheme Alpha but show it in such a way that the partitions could be easily moved - use a lot of glass, a muted color scheme, otherwise natural wood. Paint the ceiling structure black. Feed all the wiring from the ceiling. Otherwise let the furniture do the talking."

I continued, "Create some vignettes - show happy-happy people. Set up a meeting."

"Nothing like kicking ass before lunch," I thought. There was still no real resolve to hire the Tuckers. I left the office with a notebook to map out, with no further input, what I saw as the rest of the year.

***

I got back to the office at the end of the day.

"Saul is looking for you - he wants to stop by."

"By himself - he never goes anywhere without his crew - do we have enough chairs?"

Angelica knew I was kidding, "He said he was on his way to meet his wife for dinner in the neighborhood - that's all I know." Saul didn't do 'social,' not with me anyway; this was already suspicious. "I didn't find Murphy," Angelica apologized; she paused, "I can borrow my brother's *pistola* if you like," she had obviously been talking to Genevieve. She smiled and left.

Saul arrived a few minutes later. He was carrying a brightly wrapped gift box. From underneath he produced a large manila envelope. "The small one is for you."

"And the other?"

"My wife is having a birthday dinner with some friends - really a bunch of rich bitches who have nothing else to do - I'm overdue." At this, he sat down. "That's your contract by the way - Allaine's went out by messenger." Saul made no move to leave. "Sometimes it's hard to breathe."

"You want to go to the ER?"

"You know the best thing I liked about diving?" He answered his own question, "When I climbed the ladder to the three meter board, I was wearing cotton in my ears because of my sinuses - I could hardly hear a thing - I knew what I wanted to do - it was me alone - I really didn't care what the judges thought. I can't wear those ear plugs anymore; and there are far too many judges." He stood, almost forgot his gift package, and left with no, 'take care.'

"Far too many judges indeed," I thought.

I picked up Chuan's report about tents and tent fabrics to make for reading at the pool.

Saul's contract tipped the scale on the question as to expanding the workforce. Developing the group into a neatly meshed team would be another matter altogether. Tomorrow, I would call the Tuckers and set a date for them to begin work. We had just enough for a softball team assuming everyone showed up - and also assuming we had the time and energy.

I was not lying to Jose - I had played baseball a long time ago - batted cleanup - stuck in right field where I could do t he least harm on defense. When it was discovered I was seriously near-sighted, the awkward eyeglasses destroyed my timing at bat - the taunting of my mother to be careful not to break the glasses - they cost a lot of money - threw me out of sports altogether. I was another four-eyed geek, a social outcast. In those days, eyes were not tested at school. To this day I wonder how many of my classmates walked around in a blur, their parents ignoring the plight because of the stigma or the cost of eyeglasses.

I returned from my baseball reverie and reminded myself that the reports concerning the Tuckers had not been received. I was doing the, 'cart before the horse' thing which had gotten me in trouble in the past.

17

The site for the Grand Bazaar was formidable. What it presented was an immense parking area that served the former football slash baseball stadium. The sports complex was to be demolished once plans for development were approved. Because of the stadium, a complex of roads had been put in place to get thousands of cars in and out in a short period of time. Luckily, too, water and sewer and electricity were in place.

There was no remorse concerning the stadium - it had been designed to serve both baseball and football and both sports were ill served as far as spectators were concerned. The church that had somehow wound up in the parking lot could be moved once again. This was the last site in the city of this quality that could possibly provide shopping choices to a large portion of the otherwise ill-served citizens. There would be new sources of tax revenue - it was a joke to consider the financial benefits of sports teams.

With contracts in hand, we had to start producing the enhanced preliminaries. There was a civil engineer to be engaged, borings to be ordered - Allaine could take care of the foundation criteria.

We needed high-tech aerial view renderings that would excite future tenants; and get our name in the paper and on TV. Our office was not capable of turning out that sort of work. Firms in New York thrived on this business. They were quite willing to remain anonymous leaving us with the credit for the work. Benito would enjoy working with them. Maybe I could send him up there for a few days.

I would send Saul's newly delivered contract to my attorney sight unseen. She would advise me if there were any emendations required - the final signed copy would be kept safely in her vault.

"Angelica, what's the story on those Tucker credit reports and so forth?

" I'll call."

"Please see if you can find Allaine?"

"His secretary says he is in Hawaii - she gave me a number."

"Aloha, compadre?"

"*Aloha oukou.* It's six o'clock in the morning here."

"You're picking up the lingo. Is this the final college visit?"

"Final for me. You wouldn't believe what things cost here."

"Your contract with Saul is allegedly at your office.

'Who's your pick for the civil?"

"Your call."

"Borings?"

"I'll take care of that. Did you hear the news?"

"Maybe not."

"Someone I know, who knows someone I know, who knows someone I know, says that the state has ordered demolition on the Hill - they're taking bids."

"Who pays for that?"

"Apparently, the owner has an insurance policy that covers it."

"What does the insurance company have to say?"

"They took it before a judge - the judge said, 'That's why you have insurance.'"

"Really? When?"

"Could be any day - my bet is on TNT R US."

"Uh huh."

"Hasta luego. Time for the all-you-can eat-breakfast and luau."

***

I would see what I could get done before lunch.

Angelica hovered, "The reports will be faxed to us tomorrow."

"Murphy?"

"He's due any minute."

"Those faxes are private - I'm the only one to read them." I didn't want any more turmoil concerning the Tuckers.

I put in a call to the civil engineers I wanted to work on the Grand Bazaar. Saul had burned a few bridges over the years - I knew there were some firms that would have no part of any project he was involved with. But, this was a big job - sometimes that overcame previous animus.

Murphy walked in at that moment. I raised my coffee cup and motioned in a way that he knew we would be getting together downstairs.

***

We sat in our usual corner. Murphy declined coffee. "We missed you of late?"

"Are you going to fire me, Boss?"

"No; should I? Where were you?"

"Walking around the city. I just walked. I saw neighborhoods I had never seen before. I haven't slept very much."

"What's on your mind?"

"My family is driving me crazy."

"How so?"

"All of them are old - I'm the only offspring of this generation - they are expecting great things of me - get married - make a lot of money - be famous - who knows?"

"What do you want to do?"

"I promised everyone I would finish school and get my license. After that, I'm not sure what I want to do."

"Okay, go upstairs - see if anything has to be done - go home and get some sleep. And, don't walk around the city at night - it's a dangerous place."

I knew how he felt. It was foolish to fulfill the expectations of others.

"Be yourself - not your idea of what you think somebody else's idea of yourself should be.'" I had no advice - none at all. Thoreau also is quoted, from his tenure at Walden Pond, "I learned this, at least, by my experiment: that if one advances confidently in the direction of his dreams, and endeavors to live the life which he has imagined, he will meet with a success unexpected in common hours."

One could hope. There is, however, a parable to be learned of Thoreau during his solitary life at Walden Pond concerning his walking home for Sunday dinner bringing his laundry for his Mother's ministrations. One could hope.

***

"The fax machine just beeped," Angelica announced.

I waited to read the reports in their entirety, exercising patience as each page dropped into the machine's tray. The reports recited a litany of teenage foolishness: DUIs, DWIs, 75mph in a 25mph zone, expired driver's license; even more serious follies: paternity suits, bounced checks, unauthorized use of credit cards. "No jail time," I thought. All had come to a halt six years ago or more indicating things had gone for the better once they were all at Tech. That, or the judge had done some expunging.

I resisted the temptation to flip a coin.

"Mrs. Tucker - the boy's around? I'll wait."

"Yes sir," it was Jubal.

"Ready to go to work?"

"Yes sir - we lined up an apartment after we saw you the last time."

"Okay, make it Monday - that will give us a few days to rearrange the office." We had never talked about money - I knew what the going rate was and I would match that. There would have to be some small raises for some of those already on staff in order to make things equitable. I was already spending money I didn't have. I wasn't even sure of the Tuckers' worth.

***

For the next two afternoons, we all quit early and moved furniture around and sent a lot of paper to dead storage. These efforts ran past quitting time - I compensated with pizza.

Cynthia mumbled under her breath the entire time - the others were more stoic. My scheme was to give Susan some help in the residential work, set Robbie free for the tenant office work; provide new help for Benito; and to start putting together construction details for the Grand Bazaar. Angelica might be leaving and I needed to fill that slot as well. As in the past, when needed, people would float. Most of my time would be spent on Saul's work and, hopefully, some new clients that would come in as a result of public relations.

***

On Saturday, I cleaned out my own, 'stable,' reflecting on the peace and quiet. I contemplated some socialization.

The phone rang, "I need food," Dodie gasped. "What I really need is money."

"Would dinner help?"

"In the morning, I would still need food and money."

"Dodie, you don't sound like you're in good shape?"

"I can't get a break," and at that she broke into long uncontrollable sobs.

It was obvious that yet another real estate deal had gone awry. I waited her out, "Listen, here's how I will help you. There's a pawn shop on your block; run by a guy named Max - go in there and he will give you some money on my behalf - I'll call him now."

"I don't have anything to pawn," and she started sobbing again.

"It's a loan and with it is this advice which is free - dust off your teaching certificate and get a job." Making the 'big kill' is not for everyone - the temptation is great but .....

I had tried it. Ten years ago, I got the fever. The real estate market was red hot. People who had little or no knowledge of development or construction were reaping the rewards. I optioned some dilapidated buildings in the path of the new market surge under very favorable terms, procured a construction loan from a bank anxious to do business, obtained building permits and became a contractor; all this while at the same time I was running my architectural office. It was an exceptionally stressful period of my life; financial loss and the destruction of my marriage came in with the tide. The marriage part was probably already on its way for a multitude of other reasons.

Dodie was still crying when I gently hung up the phone. It was time to watch a mindless baseball game at a bar where no one knew my name. I called Max and then wrote out a personal check ready to put in the mail in the lobby.

I watched far too much baseball from the West Coast and listened to far too many guys' woes about the, 'little woman' bringing me home in the wee hours.

***

According to Allaine's secretary, he was now in a time zone six plus hours away. I placed a call from bed, "Blimey, guv - what are you doing in London?"

"Besides eating great fish and chips and getting lost on the Tube, we are looking at schools."

"What happened to Hawaii?"

"Too boring - the Continent has more to offer - and her mother will still be an ocean away."

"You think this is it?"

"Probably - it's even more expensive then Hawaii."

"When will you be home?"

"A few days - certainly not a fortnight - whatever that is."

"We need to get together."

"Will give you a ring from the aerodrome - ta ta."

***

Sunday was lost. I would not swear that the sun came up. It would have been nice to be at the beach but one would have to get dressed and get in a car - my energy level was not that high.

I scrounged for food and finally decided that an earlier then normal breakfast at the diner would have to do.

18

I was very early in getting to the office. Manuel, the building maintenance man who opened the front door for me, made an exaggerated look at his pocket watch, shaking it several times, as I headed for the elevator. The Tucker boys arrived a few minutes later carrying an extra coffee, "Manuel said you were here."

The boys looked extremely tidy - coat and tie; fresh haircuts; shined shoes - there was also a hefty combined lunch bag.

In time, I introduced Nate to Susan, "Nate is going to work on the computer at the desk next to you; give him access to all the drawings you are now working on and some recent past jobs. Let him loose at your files - correspondence, notes and the like. The idea is to establish a system that will allow you to refer back to jobs, re-use details, general notes, schedules and the like. You are the boss. I'll check back with you this afternoon."

I faked a stop at Cynthia's desk with Jeb in tow, and wound up with Robbie, "Jeb is going to set up the computer for the law firm job. Let him look at past tenant work documents for this building. You are the boss. I'll check back with you this afternoon."

Benito knew he was next. "Jubal, we are at the beginning of a huge project; we need to improve upon what we have done to date. Work with Benito - get as much as you can on the computer. I'll check in with you at the end of the day. Benito's the boss."

So far; so good - everyone was conversing - Cynthia was talking to herself - I could guess what that was about.

There was a message from Max. He knew someone who knew someone who knew someone on the school board. "Dodie could get an interview very soon."

Mail and messages took the rest of the morning.

**

Angelica brought in a few extra chairs so we could all fit around the conference table.

There was the usual eyeing of what the other had brought. Mondays were especially salubrious because leftovers from weekend repasts and of course there were the offerings from Mrs. Tucker. "Oh, look Cynthia - grits, and I believe, turnip greens - we have to try those."

Cynthia was working on some foie gras brought in by Genevieve, "I would, except that's what I had for breakfast." She was smiling sweetly.

The Tuckers were eyeing the foie gras dubiously. "Mom sent some hushpuppies," Jubal offered.

Susan looked askance. Angelica finished her peanut butter and jelly and gathered up the remnants. Most of the leftovers seemed to be fried somethings produced by Chuan's girlfriend.

***

The afternoon was spent on scheduling. We were on target for the end of the month payroll-wise. I visited the three, 'teams', but said nothing. There were no questions. Angelica signaled me that Allaine was on the phone.

"*Bon giorno*"

"Have you made a side trip?"

"No, but I did receive a call from Pasquali"

"Are we both thinking about the same Pasquali?" Pasquali was the titular head of the unionized construction workers in town. It was rumored he was, 'connected.'

"Probably so. He says he heard from someone who knows someone who knows someone that tomorrow's the big day for the Hill."

"*La grande esplosione?*"

"*Si, grande*. Take some pictures. *Arrivederci.*"

This kind of work was usually done around sunrise. It could be fun. I went into the drafting room. "Big day at the Hill tomorrow. Get there by five am - wear old clothes, hard hat and goggles. Park behind the shopping center."

***

It would be sunrise in about thirty minutes. The staff came in ones and twos as far as the gate. There were a few people from Allaine's office. Jose arrived at the gate from the interior of the site. He intervened with a state trooper who was considering sending us away.

It was obvious that Jose was   surprised to see us. "How did you know?"

"We have our own Mafia." I explained

A taxi pulled up and disgorged Maria. Jose's attention was averted.

Traffic on the main road was very light this early in the morning; soon it would be halted. Yellow flags were waving at locations around the building, whistles and horns were blaring.

"What's going on Boss?" Murphy looked excited.

"That's the five minute warning - everyone on the building site is supposed to go to the control bunker."

"Then what happens?"

"There's dynamite wrapped around the buildings' columns. It's timed to go off - the interior ones first, then the ones on the outside. The building collapses into itself."

"I see red flags."

"Get set."

There were a series of explosions, not as loud as I expected - a huge cloud of dust hid everything from view just as the sun was rising behind us. The minutes passed by slowly as all strained to see the result through the air-borne grime.

"The buildings still there." Everyone agreed that was what they saw as well.

"What happened?"

"I don't know - I've only seen this in the newsreels." It was befuddling.

I took attendance in my mind just to make sure everyone was all right. Angelica, Susan and Genevieve stood together wrapped in colorful old sheets so as to escape the dust.

"There's nothing more to see. Let's head for the diner for a recap. My treat." The Tuckers were thinking of getting closer; - I shook my head to warn them off.

Jose and Maria were not immediately in sight. Traffic started to fill the main road. Two large black SUVs with darkened windows paused to take in the site. I spotted Maria just as she let herself into the front seat of the first SUV - they slowly drove away.

Sirens sounded in the distance. Satellite-dished vans bearing TV personnel were arriving.

***

At the diner we got a better view on the restaurant's TV monitors complete with talking-head explanations. Our fellow breakfast-goers showed their usual inattention except for the traffic reports. Two of Allaine's people, who I had seen at the Hill were in a booth away from our group and watched the TVs even more attentively. Jose's face appeared on one of the screens - he was being interviewed by an attractive, somewhat scantily-clad señorita from the local Spanish-speaking station. Chico came out of the kitchen with some newly fried donuts and dispensed them, on the house. I apologized to him for the extra dust we may have dragged in and he just shrugged. Everyone was in a festive mood and it wasn't even six am.

***

We actually started work early on the day. Angelica gave me the telephone signal indicating Allaine was on the line. I had no idea where he was calling from. There was a lot of background noise on the line. "Where are you?"

"On the plane. This is one of those ten dollars a minute calls. Meet me at the airport, the British Air VIP lounge at four o'clock." And, he hung up.

While the day started on an exciting note, all routinely settled in to work. There was a brief meeting with Ms. Jones and some of her fellow lawyers in the now totally vacant space. Jeb was introduced but he stayed in the background and took notes while Robbie handled things. Otherwise, there was nary a phone call concerning the Hill. I skipped lunch in the office and walked in the park settling in with a takeout sandwich.

***

I went to the airport early, stood in line at British Air counter and after showing the usual ID, received a special pass that allowed me to be escorted to the VIP lounge. I was settled in with a drink voucher in a secluded alcove. I was soon joined by a fellow in a TNT R US jump suit. We made general conversation and I learned he was an MIT graduate who took his line of work very seriously. We stayed away from talking about the Hill. We were soon joined by Pasquali who I recognized from some TV interviews. On TV, Pasquali was the champion of the working man, his diction that of the man on the street; his influence went beyond the trade unions he had amalgamated.

He immediately cashed in his drink voucher and the three of us talked about baseball.

Allaine arrived dragging his wheelie. "Okay what exactly happened out there yesterday morning?"

"The building didn't fall down."

" I know that. Why?"

The TNT R US man answered. "Without denying any blame, I would say the structure was in much better shape than was reported. I reviewed your documents, Allaine, and studied the report that brought me to the State in the first place. The explosives should have brought it down properly," this from a MIT man - short and concise.

Allaine pondered. "Do you have the report with you?"

"They took it back - said it was highly confidential."

"Aha,"some contemplation, "Okay, Pasquali, that's where you come in."

Pasquali was confused. "Why me?"

"Because your people are out of work and their competence has been besmirched. You will lose membership. Get me a copy of the report," Allaine advised.

"How am I going to do that?"

Allaine raised his eyebrows, turning to address the beautifully coifed suite hostess, "Can we get some snacks here?" He then proceeded to give us the details of his latest college trip.

We all inspected our watches - we exchanged business cards. Allaine caught a ride with his fellow engineer; Pasquali entered a town car, illegally parked at the curb - I retrieved my Toyota from the long-term lot and sought out the local Costco.

***

I went back to the office knowing that everyone was surely gone. Browsing through the drafting room did not reveal as much as it once did. Much of what I usually looked at was now zeroes and ones. Opening the employee's computer, assuming I knew what I was doing could be considered an invasion of privacy. There were probably already passwords in place.

There was a brand new computer on my desk. A note from Angelica gave me instructions on how to turn it on. The note also said that my password was, 'boss,' and that I could change it later. I had also been assigned an email address. I sensed Murphy had something to do with selecting the temporary password. Boss should have been capitalized but I realized I was entering the world of creative spelling and abbreviations - I would have to clamp down on that.

Now, more so then ever before, if I looked into the drafting room I was unable tell if work was being done - it was bad enough with the personal phone calls, and the earphones - I now had to compare paper with time sheets to know what was going on.

I fiddled with the keyboard and mouse, soon finding out that misspelled words were not ignored but instead led me astray, taking advantage of the error to take me to somewhere else in the ether. My day had started as an observer of a building that was supposed to blow up, but didn't, and ended up by being reluctantly thrown into a new world altogether.

19

"I have the report and a U-Haul full of boxes and crates full of pieces of concrete. Also, copies of x-rays and some other tests." This is how Allaine greeted me.

"Should I ask the source?"

"The report makes sense. It would depend on whether the samples and other exhibits support the report."

"The source?"

"A guy I know owes me a favor. I'm going to have some tests run."

"Why are you doing this?"

"The latest word is that they're going to knock the Hill down with a wrecking ball."

"Pretty tame compared to TNT."

"Thanks for your support - I'll get back to you."

Allaine was on some sort of vendetta. Why did he keep me in the loop - his loop?

Allaine had made a fortune taking some outrageous risks. The engineering firm was a hobby - a profitable hobby at that. The risks involved real estate, the basis of much of the big money in the City. There was a guy who claimed in his bio that his time working off the back of a trash truck led him to owning the premier downtown hotel. And, there were the owners of liquor stores with a huge cash flow that dabbled in developing office buildings. The government had grown so fast that money was being thrown away to get the simplest things done. Allaine had a new outlet for his energies and could afford to dabble.

Allaine called back a few hours later. "I had all the stuff hauled to my friend's lab. He did a preliminary look-see. The samples, and I quote, 'are not from any building constructed in the last fifty years - the x-rays are garbage,' end of quote."

"Now what?"

"I don't know exactly how to vindicate myself. I would have to explain how I got all this stuff that was in safekeeping in the state archives."

"How did you get it?"

"Pasquali. What do you think we should do?"

"I don't know about the 'we' part. Some insurance company is paying out millions. Follow the money." With this I excused myself from any further discussion. I looked up the word 'abet' in the dictionary - it means what I thought it did.

20

For me. the Hill was like a project that never happened. I ignored the various summonses to offer sworn testimony, the lawyers were seeing the whole debacle as an opportunity to bill more fees even though there was no place to go thereafter. I kept a broken piece of concrete, a residue of the day of the demolition, on a bookshelf near my desk as a personal souvenir. The building site would eventually be built upon; for the time being it was jinxed - some might say cursed.

***

After weeks of frustrating phone conversations, back and forth, we received official notification that a contract with the Feds would commence. A list of projects was produced giving brief descriptions of the work required and budgets for same. The locations included the City and jurisdictions within a hundred mile radius. There was no commonality in the work required - it appeared we had a series of wish lists all lumped into one package. Based on a superficial review, it was obvious there were projects with totally unrealistic budgets, the purpose of this being so the politicians could say, 'We tried but, nobody could handle it for the money you are willing to allocate; no one wanted to be involved." What I had to do was help them spend the three hundred thousand dollars in a years' time and keep everyone happy.

I met with the Feds, actually a committee of officials from various departments , to discuss schedules and resources. There are many depositories of building documents and even though much of the information had been reduced to microfilm the libraries that held them were vast and not necessarily close at hand. I learned what I could as to where information was available. What I really wanted to do was identify, among those attending, a true leader - a person I could get on the phone - someone who would avoid laborious reviews - who would okay payments and who would get the job done.

Over the next few days I squinted at microfilm, ordered copies when useful, visited sites, took many photos and tried to meet the person in charge of a particular facility. If I saw in the microfilms, work that had been done by a predecessor that was appropriate and still valid. I was not averse to copying.

This fieldwork allowed me to think of staffing at home. The addition of the computers and accompanying software was starting to change how we did things.

***

"Boss, where you been?" Murphy was considering my overnight bag.

"Give me a few minutes and I'll answer your question." What I needed was another me; perhaps the proverbial evil twin. Being out for several days had created a blizzard of paper work on my desk.

Angelica stood by with coffee. "The smallest pile is of the things only you can do; the rest of the stuff I can take care of if you just tell me how you want it handled."

I noticed she had on her interview ensemble. "Another meeting?"

"Still working on money for school - it's going to take a while."

I made a general announcement to the drafting room. "Meeting before lunch today - say eleven thirty."

It was time to round up consultants. The civil engineering industry had produced a majority of prima donnas, this circumstance because of all the new environmental issues that needed to be addressed and the lack of trained professionals to handle the bureaucratic process. Fees had gone out of sight as the engineers took all the time they needed to joust with various departments of the government. Over the last several years I had worked with some young guys, part of a big firm, who had privately expressed the desire to go out on their own. I called, and left an innocuous message for one of them, ignoring the nosey secretary's, "Will he know what this is about?"

I tackled the paperwork, handing off a piece at a time and was soon interrupted by a conversational buzz from the conference room. I had made no notes as to what I wanted to say but I was among friends that would forgive pauses to hit my brain's restart button.

"Okay - lunch will start soon enough - I want to bring you all up to date on our work load.The latest news is that we have a contract with the Feds for a variety of jobs, all sizes, all types of work. We will divide this up according to your interests to start, then assign the work to get it done."

"What kind of jobs, Boss?"

"It's a mixed bag - mostly remodeling - some military - all different kinds of uses. Some interesting problems to be solved and perhaps not solved. You will learn how your government works - that's for sure. Angelica will print out the list."

"Why are we doing this sort of stuff anyway?" Genevieve's wrinkled nose expressed a look of disdain.

"It's bread and butter for our table, so to speak; the income allows us to do really interesting work, spending more time to come up with an award-winner that enhances our reputation. Any experience at this time in your careers is worthwhile." There were more dubious looks. "Most of my time will be taken up with the Grand Bazaar and shuffling paper for everything else. The problem with this business is that any job could be called off for any reason at any time; we need to be flexible and take in more than we can logically handle and hope for the best." This sort of leadership was not my forte. "Okay let's do lunch."

Lunch was a little more solemn then usual. I left after a few minutes, taking most of Chuan's girlfriends' inedible offerings of the day with me directly to the men's room.

***

I would wait a day to see how the list could be divided based on everyone's input. I thought about the running of the office. Can it be both a Democracy and a Republic?

In graduate school I took an elective course in labor slash management relations and was surprised to find out that salary was way down on the list in regard to employee satisfaction. At present, most of my people were young. They had survived a rigorous educational program and had not diverted to other occupations. Obtaining a state license allowed one to use the title, 'architect' - nothing less was sufficient to practice independently.

I finished school and married the same year. For reasons known only to my wife's family, it was thought that now that my lark was over; it was time to enter the grocery business and the only way this could be done would be from the ground up, just as they had. On the other side of my family, my efforts were considered close to useless - there was no money to be made - the ones with names in my pending profession were ivy-leagued blue bloods, dabbling if you will - and besides there were all those crude construction people; foreigners and the like.

In my own way, I was stubborn. Family advice ignored - I was on my own.

21

The Grand Bazaar project was coming together. It turned out that the civil engineers I liked had already committed to going out on their own and, for them, the chance to work on the Grand Bazaar was icing on the cake. The three principals were extremely enthusiastic. They came to the office and looked over all the preliminary documents and within a few days had prepared a proposal.

The destruction of the stadium complex had begun. There were few sentimental takers for the various sports paraphernalia - the teams were little loved and memories of long nights of poor performances created pitiful nostalgia.

We had made contact with the Italian manufacturer of the tent roof enclosure of an airport terminal in Saudi Arabia.

Saul's development people were marketing the site to, 'bricks and mortar' businesses as well as on-line merchandisers who might want to be in on the latest concept in shopping centers.

Our new computers allowed us to look at various forms for the roof. Drawings went back and forth via the internet to the company in Milan. While we slept, the tent material manufacturer was able to scrutinize designs and make suggestions.

I was constantly sniffing the air to make sure that the monies for our efforts were forthcoming. Our accounting firm had stepped in and instituted new procedures suggesting that it was necessary to do so to avoid, 'chaos.'

***

At the next pre-lunch meeting, the staff and I went over the Feds wish list towards the purpose of dividing up the projects. I had previously gone over the list and eliminated several for being unrealistic, budget-wise.

"The list is shorter now but, with these sort of contracts, new projects can be added. Also, one year can expand into two or more."

"Boss, this stuff is really dull."

"Did you see that movie - the one with the two architects, Butch and Sundance? In the finale, they're defending their design from the critics represented by the entire Mexican Army. That shows you how exciting architecture can be."

Chuan looked perplexed, "I didn't know they were architects."

"The movie is an allegory - I'll explain it to you later," Cynthia sniggered.

"Look, no one promised you excitement. You solve complicated problems, meet interesting people; see your ideas go from paper to reality, provide for the needs of humanity ....." I was on a rant, "Let's split up this list."

The Tuckers liked everything, 'military.'

Susan wanted to stay with housing including anything on military bases. The Tuckers agreed.

Chuan and Cynthia liked the health and science related projects. Robbie would handle administrative uses.

Murphy indicated his willingness to work on anything, "I need the experience."

Genevieve wanted a hand in all color selections, interiors and the like. Robbie looked confused and I told him to float.

Benito sniffed the air and he was excused to devote full time to The Grand Bazaar.

I double-checked the list. There was something at a sewage treatment plant and I took that for myself.

***

Lunch was more amicable than usual. Robbie mentioned an inspection of the law offices tenant work and I told him to grab me for the walk-through. Saul's office had called and scheduled an end of the day meeting. The law office being under construction took me by surprise. I did not remember signing the building permit drawings.

I walked around, separately from Robbie and Ms. Jones and handful of lawyers. It was hard to critique. Furniture had yet to come. The space needed people and artwork and books and signs of utility. Ms. Jones broke off and we shook hands. She passed over a check, not quite yet due, and thanked me for the 'good work.' There was nothing like a happy client paid up to date. I found a set of building permit drawings in an alcove maintained by the contractor - the signature was mine but the moment of signing I could not recall.

***

Angelica and I sorted through the new work, setting up job titles and other references.

***

When it was time to go to Saul's, I decided to walk. It was hot and I stopped a few times to take in some free air conditioning. Saul's office had the most number of gatekeepers I had ever encountered. I found all this posturing quite unpleasant. I went to the kitchenette to help myself to water and kept going so as to penetrate the inner sanctum. I did not get a great sense of organization. Soon, one of the secretaries who was obviously looking for me caught up, just as Saul and entourage appeared heading towards his office. I joined the parade.

The heat and then sudden change to excessively cold air conditioning had left me unsettled. I had no idea what this meeting was to be about. Saul's father-in-law was in attendance. Lawyer Kline sat in a corner, yellow legal pad at the ready. There was no sign of an agenda.

After an hour, every one rose to quit the office, I still had no idea what had transpired nor what the meeting was supposed to be about. Nothing came up that demanded my input and I offered nothing to the general give and go. I walked out of the office, with Saul a few yards ahead of me, both of us heading towards the men's room. When I entered the restroom I was by myself - Saul seemed to have disappeared. The access door to the exit stairs was immediately adjacent and I opened it thinking it led to elsewhere in the building. Saul was sitting on the same steps that Allaine and I had used for a previous impromptu meeting. He was staring into space and barely acknowledged my presence. I sat down a few steps below.

"I think my father-in-law is certifiable."

"I must say I didn't follow the discourse during the meeting very well."

"He tells me that the company is mine to run but he and his cronies at the country club have me on remote control. Here at the office, we need fewer old-time construction foremen and more MBAs."

"You could quit?"

"My wife would walk out - she lives for the money and her schoolgirl playmates. I would lose the kids." I was sympathetic with that - very much so. If he was looking for advice, I was not the source.

"Got to go - another meeting."

Saul's father-in-law had once told me that, "Architects are a dime a dozen," which had not helped my self esteem. The cold concrete of the steps was warning my waning rear end to move on.

I bid a loud farewell to the secretarial pool, temporarily interrupting the various personal phone calls, and hit the all-day heated sidewalk. I stopped for an iced coffee and a chance to recoup. The Grand Bazaar held me in its throes.

***

The office had emptied out. There was a knock at the door and Judy came in with beers in hand. We mused about the weather.

"Do you think my ass is getting boney?"

"There's only one way to find out."

22

The heat of the day was shimmering through the blinds. After reading all the Sunday newspapers, I ventured out to drive aimlessly around the city. One of the most redeeming features of the Toyota was its air conditioning system. The classical music stations of old were gone - CD's had taken their place. There was no longer the soothing voice from the radio to remind me of the time of day. The car seemed to know the way. I had not done this sort of meandering in a while. Neighborhoods had changed - old landmarks cropped up to keep me oriented. Deterioration seemed to be in retreat. The ladies in their long skirts and ruffled, starched white blouses, heads topped with outlandish flowery hats, walking to church, were always a sight to behold. A few fire hydrants were open in the older row-housed areas; the water steamed against the heated pavement and parked cars - impromptu blockades were in place - children scampered in the street under the watchful eyes of adults - coffee and cool drinks were being nursed. I parked at the Bluffs above the river looking down on the city.

Saul was right - the building industry of today needed different sorts of personnel - MBA's and the like. Day to day operation could not be done by remote control. Relationships were important. There needed to be a chain of command. Meetings needed agendas, time limits and written minutes. My own self- taught management style needed to be upgraded.

My stomach grumbled. I thought about my choices for sustenance on the mental route of the way home. Church was letting out and I needed to pay attention to the Sunday drivers who were given special dispensation as to parking. The neatly dressed pedestrians seemed happy, the sins of the week past washed away - the children eyed the fire hydrants now monitored by City personnel. I found a hole-in-the-wall eatery that I remembered as having sea bass - a place at the counter was just fine - the fish perfectly cooked with lemon and butter. The mood of a work-free torrid Sunday pervaded the small restaurant. There was talk between strangers about the previous evening's baseball game. The opinions of the new Cuban right-fielder varied. Back in the car again, the streets were free of pedestrians; cars at the curb, with their radios aloud, were being washed and groomed - stray dogs lazed in the shade of century old elms, the cool earth providing a reprieve. I took the infusion of good will and neatness of purpose of the Sabbath day home with me.

***

The need to get a start on the coming week led me to the dining room table and the making of lists. I noticed the telephone's answering service blinking for the first time.

Allaine's voice, "Confusion ahead. Over the weekend, Saul's father-in-law had an incident on the golf course." The definition of, 'incident' was up to me, I would guess.

***

By the time I got to the office the next morning, there were several more messages concerning Saul's father-in-law. The incident was a precursor to a funeral that was now scheduled for later this morning. There were more messages to the effect that the funeral was private but there would be a memorial service afterwards; time and place to be announced.

I wrote a personal note to Saul and his wife. Memorial services were like zoos during a holiday; too many strange people in a confined space.

***

Allaine, of course, went to the service.

"So what was it like - did they cut off your tie?"

"I have a drawer full of ties for funerals. I pick them up at yard sales."

"Any speeches that I could draw inspiration from?"

"You don't play golf - it would be hard to explain."

"Uh-huh."

"This may disturb you, however. Someone who knows someone who knows someone tells me that Saul's wife actually inherits the business." I hung up. There was only so much I could handle.

***

Angelica was staring at me, coffee cup in hand. I thanked her for the coffee and silently indicated that I was going to review the paperwork on my desk.

Actually, I just sat there. Then I called the civil engineers; they did not seem to be worried; likewise, for Allaine's people. So, why was I worried? Maybe it was that meeting with Saul in the stairwell.

23

"Benito, you're on your own - full speed ahead but do not pull anyone else in the office away from what they're doing.

Print out what you have done to date and put the drawings on my desk. Call the tent guy in Milan - have him send all the drawings he has done to date. Print those out as well."

***

I bailed out of the office and drove to the site of the Grand Bazaar. From the top of one of the closed off access ramps, I took in the work in progress of clearing the area. The church structure was jacked up on cribbing and stood ready to be moved. The church had been offered for sale for one dollar but so far there were no takers. Construction trailers were in place and more were being added. Survey crews were confirming information taken by satellite. A boring rig was at work. Asphalt paving was being ripped up and sent to paving companies to be recycled.

I convinced the security guard as to who I was and I drove down to the cluster of construction trailers. I knocked on the door and entered the most important appearing trailer.

"*Nos encontremos de nuevo?*" Sure enough, it was Jose from the Hill.

"*Al igual que una moneda falsa,*" Jose offered his hand in greeting rising out of his chair rescued from the Hill.

"Who are you working for?"

"For the time being I'm the chief honcho as long as there is concrete to be poured."

"Anything I should know?"

"No, I'm doing what the main office tells me to get done. No surprises."

Switching gears, "Any repercussions from the Hill?"

"Nothing that affects me."

Shifting again, "How's Maria?"

Jose knew I was digging deeper than projects past and present. "Back in Cuba, I think."

"Uh-huh."

"I don't see anyone working on the demolition of the stadium?"

"They're ahead of schedule."

"Uh-huh."

I borrowed the key to the church off the trailer key board, "I'll bring it right back."

I walked over to the church and opened a padlock that let me in through a side door and into the sanctuary. The interior was a single room, more a chapel than a church, ceiling following the slope of the roof, with a small balcony over the main entrance, roughened cream painted plaster and natural oak trim, original first growth wood floor, no decoration or religious symbols, the windows ungarnished plain frosted glass. My suspicions about the building starting life as a synagogue were confirmed by the aura I sensed when standing below what was probably the original 'bema.' It may have been the first synagogue in the City.

***

Driving back to the office, I thought about what could be done with the 'church' and tried to recall the name of an urban archeologist that owed me a favor.

***

I was on the line with the local historian, "We know the building - it keeps moving around." A polite laugh, "I didn't know it was now in the stadium area. It is, or was, a synagogue, built around 1840 to serve a religious enclave up on the Bluffs. The congregation moved into the downtown just before the Civil War. A group of Shakers took over the building to use as a hospital during the war and then they moved on; it became abandoned for a short time and then served a congregation of freed slaves. That African-American congregation morphed over the years. I'm not sure who actually owns the building nor is there any record as to who moved it. Someone has performed maintenance during all this time or else the building would have collapsed. As a religious facility, it pays no taxes so there are none of those sort of records. The church always seems to wind up in the corner of some public property so the City thinks some Federal Agency is involved or vice versa." He added, again with a polite laugh, "Now that we know where it is, 'today' we'll keep an eye on it."

"My client is offering to sell it for a dollar."

"Sounds like a good deal. Am not sure it will be that easy to find a piece of land to put it on, however. If it is to be a place of assembly, it would have to meet all the current codes. Our Society could place it on the register and there could be some tax breaks."

He was right. The paint on the building was in good shape; likewise, the windows and roof were serviceable - the interior was dusty but otherwise clean. I thanked the pleasant gentlemen, made some notes and set up a file - where I was going with this was a mystery to me.

I left a phone message for Jose telling him that the 'church' was to be protected.

***

"Those drawings you asked for are in the conference room - also, the latest from Milan." Benito was on his way out the door with the rest of the staff following suit.

The office was as well organized as I could have only imagined several months ago. I could devote most of my time to the Grand Bazaar - the old synagogue was a diversion.

24

I looked over the project roster. Work was moving along, or so I hoped but - it was best to see and hear first hand. The Tuckers were my chief concern so I started with them.

"Them Army bases are really cool." Jubal was reporting on the largest of the military projects.

I decided to ignore the grammar problem for now and just admire his enthusiasm. "How so?"

"There's all those folks marching around - some of them are girls - and there's the helicopters landing every which way - and lots of guns."

"Lots of guns," Nate chimed in.

"Major something another takes us around. We ate in the mess hall."

"Learn names. It's important. Tell me what's going on - here at the office."

"The job description calls for a new barracks building - for NCO's, both men and women. The temptation is to make it like a motel but we have a better idea."

I put up my hand as would a traffic cop. "You are dealing with the Department of Defense, DOD for short - get used to acronyms; the government loves them. And, we have this job today because several eons ago the DOD put their act together and obtained permission from Congress; the President concurred. Our President is also the commander-in-chief. Think of the chain-of-command all the way back from the Prez to Major whats-his- name. You will not live long enough to see your 'better ideas' even considered. Stay the course. What else you got?"

I had some of my own memories of the military, specifically the Army. Losing my student deferment, upon graduating architecture school, brought me to the top of the

Selective Service most-wanted list. I joined my local National Guard unit to theoretically reduce my exposure. The basic training unit at Fort Knox was full of people like me. Many had recently left college because of poor grades; there were some high schoolers who just wanted to get it all out of the way; and there were recently signed professional football players who did not want their careers interrupted - we were all reluctant warriors. The Army knew who they were dealing with and assigned leaders with some sense of humor and enough instinct to keep us from firing an M-1 into one another's foot or worse.

Back in Appalachia, the authority of the military translated to the familiar, 'not-one-of-us.' So much for the fellowship of the common cause - my sense of trust never returned.

"Boss - you okay?"

I had drifted. It was not the first time of late. "I am. Print out what you have done to date for the new barracks."

"We can't seem to get the other jobs going."

"That happens. The locals don't agree with the scope of work - not a big enough budget or don't want to do it at all, or some other reason - give me the list and the names of who you talked to." I needed closure. "And, the female soldiers are women, not girls. You will soon run into more than a few with a lot of authority.

I wanted to do more but felt weary. The documents for the Grand Bazaar lay before me. The designers in Milan had really produced.

Angelica hovered. "Saul called." The number on the slip of paper was not a familiar one.

The phone was picked up on the first ring but with no greeting. "Saul? "

"Just wanted to make sure it was someone I knew." The voice echoed.

"Where are you?"

"In my new conference room, next to the men's toilet where you and I met the last time."

"I beg your pardon?"

"Things have been hasty since my father-in-law died."

"Uh-huh."

"My wife is moving fast. She has a brother, a total loser, who she has put in charge of the company. She tells me to, 'hang in there' as she sorts out her inheritance."

"Speaking for myself, that does not sound good."

"I'm still on the payroll."

"I'm speaking specifically about the Grand Bazaar."

"I don't think she has a clue. I'm still the only contact with the investors - through Lawyer Kline."

I had no idea what to do - Calling Allaine was a   possibility - he probably already knew all the details. "Why don't you take a few days off - go to the beach and clear your head. Let the dust settle." Two cliches should do it.

Angelica was hovering again. "Call Allaine."

"The brother-in-law is a real nogoodnick."

"Should I guess who you're talking about?"

"I'm taking a few days off - going to the beach."

"Uh-huh."

"By the way, chappie, my daughter was accepted to the London School of Economics; I didn't know she had it in her."

"Congrats. Ta-ta."

The beach, why didn't I think of that?

25

Someday, going to the beach will be like Star Trek, rearranging the body's molecules in a transporter and depositing them at the surf line of a chosen ocean. For now, the drive was necessary. The Toyota knew the way; even knew the cheapest gas station on the route. I kept a bag with beach clothes and sundries in the Toyota's trunk. Otherwise, all I needed was a credit card.

My thoughts wandered back to the doctor's appointment made for me the previous day. Angelica, in her role as mother hen had found me staring into space after my abbreviated review of the work in progress and subsequent telephone call from Allaine:

"You don't look so good Boss - maybe you should see your doctor?"

I could not confirm that I felt ill, "I've run out of doctors, Angelica."

"There's a new practice in the building - down in the arcade." She was checking a flyer on her desk and dialing the phone. "They can see you."

"When?"

"Now, if you want?" She was opening the office door.

***

How many times had I filled out the history questionnaire the receptionist handed to me? My weight was down; I was shorter than when I remembered; blood pressure was at all time low - I felt like the incredible shrinking man.

I found myself gawking at the usual framed documentation on the wall as the doctor reviewed the questionnaire. 'University of Chicago, Georgetown School of Medicine, State License in Internal Medicine,' - the name on each indicated a female but the person sitting before me appeared to be of the opposite gender.

"Should I guess what you're thinking?"

"Is there an extra charge?"

"I am a lesbian - does that bother you?

"I'm a heterosexual - how do you stand on that?"

"Some of my best friends are straight." She paused, "I think we can skip the cognition exam." The stethoscope came out.

"Breathe deeply."

"And?"

"We're going to draw some blood, take a few x-rays - the usual stuff - I'll call you.

***

The traffic brought me back to the moment. I was soon coasting into the parking lot of my usual hotel. There was no need to change clothes. I patrolled the boardwalk, breathing in the salt flavored air; watching the sun recede and the throngs diminish, signaling dinner time. Perched on a coveted bar stool at the, *Smoking Dog,* I nursed a draft, munched on chips, telling myself that I had all the food groups covered. There were no revelations as to the world I just left. Out of the corner of my eye I spotted Beth just as she spotted me.

"I've been looking for you."

"Here I am."

"Party tonight - here's the address. No three-buck chuck this time. Give me two twenties. One of the Jacksons is for your friend." At this, she motioned to the back of the 'Dog' where Saul sat, half hidden by a fake palm tree.

I nodded to Saul, but he chose to stay put. He could use the solitude.

There was a few hours to go and I used the time to watch the after dinner parade. I needed to shower and change clothes and little else.

***

The party was in one of the beach's newest high rises. The view from the top floor apartment's continuous balcony was of sand and water as far as the eye could see. The warning lights of returning sailboats twinkled at the horizon; otherwise there was no sign of man's transgression on this part of the world.

Unobtrusive jazz emanated from hidden speakers; soft lighting displayed academic seascapes on pastel colored walls; simple contemporary furniture was scattered about in a minimalist manner - the high ceilinged room was a place for relaxed socialization. The two twenties had provided for elegant food and wine though I think my contribution was a minute part of the whole.

Beth introduced me to the hostess, a gracious, perfectly groomed woman of undetermined age, clothed in what I assumed was the latest after-six beach wear in gradations of white, displaying a healthy tan that I imagined uniformly covered all beneath her attire; no jewelry, no wedding ring, "Beth and I go back to college days."

"We were neighbors at one time - she looks after my interests here at the beach." I was not sure what I meant by that,

"You have a beautiful home here."

"Three divorces later, I finally got it right."

There was bait there, but I was unsure what to do with it, but spotting new guests, "Thanks for the invite - I'm going to mingle."

I located Saul talking intensely to an attractive petite female. I left them alone.

Circling the room and balcony, I soon realized there was someone in my wake.

"Unless you get a better offer, I'm staying the night, in the suite at the end of the hall," Beth motioned towards a discreet passage, and then turned back to some newly arrived guests

I was watching the moon rise. I thought about Greece. How long ago had it been? How much longer had the moon brought this sense of wonderment to mankind? The illusion embraced me - I wanted to bray.

**

Saul appeared on the balcony - alone.

"How did you get away?"

"Big, unannounced family powwow - I excused myself.

"Uh-huh - who is she?"

"We went to college together - she was on the women's swim team."

"Divorced, widowed, married, single, gay?"

"All of the above - maybe - she appears to morph as the situation suits her."

"What's in it for you?"

"I may be able to morph myself."

**

The evening gathered even more merry makers, many tipsy from other social gatherings along the boardwalk. The discreet jazz lost out to the circumspect ballads of yesteryear offering opportunity for couples to embrace in the appearance of dancing as prelude to something more.

For me, there were also some same embraces. Beth cut in on a loosely clad woozy partner, "Now?"

"Now." We headed towards her suite.

**

It was pre-dawn as I padded to the balcony. I smelled coffee. Newly arrived food was available in the kitchen. My hostess, in an abbreviated robe, was apparently the only other person up and about, leaning over the balcony railing to take in the sun's first lighted scene below. Thinking there was something of actual interest, I joined her, probably closer than necessary.

She turned and took me in over the rim of her coffee cup, "Sleep well?"

"You know the story about sleeping in a strange bed."

"Or, not sleeping. Try the coffee - it's my special blend."

When I returned with the ballyhooed brew, my hostess had stripped,

"Early morning sun is the best to maintain a tan."

The moment was inspiring. I went back to the suite to say a belated goodbye to Beth.

***

The drive home was uneventful. Despite having to reverse course and utilize a narrow, potholed service road, I stopped to eat and have the Toyota filled with bargain gas. My favorite diner had room for one more.

***

Once home, I ignored the Sunday paper, at the welcome mat, with the banner headline - "THREE PART SERIES STARTING TOMORROW - THE REAL ESTATE INDUSTRY IN CRISIS," and went to bed .

Dreams came in fits and starts. The struggle between Hedonism and Responsibility was waged over various battle-fields - I watched it all from my ivory tower. My new doctor appeared in a supporting role. There was a cast of thousands. It was in 3-D, no special glasses required.

Then, the alarm went off.

26

Angelica's offer of coffee was in a paper cup from the shop in the building lobby. "Is there something wrong with our machine?"

"It's being replaced with a super deluxe, 'Chico' model - there's a supply of coffee included I never heard of - we didn't order it - it's a gift - I think. They were waiting in the lobby when I arrived this morning." She seemed excited.

"Why do you think it's a gift?"

She produced a scented monogramed envelope, the seal essentially broken, "She's famous - her name is in the Style Section all the time."

Cynthia came forward with a gold-wrapped package of the coffee, the scent somewhat familiar, "You know much this stuff costs - I want a raise?" Cynthia was an expert.

I did not know where to start. Angelica waved the phone at me, "Allaine."

"Did you read the paper this morning?"

"The comics and the obituaries. Do you remember that guy ....?" The line went dead.

There was too much to do. I stepped into the kitchen to admire the coffee machine, listened to a short lecture on its operation, none of which I understood, thanked and tipped the installers for their hard work and handed the manuals to Angelica.

There was no comprehension on my part as to this largesse - I would need to write a thank you note - saying what though?

The conference room table was piled high with drawings. I told the staff to take lunch on their own or better yet eat at their stations, and be available as I dug through the mound. I would eventually need explanations as to what I was reviewing and determine what was needed to finish. I planned to stay well into the evening. Angelica had wanted to interrupt me on several occasions but I waved her off.

I was coming to the conclusion that the work for the Feds was a drain, with only the cash flow an incentive to keep going.

Cynthia went over her projects with me, "What's with the coffee machine?"

"Is it okay - you're the expert?"

"State of the art - there was nothing wrong with the old one."

Her shot about a raise was fresh in my mind. "The funds did not come from the payroll account - it was a gift."

"Uh-huh."

***

This was a multi-faceted conversation. It had little to do with coffee. Cynthia had come to me through a circuitous route. Fragments had been revealed over the years and I was sure I didn't know it all nor did I want to know as much as I did.

Born in the rural South, she came to live with her 'Aunt' here in the city, an opportunity to escape a depraved childhood, with further opportunity for the otherwise childless aunt to raise a child in circumstances that promised a future. It was not an uncommon arrangement.

Adulthood came with a price - the same syndrome that effected many adopted children. The city was a complicated place to live for the less affluent. Residents came and went. The turns of events in the real world seemed to be concentrated here. She learned drafting in a trade school environment, took some night courses and latched on as a draftsman during a period of serious labor shortage.

The world had turned full circle and now she was an 'aunt.'

"Things are working well for the office - hold out until bonus time."

"Okay, Boss." I knew she was not placated, but it was the best I could do.

Angelica took the opportunity to seize the lull, "A secretary for a Chester something or other called and said there's a meeting this afternoon."

I ignored the opportunity for my usual admonition as to getting names, "Find out who Chester is - tell them I'm not available; and to send us an agenda and a list of who will be there - if I need to attend at all."

Angelica winced and let me get back to work.

***

I snuck out to get my own coffee but, being late in the day, there were only dregs. I tried to remember the instructions given only this morning. Angelica intercepted, "Okay, you make it, some for yourself if you like, and catch me in the conference room."

I soon became aware that coffee was not forthcoming.

Angelica was at her desk - she had obviously been crying - sobbing really - she was being consoled by Cynthia.

"What ....?"

Cynthia gave me a look that sent me scurrying back to my work.

A few minutes later, Cynthia and Angelica entered, hand-in-hand. I waited for an explanation. "Sorry Boss," Angelica seemed calmer.

"No need to apologize - if I get my hands on those mothers, they'll be the one's apologizing."

"Would anyone care to tell me what's going on?"

Cynthia started to speak. "No -from Angelica - no interpretations."

"I called to find out who Chester was and to deliver your message," more composed now, "It turns out he's Saul's brother-in-law - and then this woman started yelling at me."

"Yelling - why?"

"I told them you couldn't make it and wanted to know what the meeting was about - like you said."

"That's it - you didn't say anything back to her?"

"No - after ten seconds or so I hung up."

"Okay - not okay - I'll make my own calls from now on - you didn't do anything wrong."

Something was fishy. As much as I hated gossip, there were rumors about that the secretarial pool had been selected by the father-in-law, now deceased, and that their individual talents went beyond typing. The floozies were probably a little nervous now that there was new management in place.

I shut myself in the conference room once more and continued the marathon. I took no more telephone calls. In my comings and goings, around our office building, several colleagues broached the subject of the newspaper series but I feigned ignorance.

Eventually, I read all three parts of the newspaper series in one sitting. No Pulitzers would be forthcoming. The various concerns revolved around what happened with the Hill. The deconstruction of the project and the monies dispersed in directions unknown, made for a good read. There was a lot of mystery - and conjecture. I could see possibilities for a movie. While I was personally cited as far as the Hill was concerned, I didn't feel my reputation was at stake. Overall, the article showed complete ignorance as to the strategies involved in construction.

It was time to call Chester.

27

I punched in Saul's old private line number, guessing that the phone system had not been altered, "Chester, here." I introduced myself.

"I didn't get your message - my sister is the one who

wants the meeting - she told me it was to advise everyone of our new organization and so forth."

"Everyone? So forth?"

"Really, the Grand Bazaar."

"My secretary called recently to get some information about a meeting, maybe this is the meeting you're talking about - she was treated quite rudely for some reason. Maybe you can check that out - and - let me know when you want to get together on the Grand Bazaar?"

"I'll call you back."

***

The much off-again, then on-again meeting was on again. I walked despite the heat.

***

The secretarial pool was devoid of personnel - the one receptionist looked new. "Where is everybody?"

"I'm everybody and I just started - there used to be three other people here until an hour ago," pointing to the empty desks. "I don't know what they did all day."

"Me, either. I'm here for a meeting with Chester?"

***

The person who I assumed was Chester was standing at the room's conference table. The aircraft carrier sized desk was gone. The room had been streamlined to only include the large round green-felt covered table and its functional chairs with some side chairs against the wall to handle a possible overflow. The table possessed discrete electrical outlets, a salute to the electronic age. A projection screen took up one wall. This layout was a far cry from the throne and mismatched furniture of several weeks ago.

I introduced myself to Chester and we briefly talked about the weather leaving him time to greet the newcomers to the room. Some I recognized. I assumed the only woman present was Saul's wife - Chester's sister. We never quite maneuvered to greet each other.

At the stroke of the announced time for the meeting, the new receptionist entered and handed out what proved to be agendas. Saul was not in sight.

Chester made a deliberate show of turning on a recording system - a red light illuminated above our heads. "It is my opinion that worthwhile meetings should last no more than an hour."

Allaine, who I had noticed slipping in at the last moment, nodded his head in approval.

"Now I'm going to break that rule," the red light went off. "I assume the newspaper article of earlier this week has been read by all here." There was affirmative nodding. "This is one of those instances I can truthfully say, 'I only know what I read in the papers,' and none of that has to do with the Grand Bazaar.

Allaine was looking for something in his briefcase. The room was silent. The red light went back on.

"Item one - Progress Schedule," At this, the projection screen illuminated, "Up till now we had no real schedule because there were so many uncertainties concerning the site. There do not appear to be any more mysteries. The old church still sits there however; the Feds have slapped a historical marker on the building including a notice of how much the fine and jail time is for doing the building any harm."

I smiled at this news.

"Item two - Building permit?"

I stood up - better to see everyone. "It's in progress - we're within the usual waiting period - I"ll go down tomorrow and try to push it along. Be prepared to write some large checks."

"Item three." Chester now stood up, "Prospective tenants. There have been some nibbles. We may continue with marketing on a larger scale - perhaps construct a few retail outlets so the picture is clearer.

The hour was up and though there were a few agenda items left, the meeting participants gladly rose to their feet and were gone. I headed towards the men's room, ignored the need for the facilities and entered the stairwell. Allaine was already there talking baseball with Saul. Saul offered me a cushion. We arranged ourselves on separate tiers so we could stretch our legs and see each other.

"Saul was just telling me about his new position," Allaine was still fiddling with his briefcase.

"I am director of long-range planning."

"Uh-huh."

"Any idea what that entails?"

"Not a clue. There's no pressure and I leave at five every day."

"Do we have to continue meeting here?"

"Probably a good idea - my sister and Chester have offices with their own private restrooms at the other end of the floor - the new receptionist enjoys the intrigue and keeps me informed; otherwise no one is looking for me. It would be best to be available here, not out in public."

"Damn - found it," Alan cleared his throat. "I have some new information on the Hill. "You wouldn't believe how much money went up in smoke - not really in smoke - someone is enjoying tens of millions of dollars - the IRS hasn't a clue."

"Since none of us are any richer, where do you think it went?"

"The young man's family, the fellow who was killed when the bucket fell, collected, and that's as it should be. Most of what I learned is where it came from. The insurance companies took a big hit, the unions sued for defamation - thank Pasqualli for that - Miguel's family sued - other stuff was just settled because the whole thing was considered a nuisance and they didn't want their names in the papers - it all adds up. Because the same cast of characters is involved in the Grand Bazaar and you can be sure there are a lot of antennas up out there - or is it antennae?

"Are we all being scrutinized? I thought about my actions to date, "I'm not going to do anything different then what I'm doing now."

"This doesn't come under long-range planning, but I'll keep my ears open."

Allaine packed up, dusted himself off, noted, "The stairwell could do with a fresh coat of paint," and was gone.

"You okay Saul?"

"Sure, why do you ask?"

"No reason, I guess. Maybe, besides a more cheerful decor in here, some sun lamps could be added." And, with that, I was gone.

28

Except for having a root canal procedure, visiting the Building Department was my next most favorite activity. Think of your least favorite bar, a smoking ban is in effect, it's raining outside, the big ball game has been called off, the soaps are all repeats and the beer pumps have broken down. Hostility abounds. I took a number. I waited. Luckily, I spotted Cleve coming back from his cigarette break and guided him towards an empty workstation. "How's the wife and kids?"

"It's not ready."

"When?"

"The chief is worried about the roof material."

"Any suggestions?"

"You'll think of something."

"Do you know anything about that church cribbed up on the site?"

"Say again?"

"You're an old-timer here," I showed him a picture.

"Go upstairs, see Brown in the mayor's office - don't mention my name."

I walked the three flights up, telling myself it was good for my heart. The fire stairs were supposed to be locked against such purpose but it was too convenient to use them to avoid the public elevators. By doing so, I skipped the entire front office and would up in the mayor's domain. Our mayor was an affable fellow, not a workaholic by any means - he walked me to Brown's office with his security detail in tow.

***

"Cleve called."

Why did I feel this visit was being orchestrated? "Yes, it's about that abandoned church over in the stadium parking lot."

"I know it well. I asked the Mayor to have it put there several years ago." I waited him out. "It's a legacy - Divine Revelation; from the Old Testament, you know."

I stared at Brown - I had no idea what he was talking about. I simply said, "I don't understand." The city was full of churches, some of familiar denominations, others based on the beliefs of so called messianic ministers - I didn't comprehend all the differences - I wasn't interested.

"My father, and my grandfather and a small group of followers like them have always taken care of the church - it has been a multi-generational promise. Unfortunately, we never had the wherewithal or the opportunity to find it a permanent home."

"And now?"

"You are our savior."

I looked around to see if there was anyone else in the room. "I am?"

"All the pieces can now come together."

In for the dime in for the dollar. "Go on?"

The area where the church was first built has come on hard times. "There are many long term tax delinquent properties. A good site would cost only a dollar plus back taxes. The building would be moved back to its original neighborhood and put to its former use."

"It was originally a synagogue you know?"

"Yes. Our congregation considers itself derived from one of the ten lost tribes - we are all Hebrews."

"Uh-huh."

"You are not only our savior, you are our shepherd."

I took a long look out the window and verified I was still part of a modern, urbanized civilization - no sheep in sight, "What do you see happening?"

"The Mayor will accelerate the sale of properties on the Bluff. The appropriate property will be purchased. The necessary permits will be applied for that will allow the building to be placed on a new foundation - water, sewer, electricity and so forth arranged. Our church will live on forever - praise the Lord."

I had never seen such enthusiasm in City Hall. "This will require some funding," a lot of funding for sure, as I added up figures in my head.

"You are our shepherd, Mister. Architect - you can make it happen!"

The door opened and the mayor entered, as on cue, "I need Brown for a meeting. I hope he was able to help you. We public servants are here to assist and make our city great."

I was alone in Brown's office. I scribbled some notes - looked out the window viewing the fountain and the statue of the city's Founding Father - I did not retrace my steps by way of the stairs but took the Mayor's private elevator down to the street.

***

Angelica greeted me, "Remember, the new law office is having an open house this afternoon - we're all invited." She appeared especially well dressed - I was my usual casual self and thought about going home to change but didn't have the energy. Genevieve and Robbie would be the stars and they were dressed for the occasion. The Tuckers seemed edgy but eager.

To the group I said, "There will be lot of good booze - think moderation," I was really addressing the Tuckers.

***

I had not recently visited the space - there being no concerns or complaints - Robbie had it all in hand - this had made me complacent. Now in use, and populated, I was pleased with the results, there was a feeling of prestige as well as the atmosphere of quality cutting edge services.

I nodded to a few people I knew by sight - the building management honcho shook my hand - many elegant women disregarded my presence, all good for my self esteem - finally I found Lawyer Kline and his minion tucked into a corner far away from the refreshments.

"May I have a word?" I stared down his assistant until he excused himself, "I need some direction? Let me tell you a story without interruption." I told him what had transpired at City Hall earlier in the day.

"Cleve is one of your people - I don't know this fellow Brown - everyone knows the mayor - what do you think this is about?"

"For me - it's getting the building permit - I don't do bribes - for you, it's building the Grand Bazaar and that's another matter altogether."

"You have obviously thought about it - lay out your scenario."

"First, what's done has to be separated from the Grand Bazaar."

"Agreed."

"I should have said, first is the money - the technical aspects can be accomplished but it takes money. Someone needs to purchase a piece of property on the Bluff at next weeks tax sale. I'll point you towards the best one. In the mean time, someone needs to create a non-profit, something with 'ecumenical' or 'historical' in the title - maybe both; then, enlist a group of do-gooders to announce the purchase of the church and their intentions - try to get a few Hebrews in there. I'll see to the drawings, permits and so forth - no fee - just expenses."

"You make a good shepherd."

"How's the wine?

"So-so. Come back to the partner's office - that's where they keep the good stuff."

I shook hands with Kline - the party seemed to be just beginning - too many people I didn't know - it would be easy to disappear.

I noted the Tuckers hitting up on a gaggle of paralegals.

Ms. Jones caught up and introduced me to several persons who she thought could be important to me. Cards were exchanged. "I am very happy as to how it all came out - I never participated in anything creative before." She walked me towards the door, "Cliff is pleased - I sent him some pictures."

I missed what she said after that, when I spied Maria standing alone, only twenty feet away smiling at us - at me? Leonard Bernstein's score roared through my head, amplified by the wine - the traffic at the door swept me into the hall - it had been a long day.

It was time to make a summing-up. I thought about the last meeting with Saul, and Allaine's admonition that we were being scrutinized - maybe the business with the church slash synagogue was out of bounds. It was a setup, thinly disguised, to appeal to a conscience that needed stroking - how could anyone deny God?

I felt confident enough to drive home.

***

Marcie signaled me from inside the pool enclosure which I interpreted as an offer of food and drink.

"Tough day at the office, honey? She asked this in her imitation sit-com voice.

"Yeah. How was it here at the pool?" Marcie was nursing unemployment checks and sometime alimony.

"Boring. Why don't you come by later and tell me all about your day - or something."

"This is a great spread - I owe you one."

"It's nice to depend on the kindness of strangers."

29

At the diner the next morning the TV news droned on:

"The trial of Patrick, 'the Plunderer,' Smith, accused as the ring leader of a gang that burgled construction sites throughout the area over the last several years came to an abrupt halt yesterday when his defense attorney, in opening remarks, indicated that his client knew who had, 'murdered,' a construction worker on the now defunct Hill project. He alleged that a bungled burglary, the night before, led to the murder and that his client was not involved. The judge dismissed the jury and the trial has been suspended. More at six o'clock."

The Hill was not going away. My favorite waitress was refilling the still full coffee cup. "What's a plunderer, Boss?"

"It's sort of like a pirate - a robber - it's another way of saying, 'thief.'"

"Can you say that on TV? Maybe I should have a nickname - what do you think?

I thought about, 'five thumbs' but I only thought it.

***

The drafting room was humming - everyone diligently at work - I let it be.

Angelica brought me the latest time sheets. "Looks good, Boss." "There's billing and there's collecting - but you're right, it looks good."

I made a bet with myself as to how long it would take Lawyer Kline to put the 'plan' in motion. I made a second bet as to when the Grand Bazaar permit would be ready. A third bet was as to when Allaine would call concerning the trial that nobody knew about before today, now publicly announced and then put on the back burner. There was always something new to brood about - superseding the old stuff that doesn't completely go away. Several hours of paperwork later, it was time for lunch.

"Where are the Tuckers?"

"They're in love." Cynthia smirked, "Some babes from the lawyer's office have caught their attention. It's picnic time on the plaza."

"Hopefully the ladies will enjoy grits and gravy - the Tuckers are not big on salads - it will be hard to swap around."

"What's doing in your love life, Boss?" Murphy was peering over the top of his sunglasses.

"I guess I could take that as a personal question; but I won't. Let's just say it could be better - I'm working on it."

A good question, indeed - working on it - probably not? First of all - you have to define love. What did the people in Hollywood say? 'If you want love, buy a dog.' I'm not that cynical. Of course, Murphy's definition of love could be more oriented towards the 'free' variety but I think for me he's saying, 'Get a life.' Good advice - hard to implement.

Chuan chimed in, "You probably don't want to be in my position. My father is coming to the States on leave from OECD. According to my brother, he has a secret for me - a bride that he plans for me to marry and return home with. My girlfriend is very upset - my mother can't talk him out of it - my brother is laughing his ass off - I will probably leave town."

"They can't do that - can they?" Susan was perplexed.

Angelica was joining in the cackling and reluctantly picked up the phone, "A Doctor Tabershaw?" I shook my head as to the name but headed to my office.

"Got your name from Chester."

"Okay?"

"You sound like you don't know who I am?"

"Yes." I regretted not finishing lunch.

"I have to get back to the surgery - can you meet me at City Hospital at six?"

"What's this about?" The line was dead. I could call Chester. Better not. - I remained paranoid about everyone in that company.

***

There were some dregs of lunch left. Chuan was at the table alone. "Do you think my problem is funny?"

"No, I don't."

"If you were me - what would you do?"

"I'll tell you what I would do but you have to realize that this is coming from someone older, maybe older than your father, a natural born citizen of the USA with no ties to anyone, anywhere." Those were as many qualifiers as I could think of for the moment, "You have to say, Dad, I'm a young man who has my whole life ahead of me - I need to find my life's work - there will be a phase when I marry - it will be for love and I hope it will be to someone who will respect you as I do.'"

Chuan was scrambling for pencil and paper.

"It's not a script, Chuan - go back to work. And, respect the young lady when she arrives."

Angelica was soon hovering, "Do you believe that will work?

"I had a building blown up recently - how would I know?"

***

City Hospital was on the other side of the city. I left plenty of time to get there - the streets were unfamiliar but the route was marked with rusting 'H' signs. Cynthia had given me some landmarks. It was an old building with a few signs of renovation - worn and pock-marked from years of air pollution. Parking was plentiful.

There was only one entrance - emergency services did not seem to be available. At the reception desk, I asked for the doctor and was given immediate escort down dimly lit corridors, through several doors marked, 'Do Not Enter,' and wound up in a recently used operating theater. A few observers were just dispersing from a glassed in balcony above; the area was being cleaned and scrubbed. A gentlemen in blood-stained scrubs, unlighted cigarette between his lips beckoned me to follow him.

"Doctor Tabershaw I presume." He was just peeling off blood-stained gloves so I deferred shaking hands, "What can I do for you?"

He whisked off all his clothing, which he promptly picked up and disposed of by tending orderlies. He entered the room's shower with lighted cigarette aglow. Upon exit, the cigarette was down to a lighted stub. He wrapped towels around himself and took the room's only chair. He saw me glancing at the several, "No Smoking" signs on the wall.

"Don't worry, there's nothing in here that can blow up - besides, I own the hospital. I only have a few minutes, so let's talk."

I raised my palms in a sign of futility, "What about?"

"Didn't you talk to Chester?"

"No."

He scrutinized me through the vapors of a new cigarette, "I need to do a short procedure; starting now - I'll meet you up in my office - help yourself to a drink."

***

Besides never before having been in among so many sharp instruments, with a naked surgeon, there was not much to say about the last few minutes. I was sure the venue would revisit me in my dreams. Tabershaw's age was hard to judge - he appeared fit - there were numerous scars on his body - some looked like old gunshot wounds.

An orderly opened the office door for me, turned on the lights and disappeared. I found the bar and refrigerator and poured out a club soda. The couch furthest from the monstrous desk looked comfortable.

I dozed off.

***

"I fall asleep there myself quite often." The doctor had on clean scrubs and appeared quite fresh.

"Things went well?"

He helped himself from the bar and perched on the edge of his desk, "I have done the same procedure too many times. Let's talk so we can get you home at a decent hour. This involves the Hill."

"Okay."

"I have purchased the property and plan to go ahead with the entire project."

"its a huge undertaking - a full-time job - for a lot of people."

"I am strictly an investor - the heavy lifting will be done by others." At this point the office door opened, "Ah, my wife."

I politely stood and was astonished by a familiar face and figure.

My recent hostess from the party at the beach showed no recognition, displaying a cool reserve usually utilized for servants and shop people. I shook hands - she pecked the doctor on the cheek and seated herself at the bar.

The doctor continued, "You need to talk to Chester?

"How do you know Chester?"

"My family and his go way back. I went to high school with his sister."

"You know, the site is cursed." Both laughed, almost hysterically.

"Talk to Chester. The security guard at the front desk will see you safely to your car."

Back through darkened corridors, a briefly brighter exit and then to the Toyota, I thought about the last hour. The security guard watched as I left the premises. The streets were deserted - it had poured while I was in the hospital - a hard storm bringing down diseased tree limbs.

It was best not to make light of a curse.

30

It thunder-stormed all night. The air conditioning cranked to keep up with the increased humidity.

At the diner, the TV covered the eight hours of unexpected hard rain from every angle. The weather front was almost over, the roads would be clear for evening rush and, more importantly, for traffic to the beach. Summer would continue to be with us.

***

Angelica had left a note the previous evening, 'Your doctor called.' She reinforced this, in person, "Your doctor called."

"Okay."

"She said to come by any time."

"Okay."

"I'll call and see if she's free."

It was clear that my staff was concerned about both my physical and mental well being. I spent some extra time in the men's room scrutinizing myself in the full-length mirror and more closely to the reflection of my face.

"She will see you now." The emphasis was on 'now.'

*　*　*

Again, the doctor went straight to the point. "You are run down."

"Run down - is that a medical term?"

"All your tests are within normal parameters." She referred to several pages of numbers in small type. "Are you sleeping okay - do you wake up tired - are you sleeping alone?"

"Say again?"

"Man shall not live by bread alone."

I pondered this, "That's it?"

"Do you have anyone you can talk to frankly - a good friend, a colleague, for example?"

"No - are you suggesting a shrink?"

"No - come see me in six months so I can see how you are doing."

"Do you know a Richard Tabershaw?"

"The surgeon - I know of him. Are you planning some elective surgery I should know about?"

"What do you know?"

"Only what I read in the papers. He has become very rich - travels in high society - many of my colleagues envy him."

"That's it?"

"Yes."

Yes - I knew Tabershaw all too well. In high school and college, fellow comrades of both sexes had their appeal - I exploited this lust - prudently - I did not choose to be popular or well-liked - it was fun and I was happy. Medical School was different - most of my class-mates were men - the doctor-teachers mostly men as well - Richard Tabershaw was one of those teachers - the stress of the curriculum was unbearable - I needed a mentor - he soothed my angst - he told me be a 'man' - I took it literally - he saved my life.

***

Angelica looked at me inquisitively. "Angelica - I think you need some help - find someone to act as your assistant."

"Are you firing me, Boss?"

"I'm trying to help you to help me - that's all - it's not that complicated. Show me some resumes."

I was already, vaguely, doing what the doctor suggested. It was like the blind men and the elephant. Acting as a foil to Allaine's sardonic humor helped me - Saul in his confusion was useful - my several bed-mates never took anything I said seriously and that helped in its own way.

All of it was supportive.

If Tabershaw had known Saul's wife from high school days, then maybe Saul knew some of the doctor's history. I called Saul's personal phone but there was no answer. I redialed the switchboard and learned from the receptionist that he, "was gone for the day." She then whispered, "Try the beach."

Allaine's personal secretary told me, confidentially, that he was at the beach and that's all she knew.

All my instincts told me not to call Chester. The beach beckoned.

I spent the rest of the day getting brief reports on all our projects, okaying paychecks and signing and sealing forms that I was told were absolutely necessary for first thing next week. No bells rang during the status reports. The contract with the Feds was falling into place - there was the risk that the contract would be extended. Work was getting done.

I saw everyone out the door and sat at my desk contemplating what the doctor had advised.

Allaine was on the phone, "Heard you we are looking for me?"

"How's the weather at the beach?"

"Horrible - ditto the traffic."

"Do you know a Doctor Tabershaw?"

"Planning to finally get that scrawny neck fixed?"

"Not exactly."

"He did my daughter - can't go to college without creating a new persona."

"Uh-huh."

"His hospital is a surgery mill - lots of elves working there besides the Doctor."

"Money to be made?"

"I wrote a big check."

"You think he has enough oomph to resurrect the Hill?"

"I'll find out."

That was worthwhile.

Looking near term, the city and beach offered a rain filled weekend with traffic milling about with lots of house bound families trying to find something to do. For me, some extra sleep would be helpful.

"Sleeping okay, waking up tired, sleeping alone?" That's what the doctor asked.

Beth was on the line "You are not in your usual haunt off the board-walk.

"Very true - I hear the beach is a mess."

"It is - I'm coming back to the city late tonight - very late."

"I'll leave the front door open."

"Is that an invitation?"

"It is." Just what the doctor ordered I thought.

I showered and fell asleep when my head hit the pillow.

She slipped into bed quite stealthily. I had not heard the door open and shut nor the shower run "Did you bring some cotton candy?"

"Sure did - check it out."

"Can't wait to see my doctor in six months."

"What's that about?"

"Let me ask you a question?"

"I'll try - especially if you do that thing with the feather." I was happy to oblige.

She seemed content, "My wall safe combination code is tattooed under my left arm pit - what else do you need?"

"Your former college classmate - the one with the penthouse at the beach - what do you know about her husband?"

"The doc - not much - the two lead separate lives."

"Uh-huh."

"Where were we?"

31

I gathered everyone together before the routine of the day began, "Big holiday weekend coming up - before Friday make sure you have dumped whatever you have on the other guy's desk."

"I'm still waiting from the last submittal."

"Do it again - let the other guy worry about Tuesday."

***

Allaine was on the line, "I called my stockbroker - the doctor is not one of his clients - he says the rumor mill has it that the doc is as rich as Crocus - who the hell is Crocus?

"Crassus - a former Roman emperor - thought to be the richest person in the world - ever."

"How do you know that?"

"The benefit of a liberal arts education - Crassus was not a nice person - I'll get back to you."

So much for research before calling Chester.

"I've been expecting your call."

"If you mean about the Hill I'm available for a meeting."

"Four today would be good."

Things could not be more obtuse.

"Everybody's talkin' at me -
I don't hear a word they're saying -
Only the echoes of my mind ...."

"Are you singing, Boss?"

"I am Angelica; I don't know why."

"....Going where the sun keeps shining ....
Sailing on a summer breeze ....
Skipping over the ocean like a stone."

"Don't worry Angelica - I'm okay. Let me have what you have in your hand." I added, "Any resumes, by the way?"

The end of the month bills were in a neat stack, payment checks attached, wanting for my signature. There was money in the bank to cover it all and that was a good feeling.

***

I ran into Lawyer Kline in the arcade at lunch time.

"Watch the Sunday paper for an announcement by a new non-profit."

"This Sunday is a holiday, no one reads the paper on holiday weekends except for the ball scores."

He smiled, "Have a good one."

***

I pretended to read the mail. My concerns were elsewhere. I thought, that as an outsider, I knew as much as I could about the Doctor which was nada. Chester was an enigma to me; his sister more so. I don't know who would be at the four o'clock meeting - nothing like being prepared.

I walked despite the heat and humidity.

The friendly receptionist was still by herself in a pool of empty desks, "Go right on up."

***

Chester's office was full of people milling about - only half of whom I recognized. I shrunk to a corner of the room and watched the hubbub. There were not enough seats. No secretary appeared with an agenda. Chester had to shout to gain order. No red recording light appeared at four o'clock.

"We have a new client who is ready to restart the Hill."

I looked more closely at the excited group. A majority of those present, based on closer scrutiny, appeared to be subcontractors and material suppliers always anxious for a new source of boat payments. The Doctor was not present. Lawyer Kline, his legal pad in his lap, looked bemused. "I have set a startup date of one month from now." Chester was feeding the frenzy. He looked towards me, "That's not going to be a problem, is it?

"Not for me; maybe for the next architect. I don't have a contract to do anything after the first building was demolished - I don't even know who the new owner is."

Things became very quiet. Chester needed to recoup, "Okay, I appreciate everyone's enthusiasm - I'll be in touch." The room emptied. Chester's sister was the first one out the door.

I headed for the men's room and the adjacent stairway. Opening the stair exit door, I noted the new robin's egg blue paint on the walls and canary yellow railings. Sun lamps had been jury rigged to the emergency lighting system. The space was empty.

I queried the receptionist as to Saul's whereabouts. "He's on a leave of absence."

***

The heat and humidity was even more unbearable. The walk back included stops in a coffee shop, a used book store and a bodega. I spotted Saul looking through the extensive supply of designer waters. We made our purchases and sought out the shade in a pocket park next door, away from the street.

"Looked for you just now."

"How do you like the decorating?"

"Very homey."

"I put in a work order, forged my wife's signature and it was done the next day."

"Uh-huh - I heard you were on a leave of absence."

"You could call it that."

"What should I call it?"

"It would be hard to say - my wife says she is disappointed in me - no real definition of that; I'm not fun - ditto lack of definition. It's confusing. I see the conclusion as me being out on the street."

"Uh-huh."

"Got to go - picking the kids up at school."

Why did Saul's despair seem so familiar?

***

The office had cleared out. There was the usual paperwork on my desk plus a small stack of resumes with the title "Office Manager" in their headings. Angelica was going for the big time. I wondered if I would hear from Doctor Tabershaw once he learned of the fiasco of Chester's meeting.

***

At Costco, I watched the flow of third world immigrants enjoying the American dream blissfully unaware of what lay ahead for the next generation. I imagined my grandparents looking out from their tenement windows on the cornucopia of carts in the swarming streets of lower Manhattan, likewise feeling safe and at peace with the world.

The Caesar salad and hot dog seemed to be the only constant in my life.

32

I had made an appointment to take in the Toyota for a check-up - I was prepared, if necessary, to abide by my mechanic's decision if he said to let it go. On the way to the garage, I did not dwell further on the potential loss of an old friend.

"Anything you want to tell me," Rick and my vehicle went way back. He sort of understood my attachment to the car, but didn't want to jeopardize his professional responsibility. "You need new tires for sure."

"Okay."

"You sure?" He had made this recommendation before.

"The whole nine yards."

"The tires and other stuff you probably need will cost more than the car is worth."

"You cannot measure friendship in dollars and cents."

"Very true - it's a car you know - a very old car - not an antique - just old."

"I understand - it's run down."

***

The role of Angelica's assistant, now seemingly elevated to office manager, needed to be evaluated. I read all the resumes looking for a commonality as to what these people thought the job entailed and the experience they would bring to the table. What I needed was another me plus Angelica.

"What was the source of these resumes. Angelica?"

"A lot of my friends work for banks - I asked around."

"We need another approach. Talk to Cynthia - she knows everybody."

***

A phone call from Doctor Tabershaw was inevitable. I decided to preempt it. After being passed through several administrators, the doctor himself actually came on the line. "I have just have a few minutes - I understand things did not go well yesterday?"

"You would not be exaggerating - I could not catch Chester alone. This is an immense project, Doctor, we need to create some structure - I don't know what you invested in, in the past, but it would be safe to say the Hill is different."

"And, there is the curse."

"That too."

"Got to go."

A surgeon with a sense of humor - that was a good sign.

***

I borrowed a neighboring tenant's newspaper to see if the real estate tax sales had been published.

There was a long list and it took me a while to figure out the system. A ground floor realtor in our building had all the City's real estate recordation information in his library. Cross checking back and forth, I figured out which properties were on the Bluff. That didn't really tell me enough - I would have to drive the streets of the district, look at the topography, availability of utilities and such, and see which sites were practicable for the church. The auction was set up for the following week.

While I had the newspaper, I looked for a follow-up on the 'Plunderer's' postponed trial. No news. It would probably take months for the lawyers to agree on what to do.

***

I scoured the 'OUT' basket for transmittal copies that would tell me the pace of submittals to our clients.

"Chester on the phone Boss."

"The doctor has asked us to meet him at the hospital at six o'clock - I'll drive but you will have to navigate - that part of the City is creepy." He hung up. With the Toyota being in the shop, a ride with Chester was fortuitous.

***

Chester's car had all the bells and whistles. it was difficult to determine the name of the manufacturer as there only seemed to be unfamiliar repetitious logos wherever I looked. Having someone else drive was a treat. I was sure his tires would not fail us.

"So, Chester, in one hundred words or less; who are you? He glanced sideways to see if I was joking - I was not.

"Did anyone ever tell you that was impolite?"

"Probably - so who are you?"

He unnecessarily beeped at a car in front of us, "I haven't lived in the city for a number of years. You worked for my father - now for my sister - that's my whole family. I went to college on the West Coast, and then to medical school. The career of a doctor was not for me and I dropped out. All that blood was too much. Some friends of mine and I bought a ski lodge with accompanying slopes - we never made a dime - we abandoned the business leaving various parents with a tax loss.

Never been married. When my father died, I was surprised to learn that my sister and I had been left the business. I don't know anything about construction."

"That's a few words over one hundred - let me say, I did not like your father - he's dead now so it doesn't matter. Your sister is a snob - we don't like each other and that's okay. Saul was managing to tread water on her behalf, but not any more - take a left through those gates and park anywhere."

Chester looked around, "I was here once - touring the city in a bus - in high school we had a course in Urban Studies and traced the development of the city; this was the first real hospital - newer ones were built later. This one was converted into a, 'crazy house' - it was referred to as the Snake Pit - then it was abandoned. Squatters took it over for a while; I'm surprised it's still around.

"I'll tell you what I know or at least what I've heard. Over the hill, a few miles east, is the service area for the airport. Patients from overseas who want to preserve their anonymity come in the back door, so to speak, get snipped or tucked or whatever, and leave the same way they came. Only the outside of the hospital is decrepit; the interior is state-of-the-art."

"Why is it so dark?"

"It gets darker."

***

The same coterie of orderlies, as I had dealt with before, led us through the, "Do Not Enter," marked doors. The doctor was sucking on a cigarette, his scrubs even more blood-stained then on my previous visit - the orderlies were hovering to catch his clothing once the cigarette was finished. Chester did not look comfortable - to me, without an actual bleeding patient, on hand it was so much ketchup.

"Good to meet you Chester - I'm running a little late - I need to change clothes - you two go up to my office and make yourself at home."

Chester went for a beer and I joined him. He turned on the big screen TV and surfed through the channels - on one news station I briefly heard 'trial to resume next week,' but then it was on to another channel, settling on the replay of a baseball game played earlier in the day.

The doctor entered, "Good, another fan," but he turned off the set.

"All went well, today?" It was not my meeting but here we were to discuss a multi-million dollar project, and the ice needed to be broken.

"It almost always does," he perched on the corner of his desk, "Let us start from the beginning - I have purchased the Hill property and wish to jump start construction while the market is still hot - I know it's a lot easier said than done, so tell me how we get started."

"You will have to start almost from the beginning. A new permit is required. The previous design is over three years old - codes and standards have changed - utility capacity may not be available - they haven't even finished hauling away the rubble from the first go-around."

"Maybe, one of the big boys from New York could handle it?"

"They are welcome - as far as I know my contract is dead."

"Do you think we can piggyback on the existing permit?"

"It has almost expired - every one is very nervous because of the first work being torn down." I didn't want to tell him that the demolition was unnecessary. "You need a good lawyer."

At this point the office door opened, the same time as my previous visit - the doctor's wife entered - Chester and I rose and shook hands - the doctor got his perfunctory peck on the cheek. The hairs on the back of my neck stood on end as the doctor's wife and Chester exchanged covert lingering glances during the introduction.

The doctor continued, "Can I have my lawyer call you?"

"I need a contract - I am here today as a courtesy - I got stiffed when the job stopped - I am sure you do not operate without some understanding with your patient." That was a stupid analogy and I regretted saying it.

"Have your lawyer call my lawyer." He handed me a business card which I put in my pocket without looking at the information.

Chester stood up, looking for a trash can for his beer bottle - the Doctor's wife took it from him - more electricity flowed.

Goodbyes were exchanged.

***

Despite the brightness of the day, the hospital seemed to dwell in it's own pocket of gloom. Chester broke the speed limit until he was in more familiar territory, "How about dinner - what do you know around here?"

'Take the next right - then a left."

"That's a grocery store."

"That is the undiscovered culinary capital of this city - trust me."

***

"I was wrong, it's a store the sells everything - it is a madhouse - it looks like the early pictures of Ellis Island with lots of stuff. Where's the restaurant?"

"It's not exactly a restaurant - check out the menu on the wall."

"A beef hot dog and a drink for one-fifty - how can they do that?"

"If you like pizza, I'll share one with you - maybe a salad?"

Chester was a good eater, "That's the best pizza I ever had."

"We have a branch right up the road from our office."

***

The ride back was like in a dream. 88.5 FM set the mood.

Chester dropped me off at the gate leading to my townhouse.

The sun was not quite through for the day. The heat and humidity was still oppressive. The pool was closed - the air dead still quiet. I took a few seconds to admire the mixture of colors at the horizon, then worked my way towards more air conditioning.

Marcie took me by surprise from the shelter of a pool umbrella. "Hear you're looking for an office manager?"

"How?"

"Friend of a friend and so forth - you know?"

"The answer is no."

"Why? - You don't have a jealous spouse?"

"No."

I felt guilty for eating so much. The surgical suite had its effect - life and death in real time. What was that business between Chester and the Doctor's wife? Was there going to be a murder investigation involving the Hill? Was stifling Marcie the best way to say no? How far did the curse go?

I had to remember I had no car when awakening in the morning. If I timed it right Ralph would drop me at the diner.

33

Susan caught me at the door. "I have a new client - a brand new house - great site - an unlimited budget. I have done work for their friends - they like me."

"And?"

"They want to make sure I can handle the work - they want to see the office - meet you."

"When?"

"This morning would be great."

"Okay."

***

I introduced myself and made small talk. I had read Susan's notes and the rough draft of a contract, "Why a brand new house?"

"Among other things, we have triplets and would like to raise them without conflicts as to who is getting more attention than the other - lots of room for them and their friends. We want them to grow up with the latest in everything - no, 'that's the way they did it the old days.' "

"Okay."

***

The husband took the lull to self-serve himself coffee from our kitchen. "I see you have the latest technology in coffee makers - we only made a few of those - much too complicated and expensive for the general public - how did you get this one?"

"It was a gift."

"Really?"

"I want to assure you, you are in good hands with Susan. The office is here as backup. If you need some help interviewing builders - bring them by.

The very short interview finished, "You are in the coffee machine business?"

"Not exactly - aerospace is our main endeavor - we bought a like company a few years ago - it turned out they had started out in the coffee business - even though they were now making rocket parts, they stayed with the coffee machines. It is a money-maker, so we just let it continue - we believe we will be the first ones serving coffee on Mars." He gave a self-deprecating chuckle, "If you ever have any problems with your machine, I'll send over one of our engineers."

Susan looked at me for direction. "Carry on."

***

I located the doctor's lawyer's card among various other slips of paper from my pants pocket. I called my lawyer and left a message.

A copy of the Hill building permit was in our files and I wrote down the various important dates in anticipation of her return call.

The coffee machine was still a mystery to me - there was a gift card enclosed when it had arrived - I dutifully answered - who really knows how such a piece of exotica really got to my office.

Angelica looked puzzled. "Your avocado or something like that is on the phone."

"Advocate, maybe?"

"Bonjour, Pierre."

"Bonjour, Babette; *ca va?*" Ten years or more ago I had taken a French 101 course for adults in anticipation of a visit to Paris. The teacher did everything possible to make it fun including assigning French pseudonyms to replace our real names to promote more creative conversation. This present day attorney, assigned to be Babette at the time, was as terrible a student as myself, but we laughed a lot. I did not realize she was a lawyer at the time. After going through as many lawyers as I did doctors, I called her one day for a simple matter and we developed a rapport. She had obtained some notoriety in recent years; various wags rumored she had slept with just about every member of the judiciary - both male and female - that was her business as far as I was concerned - I had my own problems mollified when I needed and it did not cost an arm and a leg.

"I know how sensitive you are about fees, so I have my telephone set - now - to turn off in fifteen minutes."

"The Hill is back on the table. A Doctor Tabershaw wants to resurrect the project. I need a contract - a large retainer would be helpful - no promises on my part. I told him the former building permit is dead and we would have to start all over. But - big but - I think present day construction can be continued - continued because the stop work order was bogus and the various reports and tests leading to the demolitions are bogus." I paused for a breath, "Unfortunately I know all this in a surreptitious manner and much hell could break loose if it becomes public knowledge. In an ideal world, the building department would admit they made a mistake and restore the present building permit, with a generous fee imposed, I would guess, and we could all pretend nothing ever happened - I have the name of the doc's lawyer by the way."

"Very succinct. I'm on my way to the beach - I'll get back to you."

The phone went dead and I called back to give the doc's lawyer information to a secretary.

***

I want into the kitchen and looked at the coffee machine. The instruction manual was close at hand - there were no clues as to who actually produced the machine - just the usual 800 numbers. The last page exclaimed the apparatus was guaranteed for life. As my father used to say - "Whose?"

"You have company, Boss."

Two black-suited men were behind me with badges and IDs on display, "Coffee gentlemen?" They declined, but spent a moment admiring the machine. I motioned them into the conference room and closed the door and drew the blinds.

"Your name came up in an investigation of an incident at the Hill. A man died in an apparent accident. The police report at the time mentions your name."

"Uh-huh."

"Do you know what accident we are talking about?"

"Maybe?"

The larger of the two men opened a folder and withdrew a photograph, time-date stamped, that showed me peering out a partially open door. "This was taken at the time our uniformed officers were investigating the alleged accident - the officer had his body camera on."

"I'm pretty sure it's me. I was on the site to sign some papers and pick up shop drawings. It was raining."

"What do you know about was going on around that time?"

"Jose told me there had just been an accident - the crane bucket had come down on a worker - an ambulance followed me up the road at the time I arrived. It was raining."

"Did you see the scene of the accident?"

"No, I had just arrived - the trailer was empty - I was waiting to talk to Jose - it was raining." I don't know why I kept mentioning the rain.

It was raining. Lee was overdue in returning my car. All he had to do was pick up his date and two other girls who had been invited to that night's party. Two policemen found me in the drafting room at the top of the architecture building - I was there frantically trying to finish a presentation due Sunday evening at six pm - I still hadn't dressed for the party.

"Yes, it is my car based on the Appalachia license plate," I answered them. Lee and his date were dead, the two girls in the back seat badly hurt - part of the road was washed away - the car was speeding - visibility was poor due to the rain.

"No, I would not be the one to do any identifications."

"Do you know anything about thefts or vandalism on the Hill around that time?"

"No."

The policemen looked at each other and closed their notebooks. They detoured to admire the coffee machine once more - I signaled to Angelica to put it in operation to fill two takeaway cups. Her hands moved too fast for me to understand the performance.

I thought about my answers to the policemen - I was sure it was best not to mention the curse.

***

At lunch, I responded to the curiosity of the staff to the drawn blinds earlier in the day, "It had to do with the Hill."

"Are we in trouble?"

"No, it has to do with an accident that some people say was not an accident. I told them what I knew - which wasn't much - I don't expect they'll be back."

"There's a rumor that the Hill is going to start up again." Murphy was a consummate conspiracy hound.

There is no such thing as a secret, I thought. "What have you heard and from whom?"

"I got to know some of the workers when I was clerk-of-the works - we bounce into each other from time to time - they heard things around the union hall."

"You know more then I do," which was probably true.

Needing to change the subject, "Chuan - any more news concerning the coming nuptials?"

"My mother received some pictures - my father is due next week."

"Cynthia was right on top of it, "Let's see the pictures."

Chuan had the pictures on his lap, apparently in anticipation of a show-and-tell and passed them around, "She has a PhD in engineering and speaks five languages. My brother says her folks are mega-rich."

At the word, 'rich' the Tuckers scrutinized the pictures more closely.

"What would she want with you?" Cynthia was her usual skeptical self, "Ask Genevieve how that works out."

Apparently I didn't know as much about Genevieve as I thought I did - all eyes turned towards her. Her face was beet red,

"I wish Cynthia had not said anything - it was a stupid personal thing - girl talk - you all are my friends - my only friends - so you all may as well know - it happened in my last year of college - I fell in love with this guy - we did all the wrong things - we got married - my parents were furious. One day my baby and husband were gone, along with all the legal papers. He had his dual citizenship and the baby was an American - it was all a plan for the future - his future."

All eyes swiveled towards Chuan.

Changing the subject had not been a good idea. "I have to make it to an appointment - in case I don't get to see you all for some reason - I have declared Friday a holiday - have a good weekend," and I was gone. The buzz, as I left, was about the beach.

I was not sure why I added the extra day-off to the holiday weekend. It was a bonus they all deserved; money would have been more appreciated. I was starting to feel nervous with all these new people in my life.

***

I headed straight home for the evening. My rejuvenated Toyota floated over the potholed streets. Rick had thrown in a car wash. I felt invincible.

The pool was mobbed, the decibel level from the near exhausted kids, fighting off the dinner hour, in the upper limits. I admired some of the mothers in the latest swimwear. "See anything you like?" Marcie was hiding under a floppy hat and oversized sunglasses.

"I thought you were mad at me."

"I never get mad for long - besides I got a new job - I'll tell you all about it - got to go."

34

On this early Sunday morning, the traffic would be at an all time low and the perfect time to slow cruise through the Bluffs, perhaps find a new diner, catch the second half of a doubleheader - pursue other benefits of staying in the city.

But first, there would be the newspaper and the article Lawyer Kline promised and then the comics and obituaries.

The phone rang, causing me to panic, imagining some emergencies that would originate a call at this time and day.

"Good morning - it's Natasha - may I pick you up in fifteen minutes?"

The voice was faintly familiar, "Say who?" The line was dead. Tabershaw's wife, the mysterious patron of the beach penthouse was who it sounded like.

I showered and dressed as quickly as possible making an expeditious decision to dress as I usually did for the office - shorts and a t-shirt would have been more appropriate for the weather.

***

A black SUV was waiting at the curb, the security barrier of the parking area actually working for a change.

The driver of the vehicle opened the rear door for me.

"Good morning - I hope I was not too presumptuous - what are your plans for the day?"

The woman knew how to dazzle. "I planned to do some research of sorts."

"We'll do it together."

"I need to get some paperwork out of the car." I grabbed the file for the church slash synagogue from the Toyota and borrowed Ralph's newspaper from his doorstep.

"My goodness - is that your car?"

"It's a beauty isn't it - twenty-five years old and still ticking?" I looked around the SUV and admired all it's features, "Do you want me to chauffeur you around today - then this fellow could take the day off - it would be more spontaneous that way?"

"I'll pass - please make yourself comfortable and direct us where to go."

"Have you had breakfast?"

"I don't eat breakfast."

"I do," and I gave the driver the directions to my favorite eatery.

***

The diner was empty. Chico was reading the paper at the counter. There were no waitresses. "Sit anywhere you want."

"The usual, Chico - the lady will have coffee - black."

Natasha took in the decor and seemed to be fascinated by Chico's ministrations at the grille. "The usual - that means you eat here often?"

Admitting it was often was probably not a good idea, "It's convenient."

"You seem to know the cook's name."

"Very observant - he's the owner as well. I usually read the paper - we can talk if you like - or we can share the paper." I handed her the sports page and the classifieds.

Chico brought everything at once. We rearranged the table, folding the newspaper into commuter panels. Natasha made my breakfast a spectator sport. Chico kept returning with coffee and to take the opportunity to observe Natasha's leisure wear or the lack thereof. Natasha flashed her credit card when I finished, "Some coffee for my driver, please - he's just outside." Chico was happy to oblige.

***

"Where to?

"We are going to a part of the city called the Bluffs," I gave the driver the address of the closest tax property to enter into his GPS, "Belay that - drive to the parking lot of the old stadium first."

"What are we doing?"

"There is supposed to be an article in today's paper that will give you a clue."

She looked through the paper as I studied her. "It will be about an old church that is to be relocated by a non-profit group or something to that effect." The doctor was a lucky man.

The article was actually a blurb, a press release, probably written by Lawyer Kline, naming various solid citizens of the city who had formed the, "Ecumenical Heritage Committee" to preserve the,"earliest houses of God" in the city. Their first project was to be the preservation of an old, "house of worship" now protected by the Historical Society.

***

The security guard at the top of the ramp knew me by now. We drove through the wasteland of construction debris to the entrance of the article's house of worship. I had made a duplicate of the padlock key. "Come in - this is part of the day we're spending together." The driver and I gave her a hand up the temporary stairs.

Our footsteps echoed off the yellow pine floors. We gravitated towards the bema or what I chose to call the probable location of the lectern. "Keep the design of the space in your mind - imagine the entrance oriented towards the west placing the ark to the east."

The driver was too curious, "The ark?"

Natasha frowned at the intrusion, "It is a simple beautiful space - I feel like I have been here before. What do we do next?"

"We look for the place for the preservation to begin."

***

The GPS took us to the Bluffs in short order. It was difficult to correlate the City's information from the terrain that lay before us. Addresses were missing on the few existing homes; street signs non-existent at many intersections - but eventually the maps and the ground started to come together.

"Okay, we are looking for a place to put that building you just saw," I pointed towards the sun, "assume that is the south, or almost so."

We drove slowly around the deserted neighborhood, checking off the probable locations of the foreclosed properties. An elderly gentleman appeared out of nowhere - he was not to be ignored - I told him we were looking for the place where my great grandfather once lived. He looked dubious but started to tell us about our surroundings.

Some of the tax sale sites were steep hillsides from which the Bluffs probably took its name and essentially unbuildable.

"There's a cemetery under all those weeds - no one comes here anymore." I thanked the gentlemen for his help and passed a few bills to him for his troubles.

Looking at my watch, 'It is high noon, that's the west - let's pick three sites and hope we are where we think we are."

***

"Ready to follow up on that big breakfast?" We had recorded all the information and had taken numerous pictures. Natasha was looking a little green. "There are some nice places down by the waterfront."

Natasha picked a white tablecloth place with a view of the water. A frosted glass of some clear liquid magically appeared at the table as she sat down. I declined a similar offering.

"You've been here before?"

"We have an investment."

We never saw a menu. A fellow in chef whites and a toque brought small plates for us to sample and it was eventually determined by him that lunch was over by offering a sample of sorbet. There was no check.

"What else did you have planned for the rest of the day?"

"We could catch the first half of the twilight double-header."

"We will do that but let's talk for a few moments. Tell me a little about yourself."

"What you see is what you got. Am sure any decent detective service could put together my whole life story. There are no secrets. If you and the Doctor believe I have any ulterior motives you should find another guy - I will take advantage of circumstances, break a few poorly written rules and regulations and manipulate people from time to time but it will be for the purpose of getting the job done - not to make myself rich.

"So, you have disdain for rich people?"

"I have disdain for lots of people - admiration for just as many - ambivalence towards the rest - money does not fit into the criteria."

"Don't you worry about your future?"

"Yes - I do not want to wind up living on the street - eating dog food - or taking charity."

"I never thought of those alternatives."

"I hope not - another alternative is 'dead' - then you have a chance to describe your life in ten words or less for posterity."

"What do you think it says on the gravestones in the cemetery we just saw?"

"It would be interesting to find out, wouldn't it?" I paused for reflection, "Let's go - I hate to miss the National Anthem."

***

At the ball park we pulled into a reserved parking space. Natasha was greatly admired by the fans arriving for the first game. At the gate she instructed the ticket taker to call the owner's box and tell him she was on her way up. She slipped some bills to the driver and waved him in as well. A private elevator took Natasha and I to the top of the stands above home plate. We were greeted by an important looking fellow - there were the cheek pecks from Natasha - I was introduced and shook hands. Some less important person was shooed out of the seat next to the owner - I made my way to the second tier of upholstered chairs just in time to order a beer from the wait staff.

The game started slowly. At the end of the fifth inning, I took the steps down to the main concourse and wandered. I spotted Jose, in the beer line, just as he spotted me.

"No Spanish, please," and we shook hands.

"Your countryman is hanging in there, his on-base percentage is up - I guess he's not being paid to field especially well."

Jose decided not to argue, "Come say hello to Maria."

I looked over Jose's shoulder to see if Maria was, perhaps, on the concourse. "Some other time - I have to get back to my party."

"I'll probably see you again soon - I understand the Hill will be starting back up."

Everyone seemed to know more about the project than I did.

***

Upon my return, I noted that the other seat next to the owner was vacant. Natasha motioned me to sit. The owner shook my hand again and inquired if I was a fan. We made small talk about the latest trades.

"I understand you are the architect on a couple of interesting projects here in town."

I acknowledged this hoping we were talking about the same ones.

"I thought about the profession once, but investment banking called me instead."

"We have some spare drafting tables available if you want to dip your toes in during the off-season."

He chuckled at my bad humor - it was easy to see why he had been so successful on Wall Street. The game ended with a whimper - we won one to nothing. Some security people appeared and escorted Natasha and myself around the crowd to the SUV.

***

"Did you have any other plans for the day?"

"No, you have been very gracious with your hospitality - you can drop me off at home."

"'Gracious with your hospitality,' is that something you learned to say from your mother?"

"I looked her straight in the eye assessing whether she was being sarcastic - she appeared to be dead serious, "No, my Dad used to say that - the ladies always took it as a compliment."

The driver opened the SUV door for me - standing at the curb I leaned back in and said goodbye. This lady was a piece of work - that was for sure.

***

The pool area was practically vibrating. Marcie had on her usual disguise and was burrowed in the far corner of the enclosure. There was no pretense as to her partaking in a prohibited alcoholic beverage - the bottle of Gray Goose and mixer were next to her chair only partly concealed by an ice cooler.

"You want to hear about my new job?"

"Okay - do you have an extra cup?"

"We can share."

I sipped, "There doesn't seem to be much mixer in here - tell me about the job."

She nudged the mixer bottle towards me with her purple nailed foot. "You were a big help."

"How so? I decided to forgo the mixer and just added more ice.

"It's with a window contractor from New York - they want to start a branch here - there will be no one in the office but me except when some big shots come down for the day. The money is good."

"And I helped how?"

"Remember that reference letter you asked me to draft and said I could sign - I did do the signature thing, They were impressed especially since the Hill was going to start up again soon."

"Anything else I should know?"

"Not really - that's a nice perfume you have on by the way."

***

The thunder claps woke me up fast. I had fallen asleep trying to finish a book I was actually enjoying but which seemed to be too long to finish.

My mind finally separated the knocking on the door from the thunder. I let in a soaked Marcie, "I need shelter." She stripped off her clothing and went for the shower, appearing, wrapped in a towel, ten minutes later, "Don't you take a shower - I want to swaddle myself in that perfume and you can pretend I'm her."

***

Natasha directed the driver to head towards the beach. She dozed - awakened - dozed.

Cliff had warned her there would be times like this. Being rich could be replaced by other passions but it was best to be rich he said. They had talked through the diamond shaped crevices of the ten foot high, razor wire topped chain link fence that separated the boys' and girls' play fields at the orphanage. They talked about little else. Her name was not Natasha then, nor was his Cliff. They picked the names together after watching a movie in the orphanage social hall one night. Soon after, both having been declared officially eighteen years of age, they found themselves working in a supermarket, rooming in a rundown boarding house. Their future prospects were as bleak as the orphanage intended.

The driver softly pronounced, "We're here," and she fell out of her reverie.

Natasha passed the driver a number of bills and excused him for the holiday.

A party was well underway in the penthouse. She waved to her friend, Beth. Most of the other celebrants seemed familiar. She went to the back of the apartment where she maintained her own bedroom. It was most definitely her own - no one entered here - not her husband or the cleaning staff - no one.

***

The room was her sanctuary. The space was a microcosm of the dormitory at the orphanage. The lighting was dim to non-existent. She had hired a TV documentary producer to make nighttime recordings of institutional spaces, capturing the heavy breathing, snores, sneezes, coughing, and cries of the dreamers, a cacophony of sounds that she identified as typical of numerous nights at the orphanage. In an antique shop, she had found an exact duplicate of the dormitory's chamber pot.

Removing her clothing she put on a thin cotton nightgown, pressed the switch that turned on the sounds of the night, slipped under the tattered Army blanket on the cot and slept. Her dreams were always the same - someday she would be rich. In the mornings, her dreams were always fulfilled - on the new day, she would leave the dormitory and walk into the luxury of a sky-high penthouse.

***

The penthouse living area was dark and empty. A storm had arrived overnight - rain pelted the windows. The sea was all whitecaps. Not so surprisingly, wetsuit clad swimmers tested the waters on the beach below. The cleaning crew would arrive in a few hours and put the apartment back together. She unlocked her study and went to work. The abandoned graveyard of the day before haunted her.

***

Several years before, she had engaged a much reputed service that utilized personal DNA to trace ancestral roots. She did not believe she would find her parents, certainly not find out why she was abandoned; but she was curious nonetheless. The report came with an optional consultation as to the findings and explanation of certain technical terms used by the science.

"We have found the genes that suggest a background that is common to people that we loosely call American Indian; also that of northern Africa as well as of a white-skinned race. The white-skinned evidence suggests Eastern Europe with markers that would suggest Semites or Jews as the source; the American Indian is more closely associated with the tribe called the Accokeek; Africa is a continent of course but it could be from the area we now call Egypt. Our data bank has many DNA samples of a similar nature. Using the anecdotal evidence from persons in our files, which is of course confidential, we can make a guess. The Accokeeks were native to this immediate area - the Jews and Africans only go back a few hundred years in this country. There are many pockets in what were the early colonies that have similar mixtures - think natives, slaves, and immigrants - Accokeek would put it closer to home."

35

The holiday storm carried into the first day of the shortened work week. The staff settled in after exchanging stories as to how they spent their extended holiday weekend. The Tuckers fully stocked the office refrigerator with Mom's home-cooking. Cynthia sniffed at these offerings in her usual dubious manner, "Hope there's something in there that didn't come out of the rear end of a pig." All the others appeared relaxed and tanned as well as less confrontational.

***

"Your advocate is on the line - I looked it up - it's French for lawyer, *n'est-ce pas?*" Angelica appeared smug as well as rested.

"The meter is running, Pierre. I had the opportunity to schmooze with some friends at the beach - no charge there - the Hill is the talk of the City - I need some information."

"Okay - what?

"You said the stop work order and subsequent demolition is bogus - can you prove that?"

"The state has all the reports, the test results and samples of concrete."

"So, if I subpoenaed all that from the archives and had an independent authority confirm that the state's conclusion was bogus then construction could continue?"

"That's the working hypothesis - but it won't work."

"Why not?"

"What you need is not in the archives anymore."

"You know that for a fact?"

"That's what I was told."

"Have you committed a Class A felony?"

"Not me."

"Do you know where the stuff is?"

"No."

"I'll get back to you."

Angelica was still hovering. "Allaine is on the line from London."

"Crikey, mate, you had me on hold for a fortnight."

"You just got back from London?"

"My daughter is homesick - she misses her Mother."

"Uh-huh."

"I hear the Hill is going to start up?"

"Maybe - where is the stuff that Pasqualli 'lent' you?"

"Gone - including the U-Haul - never to be seen again - I'm told."

"Uh-huh."

"What's going on?"

"I'll get back to you."

***

I left the office with the information from the survey of the Bluff tax properties to see if I could find Lawyer Kline in his office. We went for coffee. "These properties would all work - one, two, three is my order of preference - there's a graveyard up there - don't buy that one."

"I'll get back to you. Otherwise, any further word on the Grand Bazaar?"

"it's in your hands - the roof fabric is on it's way."

There was no way of reading Lawyer Kline's demeanor, "The tax sale is at the end of this week."

"Get back to me."

***

By the time lunch came around, I was already exhausted. Not really hungry, I surveyed the offerings. The Tucker boys were digging into a container of succotash alternating spoonfuls with slices of cornbread.

Chuan had a store-bought salad to offer, "I know no one has been eating what my girlfriend and mother have prepared the last few weeks - it has not worked out even for me. Both of them are mad at me for different reasons - and lunch was suffering - I apologize."

"Anything you want to talk about?"

"There's nothing really new - my bride-to-be is having visa problems so everything has been postponed. My brother says the delay is a ploy to make her more desirable."

Cynthia was on top of this, "I'm with your brother." Murphy nodded his head in agreement.

"What do you think Boss?"

I was lost in my melancholy. "My track record in affairs of the heart is not sterling - Chuan deserves our support - as for me, I'll wait it out - I've told Chuan, privately, what I thought early on. You all are good friends to provide your input." I left the table, forgetting to eat.

***

It seemed like I was spending my time and energy waiting for someone else to do something. I looked over the office job list to see if there was a project I could give my attention. One of the Fed jobs appeared to be stalled, or perhaps never initiated. No one had posted any time since the overall contract began.

I asked in the drafting room to make sure the file was just not up to date, "Bad news Boss - the guy in charge is a real jerk - he doesn't want anyone messing on his turf," Murphy advised.

"Perfect - I need someone to push around."

***

I called familiar name on the contact list and actually got a real person on the phone.

"We have tried making an appointment to see the building and have been rebuffed," I explained.

"The Director is very protective as to who he lets in."

"We promise to be careful."

"That's not the problem - the guy is a genius and he's paranoid - we cater to his idiosyncrasies - in the mean time, the building is unsafe."

"Right now, it's hard for us to do anything to help."

"I'll get back to you."

36

"The tax sale is not going to happen; at least not for the Bluff properties"

"What now?"

"The mayor exercised some forgotten ordinance that gives him discretion to condemn abandoned property and dispose of it any way he sees fit for the public benefit."

"What did you buy?"

"All of it - the key was the graveyard - we promised to take care of it in perpetuity."

"Really?"

"We need to record the ownership and move ahead."

"Which parcel gets the church slash synagogue?"

"The one next to the cemetery. We already have a benefactor who will pay to restore the cemetery and make repairs as necessary."

"Who?"

"Can't say - it will be done through the new non-profit."

"What's your timing?"

"Soon as possible - we need to free up the Grand Bazaar permit."

At least no one was saying, 'I'll get back to you.'

I thought about who to put in charge of relocating the building. It was time to break up the Tucker threesome. "Jubal, I have a special assignment for you."

"Are you firing me, Boss?"

"You have to stop gossiping with Murphy. It's an interesting job and requires multiple skills. You will have the backup of myself and the office if need be."

"Let me get pencil and paper."

"Good start. On the Grand Bazaar site there is a building that needs to be moved to a new location. It's an old church that has been moved before and is up on shoring. We have a place for it to go, not that far away. You need to get it done."

"I'll do my best."

"Okay - look at the map - this is the building site - this is the Grand Bazaar site - there's an old stadium being torn down at the Bazaar site - you will need to get through security - I'll call ahead and give them your name. See a fellow at the site, name of Jose, he'll be looking for you - he will give you a key to get into the church. Take measurements, lots of pictures - always lots of pictures. Go to the new site and look around. Go to City Hall and tell them what you want to do - find out what it takes to get a permit - probably several permits. Get back to me after that and I'll tell you what to do next."

Angelica was hovering as usual. "Call Grand Bazaar security - call Jose - give Jubal some petty cash. Get him a car and driver or else we'll never see him again."

"When do I start?"

"Now - don't even come back to the office until you get those things done."

"Angelica, do you have any more prospects for your assistant position?"

"I don't know what to do."

"Write up a job description based on what you do - assign some hours per week to the different tasks I'm going to do the same thing for myself. Maybe we'll get a better idea of who and what we need."

I stared at the phone.

Something actually productive would be making up a list of what needed to be done once Jubal returned from his assignment. We would need a surveyor to stake out the property and do some topo - a soil engineer to determine where to set the foundation, a structure guy to design and certify the foundation. The civil engineers would have to find out about water and sewer and gas and electric service and set the environmental standards. I would keep the historical society in the loop - they will probably need to sign off on any permits.

Now that I asked Angelica to make up a job description for herself I needed to think about my own role and what duties could be dispersed to someone else. In the good old days, I did everything - the first hiring of a secretary was a disaster - she stayed long enough to become eligible for unemployment and was gone. Temps drove me crazy - full time people came and went - Angelica could leave at any time for school - it was not a career job for anyone. The paperwork was overwhelming. There was no way I could hire someone who could do what I did.

Jubal was on the phone. "I'm at City Hall - no one will talk to me until tomorrow. I went to the Grand Bazaar site, met Jose and looked at the church for a few minutes and decided to go to the Bluffs and return to the church later. The Bluffs is the interesting story. There was a crowd at the cemetery. Folks were clearing brush and locating grave sites - the place is a mess - all kinds of garbage - there were trucks there to haul it away. An old geezer who must live in the neighborhood spotted me."

"Short guy, dressed in overalls, wild hair, one good eye?"

"That's him. He told me that the cemetery goes much further then the stone markers. People used the area long after it was an official cemetery - wooden markers are long gone. And, that's not all."

"Who was in charge of this crew and the trucks and so forth?"

"That's sort of interesting. There was this lady - really pretty - out in the middle of the mess looking at the stones and there was a fellow who asked who I was and introduced himself to me as Chester. I heard him call the lady Natasha - like in, *War and Peace.*"

"What else?"

"The old guy - he said to call him Popeye - told us that sometimes trucks pull up in the middle of the night and he thinks they are making use of the graveyard. We walked down the slope and there were some shallow graves with fresh dirt - Chester called the police and I left."

I did not know what to say appropriate to the situation just reported to me, "You read, *War and Peace?*"

"It's a great book - my Mom made all three of us read it. I have my own copy."

"Go home - get an early start in the morning - stay away from the Bluffs - don't talk to anyone at City Hall about the graveyard."

I reflected on this latest news. It would all come to light sooner rather then later after being filtered through the conspiracy mill. I wondered if Jubal had any photographs of Natasha amidst the gravestones - that would be a good one to tape to my apartment refrigerator. I was in anticipation of so much information, my head hurt.

The phone was still silent. I needed to change venues so I could think without anticipating interruptions.

***

At Costco, I made up for skipping lunch. The tumult from the shoppers, the babble that I could not understand even if shouted in my ear, was the unrivaled backdrop for perfecting my thoughts. The sustenance from the speedily obtained sandwich helped my headache better than any analgesic. I felt like I was whole again.

Saul - why didn't I think of him. He was currently unemployed - knew something about business and construction and since his wife was rich didn't need to make a great deal of money. He would welcome the opportunity to be useful. He would just handle administrative matters and keep order. He would not do what only architects are allowed to do. He would fit in with others in the office - he wouldn't need a title, just a job description. Maybe I could even design again.

I was having a eureka moment. The Asian family across from my table were all beaming, celebrating my happiness.

37

Jubal had done his first assignment well. I gave him the list of consultants to deal with directly. I arbitrarily changed the site for the relocation to one I thought was appropriate and furthest away from the graveyard. Jubal's photos were well done - the ones of Natasha in the background were not so telling - all I could make out was a figure, in Esquire's version of stylish archeologist's attire. For now, Jubal would produce an as-built drawing of the church and a preliminary site plan.

***

"Shalom, Shalom - what's new in our continuing saga?"

"You have heard about the cemetery fiasco from your man on the scene, I assume?"

"Yes - I have picked another site just in case - no harm done - I hope."

"The non-profit is making arrangements to move the church - closer to its final resting place - so to speak."

"Good idea. Make sure you keep the Historical Society informed - we need to retain their good will." I wondered if this temporary move would be enough to shake loose the Grand Bazaar permit.

I went over Jubal's notes from his meetings at City Hall. There were no surprises as far as requirements were concerned. They were treating the placement of the church like any prefabricated structure. Luckily, the building was so small and of such simplistic construction that it found its place comfortably in current building codes. I did not contemplate any difficulties except for the usual bureaucratic bickering. Anyone who read Tolstoy had the patience to wear down the powers that be.

It took me a while to find a phone number for Saul. The new receptionist, who had kept the secret of Saul's stairway hideaway, led me to an unlisted number at his home.

Saul answered hesitantly as if he didn't believe the phone actually worked.

"I miss our stairway meetings."

"Me too. The life of a house-husband is not for me."

"How would you like to go back to work?"

"Tell me what you have in mind."

"Come by the office and we'll talk."

"Angelica, I think we may have our assistance problem solved - maybe?"

"That's good, Boss - everyone working here is great and that helps a lot. We'll have it all together - don't worry.

"Allaine called."

I reflected on the concern for my disquiet in Angelica's remarks before calling Allaine.

"You are back from London?"

"The latest crisis is resolved. We got a call from Jubal - it sounds like the Tuckers are working out for you."

"He is an interesting young man."

"I'm going to pair him up with Mohammad. Between the two, we should get this thing done."

"Mohammad?"

"We're getting some Mid-East work - having the local language helps. He and Jubal should get along fine."

"Uh-huh."

***

At lunch, I brought the staff up to date on the pending relocation of the church. The two Tuckers seemed envious that Jubal was involved with, "dead people and stuff." Cynthia fanned the flames with a story about some decapitation she had allegedly witnessed. I gave her a look that suggested she should change the subject. Chuan was missing - he was at the airport to greet his father and bride-to-be. We all conjectured as to what would happen next. It was more quiet than normal - everyone was distracted by the requests and responses and comments to documents sent out before the holiday. I was glad when the lunch break ended early - I had picked at the offerings but was not really hungry.

Saul dropped in soon after with enough lunch for two.

"You missed one of our more morbid lunch hours in recent times."

"I promise not to be unwholesome - the offerings are from your favorite deli."

We moved to the conference room "This is about working here - in the office - providing administrative support." I was now hungry and paused to retrieve a corn beef sandwich and dill pickle, "We have a terrific secretary, the staff is getting efficient but, both she and I are sometimes overwhelmed."

"My father-in-law had his own way of doing things which I inherited before he died - then there was chaos when he passed away and my wife and Chester came in - there is still confusion."

"We have good systems in place - there's just not enough time in the day."

"I think I can help."

"We don't have a lot in the budget."

"I'll take whatever you offer - I don't need benefits."

"When can you start?"

"I'll give you a few hours, today, after lunch."

We mutually relaxed and talked baseball. I motioned the ever hovering Angelica to join us. "Please meet Saul. He will be working with you - you are co-workers - there is only one Boss and he plans to worry less."

"Jubal on the phone." Saul was already at work.

"I'm at Allaine's office - I just met Mohammad - who just answered our phone? We're going to look at the church together and do a slow drive-by at the Bluffs."

"Okay - get a foundation designed - include a deep cellar if necessary - sooner is better then later - a new fellow employee answered the phone - his name is Saul - you'll meet him next time you are in the office."

I called Chester to find out his take on what went on the previous day. "Yesterday was an interesting day on the Bluffs, I hear?"

"The Ecumenical Heritage Committee asked me to help clean up a cemetery they just took over from the city. I brought some guys and trucks from a job we have near by."

"Who exactly?"

"Lawyer Kline."

"Jubal tells me there was a woman there as a member of the cleanup crew?"

"That was Tabershaw's wife - she's a member of the Committee."

"Messy job for a lady?"

"She's looking for something - have no idea what - her

husband is handing us back the Hill job - we're keeping him happy."

"Uh-huh."

"Who was that who answered the phone, Pierre?"

"New employee - what's up Babette?"

"I have a meeting tomorrow with the Governor and the head of the State Building Department - please be available after lunch in case I need some information. Any chance that the material from the archives may reappear?"

"I'm told - not."

38

The diner was humming, the TVs were at full volume - the waitresses were actually running from place to place - Chico was cursing his helpers at the grille. All the booths were full so I sat at the counter. I swiveled one-eighty on the stool to view the different TV fare. A familiar talking head gave the news of the newly reopened Plunderer trial: *"... jury dismissed again as the defendant proclaimed in open court that he was innocent and that he did not murder the man discovered by the police at the scene of one of the robberies."* At least, the Hill was not mentioned. Swiveling back into place, I found coffee and breakfast on hand ready to be consumed. I waved thanks to Chico.

***

Arriving at the office, Chuan was holding court - I was sure I knew what that was about. I made a motion with my hands as if shooing geese and hung around for a few moments to make sure the dispersal took hold, utilizing my time at Susan's desk to see how the house design was coming along. I was impressed and told her so. "This one will be published - I'm sure."

Publication in a prominent magazine was the gold standard for Susan and her peers.

Saul was gesturing with the telephone hand signal, "It's Jubal."

"Everything's under control, Boss - I'll be back at the office for lunch. One thing - Mohammad and I were at the Bluffs - there was a big truck parked at the cemetery - Popeye was hanging around - Mohammad says the company, whose name is on the truck provides 'ground searching radar.'"

"Uh-huh."

Saul and Angelica had loose papers and files scattered all over the conference room table. There were brochures from companies that stored the dregs of modern day business and those of companies who safely destroyed material that was no longer viable but confidential in nature.

"We need your permission to get rid of this stuff one way or another"

"Right this minute?"

"We're running out of space"

I scanned the accumulation - so many years of stuff - too many reminders of projects not gone forward, too many fees unpaid - clients whose names I did not recognize - there was not enough of my personal time available to look at each piece of paper, "Pretend I got hit by a bus and you had to close the office - our accountant has the important financial stuff - use your discretion - keep in mind we have a dumpster in the building." Saul and Angelica were staring at me "Sometimes, the past is not prologue."

There was the usual work to face for the rest of the morning - I would look forward to lunch to hear the latest on

Chuan's destiny - Jubal would have some scandal - and then there would be the wait for a call, if at all, from my attorney.

Angelica signaled that Allaine was on the line.

"Ho-Ho-Ho and a bottle of rum - we may have buried treasure on the Bluffs."

"Is that what they're looking for?"

"I know that it costs a fortune to rent that assortment of equipment."

"Uh-huh."

"You have nothing to share with your fellow buccaneer?"

"I'll have Jubal talk to Popeye."

"Who the hell is Popeye?"

I ordered up some food from our local Chinese restaurant to add to the lunch larder.

Jubal entered with a fellow that brought all conversation at the table to an abrupt halt.

Jeb and Nate rose immediately to shake hands, "Salaam, Mohammad." Cynthia was about to say something but changed her mind. Jubal introduced me. "Salaam, Boss." The rest at the table were introduced.

Mohammad surveyed the offerings and filled his plate.

The usual gossip began but it soon turned to Chuan. "Fill us in - you missed work yesterday so something must have happened."

"I met my father and bride-to-be at the airport and drove them home. It was very quiet in the car."

"First impressions?" Cynthia had found her voice.

"She seems very sweet - she didn't have anything to say."

"The quiet ones are the best," Murphy offered.

"I dropped them off at the house - I told them I had to go

back to work - I went to my brother's and we had more rice wine then we should have and I went to sleep there."

"What do you think Mohammad?"

"I have three wives - all arranged - perhaps I am not the one to offer advice."

The woman at the table were pretending to gag, uniformly shaking their heads.

Jubal spoke of the continued activity at the Bluffs. There were no more ghoulish jokes - he offered that he and Mohammad had the permit process under control and he was, for the most part, back in the office.

"Where did you study engineering Mohammad?"

"MIT - I studied at MIT."

Mohammad took me aside to say goodbye, "I don't really have three wives - I say that to avoid being hit on by the ladies who think they can score with a rich Arab."

"I know you're not rich as well as not being married - the MIT part checks out."

"You had me investigated?"

"'Trust but verify,' is my motto."

I found myself strumming my fingers - waiting. Angelica and Saul took turns showing me documents for a thumbs up or thumbs down decisions. Eventually, a pattern was developed that allowed them to go it alone.

***

"How did it go?" It was late in the day and obviously beyond the time of her scheduled meeting with the governor.

"Not exactly the way I wanted. I'm having dinner with a judge friend of mine tonight. If I take the permit status to court, that will take the responsibility away from the politicians."

"Male or female judge?"

"Est-ce important?"

***

It was finally the end of the day. Judy knocked and brought in beers.

"Thanks." I took in her loosened blouse and tucked-up skirt and bare feet. "Did you ever make it with someone of the same gender?"

"In college - sort of - with a roommate - why do you ask?"

"For business or pleasure?"

"She had a cute boyfriend - I would say both."

"How does dinner sound?"

"Nothing kinky - I hope."

"Define kinky."

39

Another of my, 'get back to you' correspondents got back to me.

"Spoke to the lab director - he checked you out - I'll get you a special security clearance and, I'll meet you there to make the introduction. I know this sounds like an old, 'B' movie but, 'come by yourself.'"

***

The laboratory was a rambling collection of rectangular brick buildings of different stories and heights. All window opening had been filled with opaque glass or various forms of ventilation devices. Weeds and young saplings had sprouted above the roof parapets. There were signs of foundation settlement. "I should have brought my hard hat."

"Wait till you see the inside."

The director presented himself, unsmiling, and agitated. "I only have a few minutes."

"Director, we need to look around - if you don't have the

time, lend us one of your subordinates," now my sponsor was agitated.

"I will lend you Doctor Wang - she will show you around - I will catch up shortly."

Doctor Wang smiled a lot - she know her away around; nevertheless I took charge by opening doors and following my instincts as to what the complex comprised from walking around outside earlier. I scribbled a few notes for what I hoped would be an exiting discussion. The Director showed up as we arrived back from where we started. "Everything is okay - right?"

I looked at my Fed sponsor who looked at me to answer the question. "The place is a firetrap - in severe structural distress and ill-suited for human habitation and my recommendation is to tear the place down - sooner rather then later - and I'll be glad to put that in writing. Any questions?"

Doctor Wang fled the scene.

The director's face had turned purple, "Where do you find these idiots?"

Doctor Wang reappeared to escort us out.

"What is it you do here exactly, Doctor?"

She looked around. "It's difficult to explain in layman's terms. We are perfecting a method of analyzing soil to determine where it originated, who or what lived in it's domain, extracting DNA when we can - It has a long way to go."

"Really?"

We were now at the far end of the parking lot - Doctor Wang furtively looked in all directions - we were definitely alone except for my sponsor who was somewhat patiently waiting in his car. "I am actually co-director - I am here on loan from the PRC - we are working together on this research. Other countries are interested as well."

"Why are you telling me this?"

"The building is dangerous. We have plenty of money -

even in China these working conditions would not be acceptable."

Now I was more then curious, "Where does the money come from?"

"Various governments - private corporations - just yesterday some very exotic lady came in and gave us a big check along with some samples of dirt."

A car horn was now honking persistently, "It was nice meeting you," I gave her my card.

***

"What was that all about?"

"Money and dirt - I'll send you my report." For the rest of the drive, we talked baseball.

40

"How was dinner?"

"A little heavy on the protein. I'll be seeking an injunction today that will free up the original building permit - I'll be in touch.

I felt optimistic.

***

"You're not off the hook."

"Meaning what exactly?"

"The Director has friends in high places."

"Uh-huh."

"Short of tearing down the complex, we have agreed to have the place put up to snuff."

"I wish you luck with that."

"The Director likes you - we like you - we need to move forward. Doctor Wang will be your contact"

"I need a new scope of work and payment agreement. In the meantime, I'll think about it."

This job could be the cash cow of the century, I thought - there appeared to be money in dirt.

***

The Hill was stalled, but maybe not for long - likewise, the Grand Bazaar. The Fed jobs, already started, were moving along. The Fed job which I would call for ease of identification, The Dirt Lab, could start soon. Maybe.

If all of this happened at the same time, we would be swamped. Chester in his new position as top executive for the contractor for both the Hill and the Bazaar would be swamped as well - that would not be helpful for getting a proper execution of our designs.

Many of his father's cronies were still in important positions in the firm and had oversized egos that exceeded their skills. Chester's sister showed up at the office from time to time but she didn't do any heavy lifting.

"Chester, how are things?"

"We are busy but we are not busy."

"Do you have a contract with Doctor Tabershaw if the Hill restarts? "

"We have an understanding - what about you?"

"Much less than that."

"Maybe we should have a meeting?"

"Set it up - try for a place other than the hospital."

"How goes the final permit for the Grand Bazaar."

"We're working on it."

"The church gets moved to the Piggly-Wiggly parking lot this weekend."

"That will help."

"Anything else on the graveyard?"

"We're providing laborers and trucks for the ongoing clean-up - the city has taken away all of the most recent internments. Somebody is funding a search of the ground below the surface."

"I haven't seen anything on TV or in the papers, not even about the corpses dumped there during the night?"

"Somebody who knows somebody, etcetera, etcetera, has probably squelched it."

"Uh-huh."

Who was somebody I wondered - I speculated if the curse had run its course and whether we could put the Hill back on track. I thought back to an earlier conversation, ..the Director likes you .., conveyed by my Fed sponsor, and wondered what that was all about.

A few hours later I heard from Chester, "He won't leave his comfort zone - I'll meet you at the hospital at six."

***

I deliberately left for the rendezvous earlier than necessary. The hospital receptionist offered me a seat in the lobby and noting I was uncomfortable, suggested I wait in the area for relatives outside the operating theater. I was alone. It took only a few minutes for me to figure out how to get into the observation gallery. There was a huddle of people, hard to identify how many, sitting in the front rows, speaking in low tones in a language that was too hushed to distinguish. I found the furthest corner away from the group and concentrated on the scene   below. I sensed, from the doctor's body language, that things were not going well.

The doctor looked up at the gallery and shook his head left to right and the opposite several times. The huddle rushed out as one and soon appeared in the operating theater en masse overwhelming a single security guard - additional safety personnel arrived within a minute and separated the scrum of the Doctor and staff from the protagonists - the doctor still held his scalpel prepared to defend himself as he departed the room. I left as rapidly as possible to the building entrance to await Chester.

***

"You look worried?"

"Wanting to meet elsewhere was probably a good idea. It will probably be a while before the doctor is available."

"Let's take a walk - this place will always be creepy to me." I motioned to the entrance security guard as to where we would be.

"What's on your mind?"

"My sister is upset that Saul is working for you - she considers it demeaning."

"I beg your pardon?"

"Her words. She didn't offer any explanation - I wouldn't even venture a guess.

The guard opened the door to signal us to come back in just as a group of cloaked and hooded persons of unascertainable sex or age were exiting, lighting cigarettes after taking a single step beyond the entrance. Chester shuddered as we brushed against them in our haste to get back into the air-conditioning.

***

We met the doctor in the hallway at the doorway to his office. I had not had the opportunity to tell Chester what I had viewed a few minutes before but Tabershaw's demeanor announced that he was shaken. The doctor gestured us towards the bar and refrigerator and lighted another cigarette to replace the one a few seconds dead in the ashtray.

"It doesn't happen often - this last patient died on the table - I shouldn't have taken on the case - it was a futile conceit - I should have known better."

Chester and I were stone silent.

"I'll have to report it to the authorities - it has happened before - the Feds always find a way to cover it up."

There was a knock on the door. I expected to see the Doctor's wife who Chester and I both now knew as Natasha. Instead, I recognized a member of the doctor's team, who appeared to be the doctor's alter ego in the operating room,

"There's a private ambulance at the service entrance - the driver has all the right paperwork - they are supposed to take away the patient on the table."

"Check the paperwork again just to be certain we're covered - if you're sure, start the clean up so we can all go home."

The room took on a new life. The Doctor poured himself a drink. We were now comfortable enough to take him up on his initial offer for one as well.

"Okay - let's talk about the Hill?" The doctor lighted yet another cigarette.

"We are close to renewing the original permit. Close. Keep in mind I have been working on this without my firm having a contract with you."

"Chester?"

"It's the same with us - our costs are going up - we have no reason to negotiate - if the Hill design has to be upgraded because of codes or marketing strategy, we will have to start all over again. There is no incentive for us at this time."

The doctor refilled his glass. "I like people who do things by the book. Have your lawyers draw up contracts - I'll get my people to respond as soon as possible." At this the doctor looked even more relaxed. Chester and I sat back from the edge of our seats. As somehow scripted, there was a tentative knock on the office door. Natasha, as Chester and I now knew her, entered further clearing the initial gloom with her perfume and display of the latest fashions. There was the usual cheek peck for the doctor before she retired to the furthest part of the office.

"Thanks for coming here this evening - I apologize for the minor upheaval." That was our exit line which we were both happy to act upon."

***

"Did I mention that I find this place creepy?"

We were standing next to the only two cars in the parking lot. A security guard at the exit was eager to lift the gate and see us gone. "I'll race you to Costco."

41

Saul arrived at the office at his usual time, post kids-morning-carpool. There was no sign that considered the job demeaning.

I found myself staring at the telephone.

Jubal's call finally broke the ice, "Mohammad and I met the surveyors on the Bluffs - the soils people showed up around the same time."

"Anything going on at the graveyard?"

"Everyone's gone - all I saw was Popeye walking his dog."

"Stop by the Piggly-Wiggly and check out the condition of the church - then get back to finishing the foundation drawings."

Saul gestured another telephone call for me, "Benito?"

Our chief designer had been in New York City for several weeks, part of the time on overdue vacation, the rest of the days on call working with the Grand Bazaar marketing group. "What's going on?"

"I'm ready to come home, Boss. I've had the chance to work with some really smart people and I've learned lot."

"Briefly?"

"The team loves the concept - it's difficult to get the retailers to share this enthusiasm. No one wants to go first - there's nothing we should be thinking about changing."

"Okay - come on home - we all miss you." As big a pain as Benito could be some times, he balanced off myself in a positive way.

***

I was losing patience. The very unofficial conditions for obtaining the Grand Bazaar permit were well on their way to being fulfilled. It was not my responsibility to find users for the finished product - it would be nice to see some positive response, for my client's sake, but that was not in my purview. I had an itch to go down to City Hall. I stared at a sample of Bazaar roof fabric on my desk and began to have some questions of my own.

Angelica brought me a very large envelope covered with all species of official looking seals; the messenger who had brought it was waiting for my signature in the background. "Don't you want to open it?"

"I know what it is. Find Cynthia and Saul and have them meet me in the conference room."

"What's up, Boss?"

"In this envelope is a request for services from the Feds for a special project. I have been to the site, met some of the people involved - I need a fresh set of eyes to evaluate whether we should get involved - let me just say from what I know so far it should be interesting and there is some money to be made. Maybe."

"Maybe interesting or maybe profitable?"

"Maybe, for both - go to the Fed archives - there may be some relevant documents there - go way back in time - try the microfilm files - these buildings are really old - the complex could have had a different name at one time - find out if you two need a special security clearance."

***

When I first came to the City, I knew no one. Retreating from a mistake filled marriage leaving young children in the wake, I answered an ad in a professional magazine that offered me a chance to use my education and gain the necessary experience to apply for a license to practice architecture. The office was a sweat shop - the key personnel of the old school with no interest in new materials and techniques. A few clients approached me to do some small jobs on the side to gain more personal service and, of course, to save money. I was grateful for the opportunity. There would eventually be conflicts of interest and I left before I was fired. The spare time gave me a chance to spend some extra hours studying - the stars and planets were aligned, and I passed on the first go around. This brought me to phase two of my plan and I legally changed my name and brought all my past life to a screaming halt. I regretted doing this - my European ancestors would have appreciated the family name carried forward with honor but the name was too foreign, too many consonants - not enough vowels - and I wanted a clean break.

I chose a single name - Corbu. The authorities required a name a little more detailed, and I applied a first initial of 'B.' In later days, I told employees that the 'B' stood for Boss and it stuck.

I worked out of my apartment taking on any kind of work I could find. There were other people in the city operating like me and we sometimes collaborated to get the job done. The next step was some office space offering the chance to separate work and life. I created a persona for business cards, forms and the like - Corbu & Others - with only a local phone number as point of contact. To those who asked, I explained that, 'Others' was not a business partner but merely a printer's typo and the title should have read the word, 'and' instead of the ampersand and no capital, 'o' - thus, 'CORBU and others.'

The actual 'others' came later, one at a time, and with much paranoia as to the commitment on my part. The big break was the Hill. The same contractor fed us the still mysterious client for the Grand Bazaar.

***

"I met with the good Doctor Tabershaw - he said to submit a contract for services for the Hill - I would like to see a sizable retainer - his lawyers are going to look it over - he said so and I'm sure they will."

"This can get complicated."

"Does that translate to expensive?" Babette was apprehensive, I'm sure - she saw me swimming with the sharks.

"Who is going to actually own the building permit - right now, it technically belongs to the contractor - Chester no longer has a viable contract - there's no guarantee he's going to be on board for the next go around - assuming there is a next go around?"

"We had a meeting together last night - Chester will be submitting a new contract to the doctor as well."

"This is complicated."

"And?"

"Pierre, I'll repeat, this is complicated - the cast of characters is speculative at best. There are a lot of eyes to dot and tees to cross - believe me, I'll look after your interests." She dropped her lawyerly tone of voice. "I love you like a brother - let me get back to you."

I reflected on the purported complications - there were probably even more nuances to a lawyer than I could imagine as a technician; "...love you like a brother," Did that mean I was in over my head and needed to be rescued from myself? Once again, I was waiting for others to report back.

42

"Allaine on the phone."

"I'm waiting for them to call my flight - I need to bring you up to date."

"Okay."

"Mohammad is applying for a foundation permit for the church this morning - he'll get your output, whatever he needs, from Jubal."

"Okay."

"I have talked to Pasqualli - he's going to redirect some resources to the Bluffs. Chester will coordinate."

"Resources?"

"Whatever it takes to build the foundation - we'll use high early strength concrete."

"Redirect?"

"Don't ask."

"Where are you going?"

"London."

"Do I deduce problems afoot with your offspring, Watson?"

"Most assuredly, Sherlock - it involves a tattoo artist and making a new life together in the Midlands - got to go."

"Ta ta."

***

Now seemed an appropriate time to visit City Hall. First, I needed to pay some attention as to what was going on in the drafting room, now appropriately called the studio, to get up to date on how our various projects were progressing. Benito was back, and with Robbie in tow was looking at everything done in his absence to determine if the office design standards were up to snuff. I answered questions as to schedule and scope of work but otherwise stayed away from being an arbitrator. Soon it would be time for billings and things looked good. Benito was uniformly annoying to all, and I left it at that.

***

The walk to City Hall would take about an hour and would give me time to think about strategy. Along the way, I observed the ever changing neighborhoods. Once empty lots were being infilled - sometimes the new work was sympathetic to the cityscape - other projects attempted to hit for the fences and did not quite make it. I liked many of the industrial materials now being used on a smaller scale, the copious use of glass and the general feel of proudly entering the present century. The use of super graphics and bright colors at street level shook up the stodgy architecture still to be revitalized.

I window shopped the high-end men's stores, thinking that some rejuvenation of my personal wardrobe could possibly add to the city's demeanor and assist my self esteem. I had no idea where to start. Next time I was at the barber shop, I would take the gentlemen's magazines more seriously. Frank Lloyd Wright effected a cape but I did not think that was my look - memory of pictures of my fellow practitioners in the professional magazines offered no inspiration. As with my Toyota, I would, for now, 'stick with the one that brung me.'

***

The shaded entrance to City Hall was crowded with smokers - so much for the mayor's health campaign. The permit office, divided between public and private by a line of counters, showed some signs of life but as always it was difficult to catch anyone's eye; thus the public was easily ignored. During the winter months, street people took comfort in the lines of waiting area chairs to shelter from the weather. I sat, undisturbed for an uncounted moment, cooling down, catching my wind while realizing that the walk was the most exercise I had done in a long while. It was probably time to talk to my latest doctor again. I soon spotted Jubal and Mohammad in coat and tie, truly professional in appearance, making their way from station to station, processing the permit application. The fact that they had thus far not been turned away was progress.

At the last station, there appeared to be a difficulty. It was here that all the documentation was reviewed, drawings stamped for approval for construction and most importantly, for the city, the fees assessed and payment accepted. As I often repeated, "It's the only game in town and you have to go with the house rules." Jubal and Mohammad glanced back at me for the first time.

I walked up to the counter as if I was an impatient stranger and eavesdropped on the conversation." These documents don't meet code," this from an arrogant young intern-type, light-skinned African-American, an apparent weight-lifter judging from his build and dress, obviously impatient to be elsewhere.

"Maybe I can help?"

"You will have to wait your turn," he reluctantly added, "sir."

"I'm with these fellows," and from my wallet extracted a pocket-copy of my architects license, my driver's license and various expired Federal ID's from jobs past. "that's my seal and signature on the drawings - so maybe I can help you?"

"Doesn't matter - you'll have to come back tomorrow," this with a little less arrogance and more street attitude.

"Perhaps I can speak with your supervisor?"

"He's busy."

To his retreating back, "You know, it's a Federal offense to deny service - I don't want to get you in trouble, so, maybe you can find someone to give us a hand." This was an outright fabrication, but it had worked in the past.

"I'll look."

I shooed Jubal and Mohammed to the nearby seating and waited. A very distinguished looking gentlemen, in his late forties, bearing a strong resemblance to the young intern appeared. "What can I do to help?" His ID badge displayed the name, 'Ezekiel Brown.' He picked up several of my IDs and compared the pictures with my face and the signatures with the permit documents lying on the counter. "We know who you are Mister Architect."

I found this statement troublesome but said nothing. Without another word he stamped and signed for several minutes and produced a voucher for payment. I handed the voucher to Jubal who as already in possession of a pre-signed blank check and pointed him towards the cashier's window. Jubal and Mohammad returned with the permit, smiling at their success, loosening their ties preparing for the weather outside. Mohammad pointed to the amount paid for the permit on the receipt - one dollar - shaking his head in disbelief. I returned from this distraction to face an empty counter and towards the work area beyond I wished, "Have a nice day."

I thought about taking the back stairs to visit with the Mister Brown of the mayor's office but decided to let the word spread by its natural course. That took less time then I anticipated. An obvious, civilian clothed security-type person approached and politely asked me to accompany him up to the Mayor's office - thankfully we took the elevator - the stress of the walk to City Hall and the last minute confrontation regarding the permit was still with me.

***

"It's good to see you again, Mister Architect," It was truly a trifecta - the Brown family was solidly implanted at the city's payroll trough, "I heard from downstairs that you are one step closer to fulfilling our dream - you are truly our savior."

There was no reference to the Grand Bazaar - I didn't really expect such - I played it straight. "The Ecumenical

Heritage Committee has done a great job considering all that they had to be overcome. You should plan a dedication ceremony once the building is in place - hold a religious service - there's plenty of credit to spread around."

Mr. Brown smiled at the mention of credit, "You are our savior - the Kingdom of Heaven will smile down on you." That was an exit line that also offered to fulfill a promise, or so I hoped.

***

I took a cab back to the office. There, Jubal was in the midst of regaling the staff with the entire history of his efforts to successfully come away with his first building permit. I let it run for a few more minutes and then threatened, "You want to hear about my first permit?" This immediately broke up the impromptu meeting.

I left a message at Chester's office that we had the permit. Angelica made a copy for our files - laminated the original and prepared a transmittal to accompany the somehow precious document to wherever Chester indicated. Reflecting on my part in the journey of this historical building, from the desolate abandoned parking lot to, perhaps, its original location, or close enough to call home, I felt a sense of pride. I had used my professional skills as well as much of the guile I learned from my Dad.

43

"Angelica, why are those two detectives in the office again - at the coffee machine - looking very comfortable at that?"

"They are not really detectives; they are investigators."

"Again?"

"When they were in the first time, the machine really

intrigued them and they loved the coffee and since then they come back every once in a while. The tall, cute one is really interesting and he's Hispanic and he knows a lot of the same people I do."

"You know how I feel about guns?"

"They don't carry guns, they're investigators - they know lots of interesting stuff."

"Setting aside, tall, dark, and handsome, and Hispanic, of course, what do you mean by interesting stuff?"

"They told me that the Plunderer guy, from the trial that keeps getting postponed, has made a deal - the judge is sick of seeing him in court, and released him to police in California, where he will go to jail there for sure. He gave up the names of his crew and the police will be watching them."

"Any other gossip?"

"It's not gossip - it's important for the future of the Hill project - I thought you would be interested." Angelica was pouting.

"Okay. The investigators are welcome any time - keep them corralled in the coffee machine area. No guns."

Susan brought me some newly printed drawings interrupting my thoughts about guns, "The client wants to come in later this morning for a review - please sit in with me."

"Okay - anything I should know?" I was already leafing through the drawings and not seeing any surprises.

"They are concerned about costs."

"Aren't we all?"

Susan was explaining some details to the aerospace fellow's wife when the husband excused himself for a refill on coffee. I followed him out - Susan could handle bathroom and kitchen information very well without our assistance or commentary.

"I see our machine is still doing a good job. We have stopped making them altogether - too expensive and really no market - you have a collectors item on your hands."

"Anything new on your company's horizon?"

"We were working on a driverless car, but then everyone else is as well, so we moved out of that into developing a pilotless airplane."

"I thought everyone was making drones?"

"No - real airplanes - to carry cargo and, maybe, passengers."

"Really?"

Susan came to fetch us. "We need you." She did not appear flustered so it was probably about money.

Before we left my prestigious, oft-visited coffee machine, the entrepreneur engineer confided, "We need to set a budget - my wife has no limits as far as those triplets are concerned."

"Follow my lead."

***

"Sorry, we were admiring some of the features of your husband's coffee machine design. Is there anything I can add to what Susan has provided to you today?"

"I know we are both concerned as to costs," she looked at her husband apprehensively, "this will be our home for a long time, and we want the best, but everything seems so expensive."

"I think we have enough information - I'll call in a contractor friend - no obligation; he owes me a favor or two - we'll come up with some numbers and we'll go on from there."

Everyone shook hands and said pleasant goodbyes. To Susan, I offered, "Carry on."

I went back to obsessing about guns.

44

"There's a Cleve on the phone." Saul was back at work after being out for several days for no explained reason.

"Bring your checkbook." The phone went dead - I could tell Cleve was not happy - surely because his chief was not happy. i called Chester and arranged to meet him at City Hall after lunch. His sister would have to sign checks for the large sums the Grand Bazaar permits would cost. Bonds would need to be personally guaranteed.

***

Chester brought a junior attorney from Lawyer Kline's office as an advisor. I was not impressed - the Building Department's atmosphere was obviously too intimidating for her and she showed it - Cleve's crew could not be frightened by a three-piece suit and a briefcase. I stood in the background - Cleve and the boys knew I had the process down pat - I said nothing and let the procedure unfold.

Cleve explained that his Chief was still uncertain about the roof fabric and stood ready to test the delivered material in the field. This was noted in red ink on many of the drawings. It was not a condition I would take umbrage with.

Checks were written for various bonds and fees. I looked over the lawyer's shoulder to see if any stipulations had been surreptitiously sneaked in to cause difficulties at a later date. She was not happy for what she saw as my interference but after referring to her as 'honey' and 'sweetheart' a few times and calling her attention to the fact that it was my name and license number on each piece of paper - she took the hint.

***

Chester and I celebrated with an Irish coffee after dismissing the attorney with good riddance. During the second round of refreshment, I proffered my bill for the fees due at this completed stage. It was fitting that the venue was one of Cynthia's projects. As previously instructed by Angelica, I picked up a special order of coffee beans to be used in our sophisticated machine.

I thought back to the time I first engaged Babette as, 'my' attorney, and the personal demeanor she presented - she was beautiful and tough and had the boys eating out of her hand - I was impressed with her on a number of levels. I still was.

I continued my walking regime for as long as it was comfortable and then flagged a taxi.

***

At the office I announced the news to all. Benito was especially pleased - it was really his baby and he deserved a lot of the credit. I had an urge to share the news with Babette - to reminisce - she had kept me on the, 'straight and narrow' during rough and complicated times - and continued to do so - of course she was being paid - but she took my concerns seriously and did what only she could do. I was passed through to her answering service, and I left only my name and number.

I felt somewhat better - the walk was invigorating to a point - the state of the Grand Bazaar relieved certain mental concerns - and there was money in the bank. The doctor could wait for another day.

I caught Saul as he was about to leave for the day. "I need to find out what you learned about that Fed complex. You and Cynthia catch me in the morning."

"Sure thing, Boss."

45

I had hitched a ride to the diner with Ralph very early in the morning - I had actually paced briskly around the perimeter of the parking area until I spotted Ralph heading towards his car. Jubal and Mohammad were to join me for breakfast and then we would drive together to the Bluffs. I was early, and nursed a coffee and daydreamed while waiting for the two, but then refocused to a nearby TV when I heard the word, "Plunderer."

"The on-again off-again trial of the, 'Plunderer,' is off again, this time for good. Pictured here, in shackles, is the subject of the protracted court proceedings of earlier this year, at the airport last night, on his way to California where he will face trial for various Federal charges in that state. There was no comment from our local police as to any further criminal complaints involving the ill-fated Hill project."

Chico came by to commiserate about the mention of the Hill, "It's yesterday's news, Boss - the guy is being railroaded out of town."

I spotted Jubal and Mohammad at that point, "What comes next is more important. Here comes the future." I made introductions and we all ordered breakfast. There was small talk, conjecture as to Chuan's future and the like - the duo enjoyed Chico's special attention.

***

At the Bluffs there was an amazing amount of activity. Wherever or whatever was the source of, resources, it was considerable. There was a sense of cheerfulness among the workers that was not normally present on highly orchestrated budget-tight commercial construction. Jubal and Mohammad put on their hardhats and plunged right in.

I stood on a mound of crushed stone, better to see it all as well as the cityscape beyond. I was soon joined by Popeye and dog. The canine nose sniffed my crotch as I scratched his ears and we bonded. Popeye looked more dazed than usual, "Lots of different folks," he observed, shaking his head in disbelief. We both stood there enjoying a zephyr-like movement of fresh air, a climate that made this part of the city desirable years ago before air conditioning.

I thought about the mornings in Appalachia with my Dad after breakfast at the Eatwell Cafe and how much I enjoyed the startup of our latest job as the sun was still climbing at the horizon, contemplating what lay ahead for the day.

I signaled to Jubal that I was leaving and walked down the hill to the PigglyWiggly shopping center where the church slash synagogue was prepared for its final move. Walking felt more comfortable now. I found a lazing taxi with driver heavily into the sports page - we talked baseball and headed to the office.

***

I rounded up Saul and Cynthia, found the latest Fed proposal still among the debris on my desk and headed for the conference room. "What did you find out?"

"There are a lot of documents in the archives. There were many more buildings on the site at one time - some were combined - many were torn down - this survivors were lumped together and designated Building Forty-three- twenty-three - it's nickname is the Shooting Gallery - a lot of the construction predates the First World War.

"Shooting Gallery?"

"Weapons of all sorts were manufactured there and tested right on site."

"That's it?"

Cynthia was more realistic, "It's a collection of crap buildings that our government built in a hurry and forgot to tear down - now filled with tons of dirt and rocks from all over the world - some from outside our world - an empire ruled by a psychopathic director who has friends in Congress.

"It could be a money-maker," Saul was more the business man.

"You are both probably right - write up a scope of work."

***

The paperwork never seemed to end. Angelica and I went over it all, piece by piece, until my desk was reasonably clear. A general change in the background hubbub in the office signaled it was time for lunch. I had not contributed to the larder in quite a while - the visits to Costco had diminished of late - if you asked me what I ate for dinner last night, it would be hard for me to remember - breakfast at the diner was my only constant.

***

At the lunch table, I nibbled from the offerings laid out in various plastic containers. The conversation passed me by.

"Boss, what's the story on that rush job on the Bluffs," this from Murphy who was not shy when he was curious.

I told them into stunned silence.

"Excuse me - is that legal?" Murphy was tenacious.

I looked at the various faces around the table - they all showed concern - at exactly what, I was not sure - but it was a question that deserved an answer. "I don't see where any harm was done - no money changed hands - the benefits gained would be hard to put a value on. Speaking for myself, I can truthfully say, the Grand Bazaar permit should have been approved or disapproved on it's merits - but it wasn't. Every one involved had their own agenda. Did I, personally, stretch an unwritten code of ethics? The answer is yes - I was drawn in without really thinking it out. A lawyer organized it all and he didn't seem bothered. I should have never encouraged the scenario. A lot of people smarter then myself thought they were doing a public good - that's all I have to say."

An unanswered telephone broke the reverie as I escaped to my desk.

46

Babette sounded upbeat and exhausted at the same time, "We have a contract with the good Doctor Tabershaw and more importantly, a substantial retainer. You have to read the contract and sign it - I can deposit the check in your account if you want but I'm sure you know how to do that." I could picture her smiling; she reacted to my long pause to absorb her humor, "Are you still there?"

"I'm grateful for your good work - please don't take it any differently - when can we get together?" My mind was back at the lunch table - had I crossed the line and lost the confidence of the people closest to me? "Perhaps this will end the curse?"

"Are you alright? What's that about a curse? I need to make a bunch of copies - I'll be at your place at the end of the day." There was no, au revoir.

"Jubal is on the phone from the Bluffs.

I was startled, "He was at lunch a few minutes ago?"

"Lunch was an hour ago - you've been staring into space since you took that phone call - I'm making an appointment for you with that doctor downstairs - don't go anywhere," that last admonition from Angelica as I made motion to go to the men's room.

"Okay," Genevieve and Cynthia were peering over Angelica's shoulder, "a call of nature, please?"

***

The doctor always seemed to have time - I wondered if

she was that good a practitioner if she didn't have patients crowding her waiting room - I would put my investigator on it.

"How are you feeling?"

"Based on my thoughts of a few seconds ago, a little more paranoid than the last time I saw you - I have been walking for exercise and trying to watch what I eat - I don't sleep that well - I have lots of new work, some of it actually interesting - many more personalities to deal with."

"Still sleeping alone? Any time for pillow talk?"

"I'm glad you brought that up - stop me if I cross the line."

"Go ahead."

"I have known this woman for many years - she is now my lawyer - we have a sort of fantasy relationship based on meeting at a French class - again, many years ago - before she was my lawyer. She is paid for what she does on my behalf - paid whatever she bills. Our relationship has never gone beyond what I just said - a few days ago during a troubling situation she told me not to worry - she, 'loved me like a brother.'"

"There's more?"

"She sleeps with both men and woman - she is quite attractive and uses this to her purposes in business."

"Wow - she sounds like the girl of my dreams."
"Seriously?"

"What do you want?"

"A friend?"

"You two need to talk. Let me listen to the ticker and otherwise check how well it's pumping. I can't send you a bill unless I do something of a medical nature."

***

I spent the afternoon in the studio going over every project. I asked for prints for finished jobs - I still needed paper despite he fact that pencils and mylar were now obsolete. The finished product usually came out in bound sets of large sheets of paper that the contractors affectionately referred to as the, 'funny papers.'

A number of personnel had come and gone over the years and I had now assembled a group of very capable professionals. The problem was that no one seemed to be at all that eager to take the exams - the time for study and preparation was not forthcoming nor the gumption to be out on one's own.

***

"Babette arrived just as the staff was filtering out. She greeted the one's she knew by name and was politely introduced to newcomers. She declined a drink of any sort. We spread the papers she had brought on the conference room table and then gravitated to the couch in my office.

"What's going on Pierre?"

"We're very busy."

"You mentioned a, 'curse?'

"You mentioned you loved me like a brother."

"Oh good - we're going to have a talk."

"It's just what the doctor ordered. Literally."

"Just in case this talk deteriorates into something else, let's have you sign that contract and call a messenger to have it delivered to the doctor at the hospital."

While waiting for the messenger to arrive, I added a deposit slip to the envelope with the retainer check and walked it to the after-hours window of the bank at the street. The messenger was just leaving with the contract when I got back to the office.

"It's been busy here while you were gone. Besides the messenger, some bare-footed floozy came by with a six-pack." Babette's eyes were rolling waiting for an explanation.

"Describe her - we usually have a number of floozies dropping by this time of day."

"That should be part of our talk."

47

Jubal's phone call, before the appointment with my doctor, was about the status of the church: "It's done. They must have set the building on the foundation during the night. The site is clean - they even planted grass - that sod stuff - Popeye and his buddies are watering that and the landscaping right now - it looks great."

That was good news. Jubal's joyful reaction seemed to temper the response that I received from the staff as to the motive of being involved in the first place.

The weekend was upon me. Babette and I agreed, after several hours of conversation earlier in the evening, that we needed to talk more often - it did not matter where - we realized we knew very little about each other and we were both interested in learning more.

There were several calls on my home answering machine from Beth summarizing the various parties and celebrations she would be attending during the next several days - the beach was out of bounds due to a possible hurricane brushing past on its way up the coast. My refrigerator was absolutely devoid of food and drink. I looked at Beth's list of events I had jotted down, computed the distance to the closest one happening now, took a shower and dressed in the informal clothes that would provide for respectable admittance to any get-together scheduled for that evening.

***

The neighborhood of old wealth stood in the way of expansion of the city's commercial area and had so for years. There had been generational change but the same names were on the curbside mailboxes - the homes were on large lots with converted carriage houses that formerly housed servants in garrets above, these out-buildings, now multiple car garages, housing the family's rowdiest teenagers in the lofts away from the more civilized residents of the mansions. The views from the upper windows were no longer of bucolic meadows but now the twenty-four hour lighted high-rise building and freeways of downtown. Residents could walk to work; if they worked.

I parked the Toyota in front of a darkened residence on a side street and walked around the corner to the first party's venue. A discreet security person stood near the wide open over-sized front door. Beth, drink in hand, was standing beside the entrance to a room I assumed was the library - she had composed herself between two ornately framed and glass protected delicately lighted documents, one of which was the Declaration of Independence; the other the Magna Carta. They looked real to me - there was no doubt as to the profession of the home's owner.

"Pretty nice for a fixer-upper, don't you think?" Beth had all the real estate sales jargon down pat.

"I would have to look at the plumbing - what are the taxes like?"

"The taxes are killers," this from a Beth look-alike who had sidled up to replace Beth's almost empty glass.

"This is Gretchen - she and I go way back - this is Boss," Gretchen did what I would swear was a curtsey and we touched hands. I reciprocated with a couple of air kisses. High society was fun.

We circulated together. There was an abundance to drink but very little except finger food to eat. I met some interesting people - put together names from various sources with faces - many were potential clients - a few business cards were exchanged. I wanted to put the office far from my mind. It was very pleasant - I was looking to relax - it seemed that Beth and Gretchen were protecting my interests - or their interests - it was hard to say - the alcohol was diminishing my urge for food.

We left the house, cutting through backyards and opened gates to another brightly lighted manor house, acknowledging people like ourselves heading in the opposite direction. The new party offered a pop music combo - still no food - but the opportunity to grapple with strangers in a pretense of dancing. The married couples departed first, leaving the alcohol fueled divorced and singles to find companionship. There was talk of yet another party a few houses down the street but the distance seemed insurmountable.

The longer way back to Gretchen's, by means of sidewalks and driveways, seemed to be the most sensible for three inebriated persons. We hit the air-conditioning on the run, stumbling up the stairs to a bedroom suite, shedding sweat soaked clothing, finding bathroom facilities as available and crawled up the mountain to a satin-sheeted plateau - I suckled a breast and fell into a coma. Sometime in the wee hours, I raided the kitchen's restaurant sized refrigerator, drank copious amounts of water and disposed of same, led a less comatose Gretchen to another bedroom and found comfort in experiencing what we both needed.

***

The Toyota found its way to the diner unassisted. I had left Gretchen sated, I hoped - I had expressed a pat-on-the-rear-end goodbye to Beth who gave me a thumbs up and a whispered, "Next time." Chico mocked disapproval at my appearance and demeanor and sent me home with enough sustenance for the day.

48

Saturday was under way without me necessarily in attendance. I fell asleep on the couch immediately. A sixth sense awakened me hours later - the odor from my clothes from the night before had ripened, conveying evidence of having been worn on a hike through an amphibian sanctuary. Otherwise, it was a normal day-off except with food on hand for a change. The accumulated mail on the dining room table was soon all in the trash except for a, Mr. and Mrs. invitation - the dedication of the church slash synagogue would be next Sunday at one pm. The very tasteful summons was endorsed in handwritten blue ink - "Please. Brown family and friends."

***

The community pool was now only open on weekends. I wandered out in late afternoon and immediately spotted Marcie in her usual corner, feet up on her personal cooler.

"What are you going to do next month when they close the pool - I hear that the city is going to outlaw Vodka around the same time."

"Doesn't matter - I'll be living with my husband-to-be in New York."

"Say again?"

"I know you'll miss me but a girl has to look out for herself."

"Start from the beginning - I've got all day."

"I told you I was working for a branch office of a company from New York - right? Well, one of the fellows that comes down every once and a while has taken an interest in me and I like him a lot. He proposed and said as soon as his divorce is final, we will be married."

"Have you been giving out any free samples in the meantime?"

"You are being very old-fashioned."

"That's me," thinking about the previous evening, "downright prehistoric." The opportunity to give free advice in matters of the heart was tempting - after all I was an expert in the field - witness my history of the last twenty years or so - I could be a case study for Cosmopolitan as well as consult in the,

Lonely Hearts column. Probably not. "Okay, I'm going to do you a small favor - there's an investigator who works for me from time to time - she owes me - I'll give you her name and number - call on Monday - she'll check the guy out - no cost on your part."

"I'll think about it - pour yourself a drink in the meantime - you can watch the college girl babysitters and I'll keep an eye on the fathers with good haircuts."

"Fair enough."

***

I caught the special bus for fans heading to the seven-thirty pm baseball game. Many of the guys were regulars; some of the kids as well - it was a socially classless situation - no one had anything to prove - there would be some beer - wives and girlfriends usually found other things to do for the evening.

I bought my customary nosebleed ticket from a sidewalk entrepreneur and wandered until time for the National Anthem. The game started slowly - neither team was in contention for the post-season; secondary players were being given the chance to keep their jobs.

It was inevitable that I would run into Jose in my meanderings around the periphery of the infield. We shook hands. I knew how much Jose disliked my attempts at Spanish and I thought about honoring that, *?Cómo hasido buena persona"*

"Out of work for a while - I volunteered on the job at the Bluffs just to keep busy. I hear some of your jobs may be starting up soon."

"And Maria?"

"She's not here tonight - there's a party going on at her place right now - I'm going over there after the game - she'll be glad to see you."

The game ended - I was not sure of the score. I spotted a bus-mate and told him not to look for me on the return trip and walked with Jose to a nearby high-rise as the crowd dispersed in all directions. Parties seemed to be the order of the night for the entire neighborhood.

The apartment building was a series of pods, trying to reduce its scale to a human one while fighting for a share of light and ventilation. Several suite doors were open along the uppermost drawn-out corridor in anticipation of guests. Jose knew the way.

***

Maria and I sat out on the, 'Romeo and Juliet' balcony watching the game crowd disperse - then, later, the party goers - the night was declared shut down when all the field lights were extinguished. There had been a less than raucous party when I arrived. I had the idea that this was not Maria's home; there was no clue as to who actually lived in the space. Jose had disappeared early on.

"You Americans live well."

"Work hard and play hard as they say." I had no idea where this was going.

"My grandfather was an American, my grandmother, Cuban. My parents grew up in Cuba under Fidel. If I chose, I could claim citizenship in either country."

"But, you're a citizen of somewhere else?"

"Monaco. My parents sent me to Europe - my grand-father's sugar plantation money was already over there - for an education - and advised me not to come back."

"And?"

"My heart belongs to Cuba."

"I'm not going to trade life stories with you for two reasons." and, with this, I got up to leave.

"The two reasons?"

"Another time, perhaps?"

"Cliff said you would be difficult." With this, I received

and dealt two air kisses. As I thought about it on the way home, her Mojitos were excellent.

***

After the taxi dropped me off at the gate, I went over the list of weekend activities from Beth's phone messages in my head. There were some tempting parties, all of which were probably just getting into full bloom - I was sure there would be a chance to escape from reality once more but that part of my brain that decides such things said, "Another time." I glanced out towards the pool - the lights were partially left on until sunrise for security reasons - Marcie was asleep in her chair in the shadowy corner of the enclave - I brought a quilt out of the trunk of the Toyota, - covered her, and let her be - when she awakened she would be in distress in more ways than one.

***

"You owe me - water - I need water."

I had no idea who was talking.

"I went to every party on my list - you were a no-show."

"Beth - how did you get in here?"

"Some bimbo wrapped in a blanket told me where you lived and showed me where your key was in the third flower pot to the left of the gnome."

"The gnome was a gift - it really doesn't reflect my taste."

"Get back in bed."

Maria's seductive nature came to mind. Beth was after one thing - Maria seemed to be part of something else.

49

The proximity of the hurricane off the coast brought heavy rain, thunder and very soon a sodden landscape. Beth was in no hurry to leave. By late morning, I had listened to her litany of domestic problems, mostly having to do with teenagers left to her exclusive care as her ex was off finding himself far far away. I made recommendation of boarding schools even more distant from the city and a reduction in allowances - the kids were absolute brats much like the father - they deserved each other - Beth was no saint but she was fun.

***

I loaned Beth one of the many umbrellas I had somehow accumulated, and under my newly favorite bumbershoot, a souvenir of a recent golf tourney that someone else must have helped sponsor. We waited at the curb outside the gate for a summoned taxi. She whispered, "Thanks," no passionate farewell kiss - I didn't know what I was being thanked for.

She dove into the cab, "Remember - send the checks a few days late - then the kids will call more often," she laughed which was a nice thing to happen on an otherwise dreary morning.

The food supply was once again at low ebb - Beth suffered the munchies when she became more ambitious in the very early morning hours - I would have to forage.

***

Costco was the logical choice - for me; and everyone else. I became myself after partaking of several sample coffees at the store's entrance - then I hit the real sample trail until I had strength to make a shopping list and plot my course through the store.

"Make sure you fill the office list," this from Angelica with two of her hulking brothers in tow.

"Refresh my memory." I shook hands with the brothers who maintained their macho demeanor while continuing to check out the younger female shoppers.

I managed two carts so as to keep the receipts separate and probably got most of what was needed.

Angelica prodded her brothers to pack the Toyota as I held the sheltering over-sized umbrella - I gained some credence from the muchachos because of the car. She smiled and waved and was gone in a huge pickup truck to be with her family for the day.

***

The odoriferous and yet perfumed bed linen needed to be addressed so I stretched out on the couch and scheduled my laundry chores. What I really had to do was make lists. I fell asleep, of course - the lists were all in my head when the eye of the hurricane passed our close by suffering beach producing a sudden lull in the wind and lightning. When the monsoon resumed, it was necessary for me to start all over, this time with pencil and paper - the storm's ozone had cleansed the air as well as my brain.

The lists, with their various sub-categories were really only two in number - business and personal. Questionnaires often asked "business or pleasure," as if these were two separate and distinct concepts. I enjoyed my work - it indeed gave me pleasure to put it all together and actually receive a, 'thank you'. Getting paid was sometimes the only show of gratitude but that was okay.

Despite what others might call debauchery, of the last several days, my mind turned to Babette - I chose not to write her name down on a list but hold it close to my heart not knowing where our talks would lead.

50

The talk at the diner was all about the storm. The TV's talking heads could not get enough of it. Chico kept his head down at the grille. The smell of unclean wet clothes overpowered the frying bacon.

"Did you have enough food for the weekend?" Chico was totaling up my bill for today's breakfast as well as what he had supplied on Saturday morning

"Not enough - I had company."

Chico had a rare frown on his face, "Glad to hear someone had guests."

***

In the parking garage, I scrawled a few more notations to my lists. I felt prepared. At the entrance to our building, a crowd had gathered, most of its members I recognized as being fellow tenants. "Someone pulled an alarm - the fire department said to evacuate," this from Murphy who had the our staff clustered around him - I noticed the red trucks with whirling lights for the first time and heard approaching sirens that signaled more help was on the way - so much for hitting the ground running.

Doctors' patients staring at their watches, were starting to pile up. The Tuckers were taking the opportunity to socialize with the freshly groomed females of their own age group - there was little to do but wait.

Lawyer Kline caught my eye and we found an unused corner of the sidewalk so as to talk. He signaled his assistant away, "Everything seems to be in order?"

I tend to raise my eyebrows and remain mute at such open ended questions, but since Kline and I actually shared the same clients, I replied, "I think so."

He actually smiled at my unobtrusive non-commitment, "See you on Sunday."

***

Once in the office, coffee seemed to be the only thing on anyone's mind.

This led to further catchup of the weekend news and before I could review my lists, it was time for lunch. Leftovers from the weekend barbecues abounded - my shopping at Costco carried me. "We lost most of the morning so I'm going to talk business while we eat - there is a lot going on - some new assignments and responsibilities are necessary." I went down my lists

This was not my normal management style - things had just sort of evolved naturally as each of them had been hired - the staff as a whole was not usually part of the process.

"Boss, are we in trouble?"

"Murphy - you worry too much - no one is being fired." No one looked concerned. "Oh, let me tell you - the project Jubal has been working on will be dedicated on Sunday - attend if you can."

I met separately with the Tuckers, Nate and Jeb, "The Hill will be starting construction again soon - that's a maybe - by that I mean, the permit is valid - we don't know what condition the structure is in - the insurance companies sold the deal to a doctor slash investor - he has brought in more investors who I can't seem to track down - Chester says they are paying their bills which includes us so far - you guys figure it out." The young men looked stunned.

"Where do we start?"

"Gather up all the drawings and files to date - make yourself familiar - I'll call Chester and make an appointment for you to see him - meet his crew - see what they know - get names."

Saul and Cynthia were next. "Okay - the Shooting Gallery - tell me what you think?"

"Boss - its a bag of worms - literally - some of that soil has wildlife living in it"

"Saul concurred, "True - on both counts - we've prepared all the paperwork you asked for - your call."

51

Sunday promised, by the looks of the eastern horizon, every hope of a beautiful day. Babette and I had talked through many courses of Chinese food and too many pots of tea until Mister Wu flicked the lights on and off for the third time a few hours earlier. We had agreed we were still a long way from knowing each other. I walked her to her car and received a chaste kiss. The tea did its thing and left me sleepless which I decided to counteract with coffee. I carefully picked out what I would wear to the dedication and the sat back to kill the remaining hours of the morning.

***

There was heavy traffic in the area of the Bluffs. Police were handling the congestion in an unusually efficient manner. People were making an effort to be on time for the ceremony. The Toyota was sniffed at by some very affluent looking folks as I parked the car - we were used to that. A small dais had been set up on the building entrance creating elevation for any speechifier - there was a microphone with portable speakers adjacent - an assortment of folding chairs was spread in front - some of the attendees were bringing in their own seating. A city ambulance was discreetly parked in a vacant lot. The Browns' church ladies were spreading out a buffet assisted by city police and fire personnel. In miniature, there was every appearance of a major event.

The sunshine could only be described as God-given glorious considering the religious nature of the occasion. I walked around the building - the new sod squished underfoot - Popeye and his friends had been a little too zealous in watering.

"How do, Boss?" Popeye and several of his neighbors had followed me around, separating from the growing crowd. He was dressed in only what could be called, Sunday-go-to-meeting clothes, albeit of a long past era - his contemporaries, much the same, "Big day?"

"Big day for a few hours I guess - you should get your peace and quiet back soon enough."

"Folks have discovered the Bluffs - we plan to catch the mayor before he leaves today and make sure it's done right." His fellows were nodding their heads in agreement.

"Good luck on that." It sounded cynical, I'm sure, but Popeye knew what I meant.

***

Black SUVs pulled up to discharge the mayor and family, the multi-generation Brown family and a group that I wanted to identify as members of the clergy although I did not recognize any of the personages - most of these participants taking seats in the temporary seating adjacent to the building. A gentleman who must have been a heavy hitter for the Ecumenical Heritage Committee, tested the microphone and called the assembly to order. "Please come to order - we are here today to dedicate this historic building - the several speakers have been asked to be brief. The interior of the building is only available to be viewed through the front doors - unfortunately, our next speaker has not granted an occupancy permit," at this, there was the choreographed laughter, "but that is forthcoming, I'm sure."

The mayor took the microphone and asked the clergy, as a group, for a blessing. A rabbi who appeared to be spokesman for the body asked for us to give thanks to all who helped bring back to life a place of worship that had served so many of different religious beliefs over the years. His compatriots raised amens and returned to their seats.

The mayor spoke of his personal attachment to the church, noting the history of its original construction as a synagogue and attaching himself to the Bluffs where his family had lived for several generations.

A spokesman for the Historical Society thanked all who had helped and promised the structure would be protected under Federal Law in perpetuity.

The mayor thanked us all once more and asked us all to partake in refreshments provided by the lady's auxiliary of Mister Brown's church.

I looked around at the faces of those in the audience, expanding my view beyond those seated, and was pleasantly surprised to see my entire staff. All were clustered together dressed neatly in a manner fitting a dignified ceremony. Cynthia was accompanied by her ward who was fully attended to by all.

The Tuckers' mother and father were in the background as was the family councilor, the judge.

"We did good, Boss," this from Murphy who was taking on the role of spokesman,

"We all did good." All were nodding in agreement - I felt numb, "I checked out the refreshments earlier and would encourage you to take a look."

Changing the subject by referring to food and drink was a stupid thing to do - I really did not know what else to say - the whole process leading to this moment was absurd - the motives of all actively involved were filled with guile. My people were proud of what had been accomplished, even knowing of the complicity involved.

I moved with the young Tuckers towards the parents and the Judge to acknowledge their presence and make small talk - they had gone to a lot of trouble to be here - the boys were doing well, away from the nest, and becoming accomplished and self-sufficient. "This is a surprise - how are you all?" Handshakes were exchanged.

"Jubal and the boys has told us all about this project and the other work in your office - it sounds like they have settled in." The judge was doing the talking probably because we had checked each other out.

"With some more experience, they should be able to take the exams," this to assure the elder Tuckers that their investment in education would pay off. "Enjoy the rest of your stay - meet the mayor - he's quite a character - the refreshments look good."

I pivoted about to check the declining throng before bailing out myself. There was Saul with his wife and kids - I waved - his wife could take that any way she wanted - that also applied to Chester, mainly because I had passed by his sister, hoping to avoid familial conflict becoming a lightning rod for some perceived social faux pas.

The Historical Society fellow caught up with me, "Thanks for bringing her home - I can cross the building off our WANTED posters at the post office." He gave his signature warm self-deprecating chuckle. "Hope we meet again."

This left a beautiful Sunday to fill out. The lack of sleep from the night before was catching up with me - I was hungry - and I was by myself. The Toyota knew the way home.

***

The wares from the recent Costco run satisfied my appetite. I took a shower and stretched out on the rear patio chaise.

The phone awakened me three hours later.

"How did the ceremony go?"

"It was beautiful."

"And?" Babette knew my moods by now.

"I came away with a feeling of guilt which I am nursing right now."

"Why so?"

"It would be hard to explain."

"What are you wearing?"

"A towel - why do you ask?"

"Okay - I'm going to get naked and get into bed - you do the same - we'll have pillow talk."

And, that's what we did.

52

On Monday morning, I wanted to make a decision as to the Shooting Gallery. I found Cynthia at her work station but Saul was not in the office. Have you seen your compatriot?"

"I saw him yesterday - I met his wife and kids - he split off to talk to his wife alone - they seemed to be arguing. He came back, shaking his head and said to me, "It looks like you'll be stuck with me for a while. I didn't understand this and just took my leave."

Angelica was signaling telephone call. "Allaine said to find a private place to call him back."

I was immediately worried. I had seen his two associates the day before, with Mohammad, in the far background at the dedication. Those two always seemed dour in demeanor - I had mentally code-named them - Heckle and Jeckle.

"Good morning Allaine - we missed you yesterday."
"Are you alone? His voice was tearful.
"Yes - are you okay?"
"It's about Saul."
"He's not here just yet."
"I know - he's dead."
I forgot to breathe. "What?
"Last night, he went to the Natatorium at the University - believe it or not, he had keys from the time he was in school and they still worked. He went to his old haunt - the diving pool - the lights weren't on - he changed into his pool gear and took a dive from the three meter board."
"And?"
"The pool had been drained - there was only a few inches of water."
"And?"

"I think he killed himself."

"What do the police think?"

"The same - but the family will not allow to that motive."

"I'll get back to you." I thought I knew the motive - a stupid one as are most that lead to perpetual damage those around them - it did not matter.

I opened my office door to face the entire staff staring at my appearance. "You heard?"

The women were crying - the guys looked solemn, not knowing how to show their emotions, "Is it true?"

"I think so - Allaine gave me the news just now - Saul's family is calling what happened an accident - am sure there will be a funeral and a memorial service - we will close the office for that. That's all I know."

"Is there anything we can do?"

"Write a note of condolence to his wife - maybe a separate one to the kids - maybe make a contribution to his favorite charity - I'm going to take some time off to call some friends."

I didn't call anyone. Saul was a smart, ambitious person, well-liked by his peers - his wife less so. I did not wish to exchange gossip. My life to date left me with no family to be concerned with my well being. I dwelled upon my personal life choices, past, present, and future, until Angelica knocked and interrupted my reverie.

"You okay, Boss?"

"Just thinking - what's up?"

"This is like embarrassing," at this she shut the door and sat down, "I'm a good Catholic girl - I think you should know something even though I should be talking to Father Gomez - it's about Saul and Genevieve - I hope you don't think I'm a bad person."

I listened, expecting the worst - it would be what it would be.

"Saul and Genevieve have been seeing each other - more then seeing each other - this is embarrassing - she is," long pause, "expecting."

At this, Angelica burst into uncontrollable sobbing.

I brought Cynthia into my office and a soon as she saw Angelica's state, she knew that I knew. They both sobbed together for a while. I offered Kleenex and waited it out. "Okay, the best thing to do right now is to find Genevieve and take her home. Call me and let me know what's going on. She has some family in the area - find out if they are available to help." Genevieve was estranged from her parents - maybe there are brothers or sisters - maybe the parents could forgive past transgressions - maybe life choices could be adjusted.

Allaine called with the news of the funeral arrangements and the memorial service. I did not make conversation. A few minutes later, Saul's former secretary slash confidant called with the same information - she joined the host much upset with Saul's demise. No one seemed to have seen it coming and that was shock unto itself.

53

A sleepless night was followed by gut wrenching spasms - I self-medicated to get through the late morning theatrics. The morning newspaper took the easy way out, reporting Saul's passing and avoiding the cause of death.

I took a taxi to the services and waited until the last minute to take a seat. Of course, I knew many of those in attendance. I managed to maneuver to place myself among strangers. Most of the staff was there - Genevieve, Angelica and

Cynthia were not. I exchanged a few words with Allaine and left as soon as I could. I had told Murphy to advise the others to take the day off.

I waited at the curb of a nearby street to flag down a taxi - when that ride came, I would decide where I wanted to spend the day. A car pulled up and powered down the passenger side window, "You need a ride?"

I leaned in and recognized a fellow architect who I had worked with in the days of apprenticing, "Sure - anywhere there's a better chance to catch a taxi." I struggled to remember his first name. I endeavored to fasten the latest model seat belt, "How about a second breakfast at the diner - my treat?"

We drove in comparative silence, both of us having just come from a traumatic event.

Chico greeted us both - his memory was prodigious as to recognizing regulars - from this greeting my memory was jarred to recall my ride's name and much of the time we worked together. "Jerry, how have you been?"

"The big news is, I've closed my office - did you get any resumes?"

"Probably not - the new boys in town are paying better then I am. What now for you?"

"Nothing."

"Nothing - one has to eat and all that other stuff?"

"Big inheritance - from some uncle I hardly knew - I was ready for a change?"

"Change - as sitting on your rear end in a rocker?" I contemplated this experience enviously. "You married? - Kids?"

"All that is in the past," he did not look wistful.

We ate in silence for a few minutes mesmerized by the TV and the latest escapades of some, 'beauty queen.' Jerry reflected, "Do you remember Mary-Lou?"

"I do." MaryLou was the office trollop who Jerry and I , 'dated' from time to time.

"Those were different days." I did not inquire as to her fate.

"Saul was a nice guy - his wife is a bitch," this out of nowhere.

I knew what gave rise to this. Two guys without family, both newly wealthy - wealthy defined as having more money then we would ever need - reflecting on days gone by when things were actually fun - never to return - while a guy who deserved more was dead and his wife provided the provocation. Jerry did not know about Genevieve - that was in God's hands.

Out in front of the diner, the normal day was in full bloom - life goes on I thought - Jerry offered me a lift which I declined - we shook hands and wished each other well. I watched his brand new car depart and went back inside to get Chico to call me a cab.

***

I slept, unaware of the normal activity around my townhouse.

"How was it?"

"It was my second funeral here in town - same venue as a matter of fact - some of the same people - it would be difficult to rate it."

"How are you?"

"I ran into a former architect workmate - he just closed his office - he plans to live on some deceased uncle's largesse."

Babette produced her signature skeptical cluck, "Maybe we need to talk?"

"Pillow talk?"

"Maybe."

54

Angelica and Cynthia caught me in the lobby. We relocated to a quiet spot in the coffee shop.

"We helped move Genevieve to her parent's house - her folks were very welcoming - whatever happens from now on, she's not alone."

"Thank you." I just had to let it rest.

***

Chuan had returned from his leave of absence. I interrupted the resulting gossiping, gave Chuan something to do, and asked all to catch up with missed work. I had done no planning over the weekend - with Saul gone, the administrative work would soon pile up - again. The Shooting Gallery project had to be assessed - again. I felt out of touch because of this latest bump in the road - learning of Jerry's new found freedom did not help my state of mind.

"Boss, are we going to replace Saul?" Angelica was on top of what needed to be done.

"Yes - round up the usual suspects." I gave her the name of Jerry's firm, "See if you can find the names of personnel from his office - someone we would like could be looking for a job."

***

At lunch, Chuan was in the limelight. His prospective bride-to-be had turned out to be likable - even lovable. Chuan's live-in girl friend had left for other climes with a rock guitarist leaving the coast clear. The families had all met and gone through all the old country rituals. The sticking point of living and working in the United States had been overcome.

In celebration, he had brought in home country goodies prepared by his future wife. Most of us were wary but the Tuckers, who were voracious, pronounced every dish delicious and they were right.

"Does she have any sisters?" This from Murphy who got a sharp look from Angelica.

No one spoke of Genevieve. If Chuan had not just returned, lunch would have been one of the most subdued ones I could remember.

*****

I asked Cynthia to find a new partner for the Shooting Gallery and report back to me as soon as possible. Nate and Jeb had met Chester and his people and they felt the meeting went well. They had taken notes and were awaiting the structural reports to allow us to pick up where we had left off. We needed to compare the requirements of the old code to the latest adaptation to determine if we could make changes with little or no expense to the developer. Susan reported that there was a hold on the aerospace engineer's new house and she was upset. I told her to take over Genevieve's work load. Allaine left a message that the first masts would be erected at the Grand Bazaar tomorrow morning. All other work was progressing - there was some potential new work that required meetings and proposals.

I would call Saul's wife. My excuse would relate to personal items he left here in the office - person to person condolence would be appropriate as well. We were in bed with her company for two huge projects - individual animosities could prevail - she was strictly an amateur to the construction business. I was sure Saul had done what he did partly based on her refusal to let him do the work he had done before Chester entered the scene. And, there was Genevieve - eventually someone would talk too much and then what would happen? I needed more than pillow talk from Babette.

55

Allaine and I stood at the top of the remaining stadium bleachers watching the construction activity below. The security guard who let us in to the otherwise forbidden area told us to be careful and departed as quickly as possible. Mast components were spread out in what would be the parking lot, each piece bearing a colored code number as in set of Lego. There were an unusual number of building inspectors present. Cleve was taking no chances - his boss had been subverted by the mayor and his cronies - it was a nervous time.

Jose was studying the erection diagram once again - cranes were at the ready - a helicopter stood by to handle the larger pieces.

"Does anyone understand what is going on?" Allaine was growing more skeptical of his own design now that it was in the hands of others. He had probably doubled the factor of safety in his calculations in anticipation of some sort of disaster.

One of the smaller masts was put in place, "So far so good," I assured him.

The engineers directed the fastening into place with various laser powered instruments

"Have you ever thought about doing something else or not doing anything at all?"

"Are you trying to take my mind off some pending catastrophe?"

"Yes, but it's still a legitimate question." The second mast was in the air. "Piece of cake."

"I have."

"Care to elucidate?"

The helicopter raved it's engines making it hard to hear.

"Are you having some sort of mid-life crisis - I don't

handle other peoples problems very well - my personal life is a little messy right now as you know."

"Here comes number three - should one and two be shaking like that?"

Allaine put on his glasses which he only wore when he absolutely had to, "I don't see any shaking."

I took off my glasses and wiped them clean. "Okay."

The helicopter was now hovering with a cable loosely lowered to the ground. A medium sized mast was now scheduled to be put in place. The cable was fastened to the mast and the helicopter rose so the base of the mast was just above the ground and then maneuvered the mast in a vertical position to its foundation. The fastening and leveling was tedious but then the cable was released and the helicopter waved off - a cherry picker moved in to take away the cable to be used again.

Allaine was a little more relaxed. "Where were we?"

"You were proselytizing about an ashram for disgruntled architects and engineers," the atmosphere became clogged with dust and was deafening. "Okay, here comes the biggest one."

Allaine was utilizing body English to help position this largest mast. The helicopter was straining - it took amazing patience to get the piece placed and anchored.

Jose called a break to relieve the tension. The building inspectors were mingling with the workers - cigarettes were being shared - the helicopter crew deplaned - the crane operators stayed put to avoid a second laborious climb but waved to those below - the teamwork was palpable.

Allaine's pallor had receded. "To answer your question, I like what I do - too much - my personal life has suffered I admit - I'm working on that."

"Me, too."

***

It was a beautiful day - the weather had been especially cooperative in allowing the work to proceed. The heavy-lift helicopter restarted its engines stirring up the dust and accumulated debris of the site - that was my signal to leave. Allaine could handle my worries about the Grand Bazaar for now - I opted for lunch away from the office. The Toyota took me past the Bluffs - the newly placed church fit into the landscape as if it had always been there - Popeye was watering the grass - I did not stop to say hello - the view of the city remained spectacular and undiscovered.

56

I had meandered too long - dawdling - driving through neighborhoods I had never seen before - admiring some striking century old buildings by designers unknown. Much of the work had been done before architecture was even a recognized profession.

The office was emptying out. Angelica handed me lists and notes - there was no commentary - and she was gone. I thought about dinner - studied the paperwork - thought about the newly placed masts - it was a new era for me - the Grand Bazaar had been my idea - admittedly Benito had developed the concept but I felt some pride of authorship.

My professors in architecture school, who gave me little hope, while they basked as wannabes of the Bauhaus culture, would still probably be negative as to my prospects - maybe those unknown builders of the antique buildings I had seen earlier in the day had a better deal.

I dug into the pile of drawings on the conference room table. There were the usual markups - possible zoning and code problems - lack of coordination from one page to the next and, of course, spelling. I signed and sealed documents to be officially submitted for permit. Proposal letters needed to be reviewed as to scope of work. My calendar had been brought up to date regarding appointments.

I ran out of gas as daylight failed.

Judy came in - later than her usual visits. "Are you alone - the last time I came by some witch threw me out?"

"Witch?"

"Actually an attractive witch - she cast a spell - '*trollop allez,*' I got out."

"Oh, that witch."

"I understood the trollop part - do you think I'm a trollop?"

"This could be a case of the pot calling the kettle black - I think we should have dinner and cast off the spell."

***

I did not spend the night.

***

"Tell me about the masts."

"It's four o'clock in the morning."

"The masts?"

"Everything went well - Allaine was extremely nervous - I kept him company for a while - how was your day, honey?"

"Take off your clothes - we are going to have pillow talk."

We talked until my phone battery signaled death. I learned some more about her childhood, first loves, jobs - the conversation had no continuity - I gave as much as I received.

"Okay, that's enough - it is time to hit the gym."

I could not imagine myself in a gym at this hour - the diner had more appeal.

57

Genevieve, Angelica and Cynthia greeted me in the lobby. We adjourned to the coffee shop's table furthest to the rear. The women did not order coffee in sympathy with Genevieve who had been told not to partake - I could live without caffeine for the short term - we all had bubbly water with lemon - I would wait. I also remained in readiness for the purpose of the early morning ambush.

Cynthia spoke up, "Genevieve would like to come back to work."

"Okay."

"I don't want to be a problem."

"Okay."

Angelica had a need to clarify things, "Genevieve plans to talk with Saul's wife."

"Okay."

"Couldn't this hurt your business?"

"Genevieve - please don't take this the wrong way - you messed up - Saul would have done the right thing - whatever that would have been - you have a life - two lives, to take care of - please try to leave me out of it - I hope you didn't shtoop in the drafting room for the sake of the morals cancellation clause in my lease. You are on your own. Come back to work as soon as you want." I reminded myself that this was not the first time I had lectured Genevieve.

***

I caught Jubal and told him to go out to the Grand Bazaar site. "Talk with Jose - get an idea of the schedule for placing the roof fabric."

Susan advised me that the aerospace engineer and his wife would be in later in the morning. "We are about ready to call in some contractors but I don't think it's going ahead."

"I'll be here if you need me." Susan's instincts were probably correct. Cynthia and Chuan had prepared a proposal for the Shooting Gallery. I took the paperwork to review and asked them to find me after lunch.

I closed my office door and called Chester. My purpose was to clear the air before any contamination set in. "How is your sister doing?"

"She is at the beach with the kids and some of her cousins - it's blissfully quiet here."

"And?"

"A divorce was in the works I'm sorry to say - she is a different person now that she's wielding the power our father once held - her friends are a bunch of money grubbers - don't quote me on that. I actually own a piece of this business and would really like to make it work."

"Changing the subject - any word on tenants for the Grand Bazaar?"

"It's just not happening - nobody wants to be the first one on board. There are incentives on the street but no one is biting."

"Keep in touch." This would not be the first architectural gem that had no commercial appeal - I tried to think of secondary uses.

***

"City Hall wants a third party to approve the Hill as safe to resume construction," this from Allaine based on my earlier inquiry as to schedule.

"It's impossible to find someone willing to stick their neck out - the city would like to see it all bulldozed - they really want the present permit to expire."

"Any suggestions?"

"This is when the lawyers step in."

***

I found the aerospace engineer in the coffee room

inspecting the back of the coffee maker, "My wife and Susan are saying goodbye - they have enjoyed working together - Susan will tell you that we are moving out of the city - for the sake of the triplets we will start again elsewhere."

"Anything I should know?"

"I don't want you to listen to any gossip that would impugn my morals - my company has an experimental product that has been misplaced, maybe stolen - I am technically responsible - I need to get out from under the investigation - moving away is a start."

I had grown to like this tech savvy gentlemen with a quirky sense of humor and deep feeling of family responsibility,

"Will you be all right?"

"I have a lot of friends in the industry - my wife and I have family - things will be okay. I can always go back to making coffee machines - the market is out there."

***

At lunch, Chuan regaled us in the details of his pending wedding. The rituals were incredibly complex.

"Have you thought about eloping?" Cynthia could always cut to the bone.

"My cousin down in Rocky Mount eloped - he didn't get any gifts - the family was sort of miffed - they were divorced a year later so it was just as well." The two other Tuckers were nodding in agreement.

"You guys are going to be invited, but only to the third and final day."

"Is that the honeymoon - I always wanted to be the fly on the wall." This from Murphy - Angelica was blushing.

The Shooting Gallery proposal was fine - I added some more dollars in various places and told Cynthia and Chuan to get it ready for my signature.

***

A clap of thunder, so intense the double paned glass of the office windows vibrated, brought a rain, almost horizontal, against the building facade. The sounds shook my brain; a review of the engineer's attitude towards career and family, like Chuan's wedding plans, seemed like foreign concepts to me.

58

In the building lobby, a crowd gathered - no one chose to challenge the weather. There was an atmosphere of hopelessness. Building security worked their way from group to group to suggest a return to offices to wait out the deluge and most people did that including myself.

***

The staff had all returned - time was being spent talking on the phone or helping fold the thousand paper cranes required for Chuan's wedding ceremony, or both. There was a call from Jubal - he was keeping company and sheltering with Jose in a construction trailer. He reported all the still-to-be-utilized mast foundations were filled with water - everything else was okay.

I watched the paper folding process for a few minutes; I picked up a finished crane and a few pieces of special paper, and want to my office and shut the door.

"Without any wardrobe changes, are you available to talk?"

"What are you doing?"

"Origami - but I don't think I'm very good at it."

"Seriously?"

"We need one thousand cranes by next Sunday - I'm not

worried - I believe people more competent than myself are also working on it."

"Will you be home tonight - I'll call you then."

"Be careful out there."

"You, too."

Chester called a few minutes later, "Can you make a meeting with the Doctor tonight?"

"Have you looked out the window in the last few minutes?"

"He says it's important - one of my people has one of those off-the-road-vehicles with oversized tires - we'll pick you up in a few minutes."

***

The lobby's denizens cheered as the strange vehicle with its racks of auxiliary headlights, mounted the curb at the street and parked as close to the lobby revolving door as possible and then cheered more as they saw me drenched in the few seconds it took for me to mount the vehicle. The driver, Rondal, was maybe eighteen and drove as if he had no dependents to worry about. Chester had swept a variety of fast food debris to the floor to make room for me and our adventure began. The swamp buggy dived into and through stands of water containing stalled, ruined cars. The traffic signal system was down, streetlights were useless - Rondal followed Chester's directions ignoring all but the major obstacles. The sight of the hospital compound did give him second thoughts. "I'll wait outside."

The building was taking in water adding to it's foreboding appearance. Emergency lights provided the only illumination. An orderly met us at the door with clean dry green hospital scrubs and directed us to a changing room where we hung our own clothes to drain. We waded and slid down the corridor to the doctor's domain.

Tabershaw's office was a welcome refuge, normally lighted and air-conditioned with the bar fully open to greet us. Chester and I took our usual seats on the couch, drinks in hand and began to take in the scene. The doctor entered from an adjoining room with Natasha and Maria and a gentleman who was not introduced. The doctor's group was all business - there was no shaking of hands or social chitchat.

"Thank you for coming on such short notice." There was no reference to the weather. The doctor referred to notes in his hand - Natasha was fashionably perched under an overhead light fixture - Maria and the unknown gentleman sought the shadows. The pounding, drum-like rain at the windows was the only sound. "It is my intention to take a sabbatical - not doctoring for a while - my other business interests will continue. Maria and her brother will look after my affairs in conjunction with Lawyer Kline. The Hill is fully funded and I believe things should go smoothly in your good hands. I will be checking in, of course, some of our travels will be to remote parts of the world, but you should feel I am available if need be."

The doctor made motion to leave and the others followed. By the time Chester and I struggled out of the deep recesses of the couch, we had the office to ourselves. Chester helped himself to a generous second drink - made motion with finger on lips for me to be silent - pointed out that the rain had stopped and we left to pick up our clothes.

Our various garments had been cleaned, dried and ironed. We took a set of scrubs and several towels for Rondal. He was gunning the engine when he saw us exiting. "You like pizza, Rondal?" Chester directed him to the nearby Costco where he changed clothes, consumed a large pie and several hot dogs and a chicken Caesar salad, with each bite appearing less and less apprehensive then he had been at the hospital.

***

Chester dropped me off at home, "I'll call you

tomorrow," was all he had to say - he had been especially tight-lipped at dinner - Rondal and I had talked baseball while Chester was lost in thought.

***

"What are you wearing?"

"Some very clean dry clothes - how about you?

"I was soaking wet when I finally got home - took a very hot shower - am still wrapped in a towel."

"We seem to be at a clothing impasse." I told her about the recent meeting.

"Okay, that goes in the business file - hang up your new found laundered duds - we need to have pillow talk."

Babette brought me up to date on her life over the last several years. There were flirtations with, 'sex-drugs-and-rock-and-roll' - the things she never had the opportunity to get out of her system post-law school and era of career building.

59

The ceiling of the drafting studio was festooned with paper cranes. The vast majority were uniform in size and white. Boredom had apparently set in at some time, explaining the cranes whose origins were surplus shop drawings or pages from magazines. The borrowed finished crane and paper raw material on my desk was gone as well as was my partially finished attempt - I sensed I had been fired.

I pondered the carte blanche granted by the doctor in regard to constructing the Hill anew - Allaine would have to agree.

***

"Think on this for a minute - tear the building down to the footings - we'll assume the foundation is okay - we use the same footprint but design the apartments to meet code - concrete is cheap and fast - there are a lot of paid-for materials on hand - all that crap Indian steel will be gone. I think I know how to add a floor or two - all you have to do is find someone to certify the foundation."

"I'll get back to you." If nothing else, Allaine was pragmatic.

I was not that familiar with the new code. This model ordinance, prepared for international use, is reviewed and updated every three years - sometimes whole sections were left intact - sometimes the City, like others who subscribed to the service, did not agree with the changes - sometimes the Council took more then three years to work things out and approve the Code - by then even more changes were in the works - all this uncertainty gave much power to the Building Department. A visit to those who did the interpreting was in order.

***

I looked for Cleve but I was told he was not available; make an appointment. I asked for the younger generation Browns but was told they were busy. I pretended to leave but instead headed for the stairs that led to the executive suites. I was interrupted at the upper level by security people and politely invited to go, unescorted, to have coffee in the City Hall cafeteria.

Cleve was sitting in a far corner, a wan smile on his face.

"I am at your disposal."

"I need some advice - you know the Hill project better then anybody - what do I need to do to meet the latest codes?"

"Start over."

"Say I don't do that - I revise the existing permit documents instead?"

"That is not starting over."

"What's so different this year?"

Cleve sighed and looked around the room, "Not very

much at all."

I then looked around the room, "So, if I sent one of my people down here, we could move ahead?"

"We still need verification that the structure is okay - if you want to make changes to meet the latest code or any other reason, there's nothing to prevent you from doing that - getting the new plans approved is another matter."

I rose, coffeeless, from the table, "So, who's the three hundred pound gorilla in the room, Cleve?"

He looked around again, "I wish I knew."

Some entity was feeding money into the project; a lot of money - someone else was pulling strings to kill the deal - why did I get the feeling that they were one and the same?

***

"A Doctor Wang called," Angelica looked bemused for some reason.

Something was afoot and it didn't concern paper cranes, "Find her - and see me afterwards,"

I found the proposal for the Shooting Gallery in front of me on the desk, "Hello, Doctor Wang" there was a torrent of feverish language, only some words in English, as a response. I looked at Angelica who was hovering, and not offering any assistance and hung up.

"Another unhappy lady friend, Boss?"

The phone rang at once, "This is Doctor Wang's assistant - she is very upset - our building has been damaged by the rain - she wants you to fix it." His English was pretty much understandable

"That's not exactly what I do for a living."

"She says you know people - she has money - please send someone."

"I will call the man in charge of the building for the government - that's all I can do."

I gave him the only name and number I knew and kept

my promise.

I turned to Angelica, "You are way off base - I keep my personal life separate from the business as best I can. Doctor Wang is a hysterical client - not a spurned love interest. If some woman calls for me here and you protect my privacy and she gives you a hard time - let me know." I took a deep breath, "We need a replacement for Saul - hire a temp - hire two temps - maybe that will take some of the pressure off of you."

There were too many uncertainties at hand - the tension was becoming contagious.

60

I met up with Jubal at the Grand Bazaar. By the end of the day, the last of the masts would be in place. Deliveries of the roof fabric would occur over the next several days, Allaine was not present - his two associates were there however - at ground level - peering into the mast foundations - I assigned Jubal to work with them and went to my usual perch at the top of the last remaining bleacher section in the former stadium.

I had left word with Cynthia to make a slow drive by the Shooting Gallery; Murphy had been told to make an appointment with Cleve and get the precise details for revising the permit drawings for the Hill. Angelica had been authorized to pay top dollar for whoever she deemed suitable to get out from under the accumulating paperwork. The rest of the staff had plenty to do.

***

At the office, I encountered two strangers - the first at Angelica's desk who challenged my movement past the reception area, the other young woman, rummaging through the mail was hostile to me as well. Angelica came to the rescue and introduced me as Mister Boss.

"So far so good," Angelica informed me, "we are making inroads. Cynthia called - she is inside the Shooting Gallery touring with Doctor Wang and the Fed officials - she hoped you would be okay with her spending the time."

Murphy was heading out the door. "I'm having lunch with Cleve - it is at a place on the other side of the City - I'm taking drawings with me."

My desk was devoid of paperwork - actually, it was devoid of everything that had been there the day before, "My crane project is missing."

"That will not return - we are documenting everything else - you can decide what you want back on your desk tomorrow." Angelica seemed pleased. "Allaine called a few minutes ago - he's coming by."

***

"Wow, the top of your desk is made of real Formica."

"And to think I was going to trade it in for something in rosewood."

"I spoke to a friend who spoke to a friend who spoke to someone who will okay the footings - this guy is retiring and leaving the country - where he's going, they'll never find him - he wants to get paid, of course."

He named an amount. "Okay, tell Chester to write him a check."

"Maybe our man should visit the site - go to City Hall and make sure his license is valid - those sort of details."

"You know more about these sort of things then I do - send him a down payment."

"I resent your implications - it will have to be cash."

"Cash - as in small, used bills?"

"That will not hurt."

"This will require a number of ATM visits."

"I know an easier way."

"How about lunch?"

Cynthia was back in the office when I returned from lunch. "The building was a mess before - now it's a disaster."

"What did the Feds say?"

"They were arguing among themselves - I didn't say anything, and just left."

"You did good."

***

The temptation to return to the Grand Bazaar to see the final mast put in place was too great. The helicopter was just departing and I followed its course until it disappeared at the horizon - I fantasized soaring, untrammeled in the sky. Jubal was at the location of the most recent mast placement talking with Jose. I joined in the conversation and congratulated Jose on a job well done. "I saw Maria the other evening - her brother as well."

"You must be *misyaken* - Maria is *hijo unico.*"

"Mea culpa," I was sure that the doctor had said, "brother." I dropped the subject and repeated myself, "You have done well here." Jubal had nothing to report - I told him to take the day off.

***

I got back to the office in time to share a few photos of the masts in place. The housecleaning seemed to be well underway. I placed a call to Chester and left a message that Allaine would be calling him in regard to the Hill.

61

"Doctor Wang called," this from one of the temps who was otherwise stamping some forms that I did not recognize. She handed me a call back slip with the number and under the message entry several lines of hieroglyphics which I presumed was Chinese.

"Ah, so - translation, please?"

"She is grateful for you sending number-two person to the lab - please let her know what is happening."

"Really?"

"Actually the translation for, 'grateful', is complicated unless, of course, you have slept with her?"

"Any other possible translations?"

"Okay, I was a Chinese major in college - temping is the only sort of job I can get - I also do stand-up."

"I need to talk to Angelica."

"I heard. She's a hard worker - the Chinese thing was in her resume - I didn't think it was important."

"Okay," I needed to find Cynthia.

***

Cynthia was in my office placing a large brown envelope in an unfamiliar desk addition, a tray marked, 'IN.' I opened the envelope and we each took a copy of the paperwork to read.

"Well?"

"It sounds like they want to pay us a lot of money."

"Yes - but can we really save the building? Make an appointment - take Nate and Jeb and pay a visit - take the new temp who claims to speak Chinese. By the way, have you seen my crane project?"

"I'll ask Murphy."

Through the open door I heard, "Okay, which one of you college ladies does Chink talk?" Cynthia had found yet another demographic to offend.

***

"The fix is in."

"Okay?"

"Chester applied for a demolition permit - our new

consultant will be in town next week."

"Murphy is working with Cleve on revisions."

"Ta-ta, I'm off to jolly old England for a few days - I'm going to be a Daddo."

***

"The roof fabric has started to arrive." Jubal was reporting from the Grand Bazaar prior to coming in to the office. "Jose is doing inventory - he plans to start to start the roof once he knows everything is on hand."

***

I took a slow walk around the studio to look over shoulders, make comments if necessary and otherwise catch up on the work in progress. Angelica had reorganized the furniture so I now had an actual work station with reference board that I could call my own. Genevieve had returned to work - she was showing, as they say - I was still waiting for the other shoe to drop.

There were more cranes dangling from the ceiling. The general buzz of quiet telephone conversation - the dim overall illumination that benefited the computer monitors made me somnolent.

At lunch it was necessary for me to scrounge. Several were out on assignment reducing the larder. Chuan was at a fitting for, according to Jubal, "... some kind of robe that promotes procreation ..." The lone temp who had not met Chuan had no idea what Jubal was talking about, "I'll explain it to you later," Jubal added, as he took in her well-filled blouse front and petite crucifix.

Angelica handed me a list, "While you are at Costco," I realized it had been a while since I shopped.

***

"I tried calling you last night."

"I went shopping - then to a movie I have been wanting to see."

"Alone?"

"Yes - why do you ask?" There was silence on the line. "Are you there?"

She sounded more then tearful, "Yes."

"Are you angry - what's wrong?"

"You wouldn't understand." There was silence on the line and then the signal of disconnection.

I had exposed myself once more - Babette was just another nut case on whom I had wasted far too much energy.

62

Roof fabric placement began. Representatives of the Italian manufacturer were on hand to advise. The site was full of bundles of various sizes. The process began with cables being placed from mast to mast and from cable to cable, the spinning process equal to that of a spider, only the brain of this arachnid was a computer originated in Milan. Cranes and unique lifts started the process followed by workers making the final connections by means of special stainless steel hardware. The newly processed materials glistened in the sunlight. Looking at the assembly with a squinted eye and at the proper angle it was possible to imagine a black widow creating a trap for its prey.

This process took several days with occasional lulls as the Italian engineers and Jose with crew consulted. The building inspectors stood around in hopeless befuddlement. Jubal and I came and went as did Allaine's associates.

The network of cables provided the scaffold for the placement of the fabric roofing material. The pieces of material were small in comparison with the overall structure, the intermittent sudden air currents above ground level were the greatest deterrent to ease of positioning and fastening. There were no safety nets and harnesses were not useful. I was reminded of the formidable jungle gym which I encountered when I first entered elementary school.

Rain halted progress for several days. The crews all hung around the site in anticipation of respites. The Italians were somewhat aloof, mainly due to language - Spanish is a romance language, close enough to Italian - the Hispanic workers led the leap to English. Food was also helpful - a kitchen, that ignored health department standards, was set up in an empty shipping container - as always, most people like to eat and with that comes socialization; and, hence, cooperation.

Taking the food operation as an example, the marketing people were looking at converting other containers on the site to temporary shops. There was still no sign of the big boys. Chester never mentioned any wishes from the developer - my bills were paid on time without question. For reasons I could not explain, I still felt uneasy.

***

At the office, there had been was so much reorganization I thought I had gotten off the elevator at the wrong floor. There were few pieces of paper in sight. My office, while not pristine, was an example of minimalism. At my studio work station, there were notes advising me as to, "New upgrades to the server." As I sat down at the computer, Angelica and the two temps hovered. "Want to take it for a ride?" this from the Chinese speaking temp.

All three women's eyes were aglow with anticipation, "Okay." I had no choice.

After an hour of mind boggling instruction, I sent out my first 'all staff,' message : 'LUNCH.' At lunch, I was praised for my efforts with the computer. Chuan's wedding, now a week away, was secondary to glorifying my entry into the latest century, or so it seemed. Chuan was happy to be out of the spot-light - the latest count on cranes the only thing discussed. I signaled to Cynthia and the two younger Tuckers to see me after the meal was over.

***

"Tell me what you think?"

"As we say down home - anything we propose will be like putting, 'lipstick on a pig,' This from Nate with Jeb nodding his head in agreement.

"For once, I think these Crackers have it right."

"We need some facts and figures to support that decision."

"That Doctor Wang still wants to see you."

"Get the facts and figures together and I'll present them to her." I wondered where her co-director was in all this.

Murphy called in. He was at yet another meeting with Cleve. In the meantime, the clock was ticking on the expiration date for the permit.

***

The end of the day brought me home just as a torrential rainstorm began. There was plenty to eat in the refrigerator, some good books to peruse.

"I am home, safe and sound."

"That's good."

"How are you?"

"Babette, I am fine - if I said something the other night that offended you - you need to tell me."

"No - you did not - it's hard to explain."

"Should I be disrobing?"

"That would probably help."

We started from the beginning and covered all the ground she wished to divulge. I told her that my life was an open book as far as she was concerned - there was no more to add - I had done stupid things that I wish I hadn't ,but that was then and this was now.

"She sighed deeply and there was a long silence. "Could you love me?" She said it very quickly as if I could say I did not hear it.

"Yes."

"Me, too." The phone went dead. The rain continued.

63

Jose and his crew had retreated to home and family - the Italians adjourned to their hotel - the Grand Bazaar was awash. The security service for the site stayed well away from the structure - there were no reports of damage, just the usual stew of debris created by too much water and not enough immediate outlets to the river.

I thought back to an earlier visit to the Hill and the mess that too much rain had caused to the whole neighborhood. There seemed to be few places for all this valuable natural resource to go except out to the ocean.

Before I could call Doctor Wang, she had called me, panic in her voice. Temporary measures had been taken to repair her laboratory's roof but she feared the worst. I got this information, second hand, through our effervescent Sino-temp complete with hand gestures. Cynthia's team's report lay in my IN box.

The report was brief and to the point. No architectural terminology was necessary. The costs for replacing the building were astronomical. Repairs were notoriously more expensive than new construction - then there were the tons of dirt from all over the world to be dealt with. I would have preferred to put this all in a letter, but Doctor Wang had made it personal. We had a contract with the Feds - they would make the final decisions. I had my resident Chinese speaker make the call.

"She asked if you could come now."

***

The sky appeared to be clearing. Our drive was uneventful - I avoided conversation except of a general nature. The guard at the gate issued me a VIP entrance pass for the Toyota - the car ran the last hundred yards with pride just like it did after a rare carwash. We were ushered to the co-director's office, a refuge from the sordid dimly lighted endless halls that made up the complex. There was no escaping dirt. Doctor Wang's office was filled with samples in neat glass containers - her desk was piled high with paperwork - the most prominent decoration, if you would call it that - a gigantic portrait of Mao. We looked around for a place to sit but it would have required moving stuff and it did not appear to be any new home for these odds and ends. Mao's eyes seemed to follow me as I leaned against a file cabinet.

"Thank you for coming." No translation required.

After that came an outpouring with very little English to allow comprehension. My eyes left Mao's, and to my temp. "Just a general gist, please - this is not the United Nations." I waited it out for the summation.

There was nothing new. She has plenty of money at her disposal - she did not understand why the government had to be involved - she did not comprehend why it would cost so much - she was the granddaughter of the, 'Chairman' - in China hundreds of people would show up and everything necessary would be accomplished.

At this, she motioned for the temp to excuse herself. In a new voice and in good English while standing very close, her light perspiration intoxicating, with Mao's eyes diverted, she said into my ear, "Natasha said you would be difficult - we will do this again in private very soon."

***

I prepared a memo of the meeting for the Feds along

with a scrubbed version of our estimate of the cost of construction. I left out the part about the proposed private meeting.

Tomorrow would be another day - if the weather was clear by morning the structure of the Grand Bazaar would be available to be finished. The staff was leaving for the day. I waved from my newly furnished office while reaching for the contents of the IN-box.

Judy came in with beers and took in the new look of my office. "There's room for one of those fold-out couches now."

"I'll have a to run it through my management committee - changing the subject - have you ever made it with someone of the female Asian persuasion?"

"Let me say that college was the peak of my era of experimentation - I had this roommate - she was from Hong Kong - a wild thing - we fooled around."

"Is it true - you know?"

"Is this that vertical or horizontal thing - you boys will always be boys - you want to have dinner or something?

"I'll take a raincheck."

***

At home, I returned Babette's call. I was excited about the pending completion of the Grand Bazaar structure - I explained my enthusiasm, "Design has always been my Achilles heel - my professors had advised me to consider agronomy on more than one occasion - the success of the Grand Bazaar allows the firm to break away from the mundane."

"Maybe you would have been a good farmer?"

"I thought about it but, I'm a hard person to discourage."

"Yes."

"I love you Babette - thanks for listening."

"You too."

We were talking about the real world now.

64

Jubal picked me up before sunrise. When we arrived at the Grand Bazaar, the workforce was revving up the various pieces of machinery - men were swarming over the fabric already in place to test for any damage from the storm. Jose and the Italian engineers were conferring around the bundles of fabric on hand. Jubal informed me that they had known about a shortage for a week and that what was needed to finish had been air freighted from Italy and had arrived and was waiting at our local airport.

I had debated whether to stay for more then a few hours but then I spotted Allaine.

I didn't realize he was back from England - there were surely stories to tell - he caught my eye and we adjourned to our aerie.

"You first."

"I'm beginning to like England - it is so - orderly."

"I'm confused?"

"For example, if you call someone who knows someone who knows someone and a few quid changes hands, a person you hardly know can lose their visitor's visa and be put back on the next plane to Slovenia - for example."

"What about your daughter - I thought she was expecting?"

"It was a ploy - she is back in school - with various tattoos to remind her to be more careful - that took a few quid, but I handled it myself."

"You are getting good at this - Chester says our consultant will be in town in a few days."

There was a conversation-ending roar as a helicopter arrived, bringing the roofing fabric from the airport - it maneuvered next to the structure so its load could be winched down and put to immediate use. Jose and his crew stood by. A glint of shining metal, which came into focus as a small aircraft, stealthily approached as if out of nowhere and struck the helicopter - there was little sound of collision - a small flame appeared - ignited fuel leaked onto the fabric roof which burst into flames soon becoming an inferno - the helicopter limped in the sky above us and crashed into the abandoned ball field at around the former second base - the small plane was not to be seen - smoke and flames flew to the sky - everyone on the ground fled towards the surrounding neighborhood - the helicopter's crew dove out of the cockpit but did not get far before the, 'copter' exploded - the sound of approaching sirens and crackling flames was all that could be heard.

Allaine and I stayed put - we felt the heat and breathed in wisps of acidic smoke - there was plenty of fresh air as well, and the stadium perch was not combustible. The flames spread - the fabric of the roof fed the conflagration.

"That stuff is not supposed to burn." I was furious, "All the testing and research and certification of incombustibility and the zero flame spread rating was a fraud. People have surely died."

Allaine had nothing to say.

Fire engines had arrived from multiple directions - it was apparent the decision was to allow the fire to burn itself out. Police showed up and started asking questions. Jose counted off his personnel and seemed pleased that all were accounted for - based on their body language, the Italians had ideas about leaving . A policemen spotted Allaine and myself and signaled us to stay put.

A uniformed policemen and a companion in plain clothes made their way up the stairs. It was crowded for all four of us on the grandstand outlook - we all kept changing positions so as not to miss any of the action.

"Were you up here when the fire began?"

We both nodded yes and told them what we saw, all of which took place in only a few seconds.

"I'll need your names and where we can get hold of you." We gave him our business cards.

"Anything you can add - what did the plane look like - how did it act exactly?"

"It was the size of one of those small commuter-type planes - all silver - a sharp pointed nose - it had no engines or propellers that I could see. It was entirely quiet."

"Maybe a jet - a rocket?"

"I don't know."

"Any markings?"

I shook my head and Allaine interrupted. "The number seventy-seven on the tail - it's my lucky number - that's how I can remember. It all happened very fast."

"We should go down - it's not healthy up here."

Looking down on the former ball field, paramedics were tending to the copter pilots - it appeared that they had somehow survived - it was hard to imagine, but like all the events of the last few minutes, the action had gone by so fast that the trauma of being a spectator distorted reality. The TV news people were arriving in force. The police were still taking statements - the fire department was hosing down the ashes and putting out small pockets of flames - there was no holding back the assembly from peering into the morass to try to identify the object that had started it all. The Italian engineers were nowhere in sight.

I found Jubal who had escaped with Jose and the building inspectors. Jubal And I drove together towards the office.

"Do you want to take the rest of the day off, change your clothes or whatever?" Jubal appeared disoriented, "I can catch a cab." His attention to the road was marginal. "We could use some breakfast."

***

At the diner, all of the TV stations were featuring the Grand Bazaar - the various talking heads conjectured as to what happened without any real information - Jose was having his fifteen minutes of fame. Chico personally delivered our 'coffee' - there was an alcoholic aroma that gave me a clue that he was playing mental health care provider - Jubal took his all down in one swallow. We ordered breakfast and turned our backs on the TV.

Getting ready to leave, it was difficult not to watch the latest pictures from the Grand Bazaar. A few of the masts were still standing. A machine with a multi-toothed claw was gingerly stirring the debris allowing the smoldering remains to be hosed down by awaiting firefighters - finding the remains of the aircraft was probably a goal as well.

Chico collected on our check. "Saw you on TV earlier - glad you are safe," He turned to Jubal, "You too, muchacho."

In the parking lot, I verified Jubal's eyes for signs of Chico's special 'coffee.' Under way, Jubal had the local news station on immediately:

"A terrible tragedy at our former baseball stadium early this morning. In the last few months, the stadium has been demolished and erection of a new state of the art shopping center begun on the former parking lot but fire of an unknown origin has wiped out all the new construction. The matter is being investigated - no casualties have been reported. Keep tuned."

Jubal glanced over at me, "There's more to it than that."

"The TV gives you the visuals but little real information - they want you to keep your boob tube on all day - watch the soaps, bombard your brain with lots of ads - the radio metes out information that it knows and waits it out."

"What's going to happen now?"

"I wish I knew."

65

Jubal dropped me off and went to park his car. Lawyer Kline was leaving the building on what appeared to be an important errand but stopped when he saw me. "You okay?"

"Yes," I did not offer any details or express any emotions of the mornings experience.

"We'll talk," and he was gone.

***

I had to shove the office door open - a mass of humanity awaited just inside - Judy and building acquaintances as well as staff filled the reception area - Jubal came in immediately thereafter.

"You okay Boss?" Murphy was in the lead once more, "What happened?"

I told them what Allaine and I had told the police, "It all happened very fast I was up in the abandoned stadium cheap seats with Allaine to watch the finishing of the roof - it was all over in a few seconds - the police are investigating - I don't think anyone has the whole picture - Jubal and I appreciate your concern - I don't know what else to say.

Judy squeezed my arm on the way out - the other building workers filed out giving a thumbs up. To the staff I said, "Jubal was in the most danger - I'm sure he will fill you in." I retreated to the safety of my minimalist office.

"The latest word is that the mayor is on the warpath," this from Allaine.

"And?"

"He sent the police to the airport, had the Italians arrested, arraigned in court, and he personally destroyed their passports. He is really pissed."

"Can he do that?"

"Probably not - have you heard from anybody"

"I'm sure I'll hear from Cleve when the permit is revoked."

"Keep in touch."

***

"You could have called."

"I'm sorry Babette."

"Don't do it again."

She hung up - maybe she really cares.

At lunch, the main topic of discussion was Chuan's pending wedding.

The thousand crane quota had been achieved. The ladies kicked around what to wear and decided to have a combined shopping spree; the guys chose a practical wardrobe that would suit the occasion and not require any expenditures. I would need to look in my closet - I was with the men as far as spending - Chuan would get a nice wedding gift and a week off with pay. No one spoke about the Grand Bazaar.

***

The late evening news reported that the fire was out and the remains of an aircraft had been found - the aircraft had been incinerated - no bodies had been found - no one was reported missing thus far - the investigation would continue at daylight the next day.

***

"Incinerated?"

"That's one way to go - everyone I know is accounted for."

"Any problems - anyone bothering you - this is your lawyer speaking."

"My only immediate problem is what to wear to a wedding on Sunday."

"You could go shopping - that's what I would do."

"No shopping - would you go with me?"

"Shopping?"

"No - to the wedding."

"You mean like a date?"

"It's a wedding."

"Okay."

66

The other shoe never dropped. Clean-up at the Grand Bazaar was now shielded from view - those participating were tight-lipped. Police guarded the site night and day. Whatever was taken away was done so in secrecy. The media grew tired of the story. No one had been reported missing.

***

I studied our Project List - we needed to redistribute personnel. The Grand Bazaar would probably not be rebuilt - the Hill was stalled - those were the big ones for us.

Susan was at the doorway, "Good news, I think - the aerospace engineer and his wife are coming in - it looks like the house is on again - will you be around?"

"I'll be around." This was curious - his family leaving town seemed so definite the last time we talked.

***

As if he never left, the engineer was inspecting the back of the coffee machine, "Yours is the only one I've ever seen in use - I still think there is room for improvement and cost cutting."

"I thought you were leaving town?"

"My higher ups admitted to a big mistake - one of my fellow engineers was responsible for stealing the prototype I was working on - he was let go - they never found the aircraft - I actually got an apology and a raise in pay. I will have all the time I need to create old, 'seventy-seven,' all over again, and maybe work on the coffee machine at the same time."

Susan and the engineer's wife came in for coffee and beckoned us to the conference room.

"We're back on track - there are some changes but then we'll interview contractors as we originally planned." Susan was pleased.

"Seventy-seven - you mentioned that number a minute ago?"

The engineer's wife spoke up, "That was the number on his MIT football team jersey - I met him there in Cambridge - it's a sort of an inside joke."

"Uh-huh."

***

"The Mayor is a little crazy but so far everything seems almost kosher"

"Uh-huh."

"The honcho at the Italian consulate and his lawyer made a visit to City Hall threatening action in the courts - they did not make an appointment."

"Uh-huh."

"The Mayor ordered the water turned off at the Consulate and for the Street Department to dig up the paving in front of their garage trapping everyone's car inside."

"That'll show them."

"The Health Department noted there was no water - made a visit and closed the Consulate due to unsanitary conditions."

"What is the purpose of all this?

"The mayor wants someone to make restitution for the results of the fire and he wants to put someone in jail for lying about the fabric," Allaine was laughing.

***

The Shooting Gallery project was in, 'no-man's-land.' We believed the costs would be exorbitant, and had told the Feds so - they had not responded - we still had a valid contract. Doctor Wang said she had plenty of money but there was no definition as to amount and I wasn't sure she had the authority to spend it even if it was sufficient. It was a quandary.

Looking at my list of personnel and payroll obligations, I decided to move forward.

"Cynthia, round up your team, we are going ahead with the Shooting Gallery." I had some ideas just like I did with the Grand Bazaar - the concept was there in my head - the images could not break through as sketches - I needed to verbalize and let others bring things to fruition adding their educated input.

"Here's what I see," Nate and Jeb were locked in - Cynthia, actually taking notes, "We can restore the building; actually rebuild it a piece at a time - we need to find a new home for all that soil - a new filing system so to speak. We move the dirt into special shipping containers, color-coded, maybe, lot's of super graphics, and stack them in a sculptural manner - the lifting devices for moving them about will be part of the architecture - maybe a big open shed over it all, like the old Paris train stations. After you study it in depth, get Benito involved."

And, to retreating backs, "Let me handle Doctor Wang."

The rest of the day was routine. Paperwork filled my IN-box. I did not even note the staff leaving at quitting time.

***

"You still look all tense."

"I am okay - I never even thought of the danger at the time - Jubal and I even had breakfast before coming back to the office. Its on my mind, of course."

"Doctor Judy knows what's best."

And, she did.

***

"I went shopping anyway."

"What did you get?"

"The dress is flowered and long - sort of Asiatic - you'll like it."

"Any new lingerie to go with it?

"Of course - you'll like it as well."

I was now totally relaxed.

67

The wedding was at a non-denominational chapel in the suburbs. The immediate families were present as well as relatives from afar. The bride's Father was in attendance having flown in from some Far Eastern country the night before. I met Babette under the chapel's entrance awning and we made our way to the, 'friends of the groom,' side seating. Babette took my arm - she was stunning, almost regal in no way resembling her lawyerly demeanor. The staff was all sitting together nearby - I could pretty well guess what all the whispering was about.

The ceremony, despite all the pomp and circumstance, was blissfully short. I noted the resemblance to other weddings I had attended - some of them had been so long that I forgot why I was sitting there. Chuan and his bride looked nervous and very much in love.

While lost in reverie due to the unfamiliar language, I noted that my partially finished crane was among the thousand or so hanging from the ceiling.

A reception was set up in the chapel's garden. The line of bride and groom and parents and significant relatives were to be congratulated of course. I introduced myself and Babette to each - I shook Chuan's hand vigorously - Babette kissed the bride and murmured a few words in Mandarin - I was astonished at this previously unknown language skill. I met Chuan's brother for the first time after having heard about him at lunch on more than one occasion.

There was champagne and many bite-size tidbits to partake of. A string quartet played American pop suitable for dancing. My staff was grouping once more and moving in a bee-line towards Babette.

Cynthia and her ward led the pack. "I'm Cynthia and this is Samantha and you are?"

Murphy was snickering - I noted he was holding Angelica's hand.

Babette was a little startled, but recovered very fast, "My name is Babs - I'm a friend of Boss."

"Uh-huh."

The remainder of the troop introduced themselves and engaged in light conversation, ignoring me entirely. Angelica, still clinging close to Murphy, hung back, "I recognize her voice from somewhere - after a glass of champagne I'll think of it." I think she already knew.

The caterer advised us as to the contents of some of the food offerings and we selected carefully. We took seats at a table with Chuan's brother, Cho, and family and some of Chuan's friends and made smalltalk. Cho was as humorous and sardonic as I imagined. The champagne flowed - the dance music became enticing - I offered my hand to, 'Babs' - I became aware that this was the first time we had touched - her face expressed the same emotion.

Our dancing was chaste, "Should I be referring to you as Babs from now on?"

"If you wish."

"And, the Mandarin - is that something you forgot to tell me about?"

"I have some Chinese clients - they appreciate my

attempts - any other inquiries."

"The color of today's lingerie?"

"Red - always red," she moved closer, "you can check out my wardrobe at home later."

***

I had checked out her lingerie drawers - the inventory was extensive and definitely all red. We lay together in bed, champagne fueled, blissfully naked, and did pillow talk - there was no sex.

***

"This day was what life is all about," this addressed to the dashboard of my Toyota on the way home, "It's a journey, not a destination." The Toyota had heard it all before and made no reply.

68

The mayor and the Italian government were at an impasse. The local police and various Federal authorities had finished their investigation. No conclusions were announced to the public. This did not deter City Hall from going after the fabric manufacturer, safely in Milan, by placing the engineers back in jail, setting a multi-million dollar bail for each and asking for a speedy trial. "Lying in the pursuit of a building permit application is a felony - public property was destroyed - these people will be prosecuted to the full extent of the law," this announced at a news conference held just before the last baseball game of the year.

The Italian ambassador had given up negotiating. The Feds said it was a local affair - perhaps the people in Milan would like to, "apologize and provide restitution?"

Personally, I had not heard a word since the police interview at the Grand Bazaar. This was disquieting.

***

It was the last game of the year. The crowd booed the other team's Italian named catcher at every opportunity. Allaine had invited me to share his box.

"I did not know you were a fan." Allaine had on a cap three sizes too small.

"My daughter is visiting - she brought some friends who had never seen a baseball game before - I, of course, made all the arrangements."

"As to this Italian snubbing, I am boycotting pasta in all forms."

"Seriously, something is afoot - watch out who you talk to."

***

I needed to get back to architecture. Thea work station in the studio became my domain. I told Angelica to take all calls - I would look at them at the end of the day. Instead of letting the non Chinese speaking temp go, I set her in my office and told her to work from there - she could pretend to be Boss if she chose to - alone that got past Angelica could deal with her. I dug into the work being printed for my final approval .

Spelling had improved but not by much. Some detailing was sloppy and left room for interpretation. Consultants were not coordinating among themselves. I started working more closely with all the staff. Benito's ego was still a drag but I had learned to live with it.

After lunch, I browses through the arcade, stopping at my doctor's office to make an appointment. The receptionist told me to come back at three.

***

"I don't know how medical this is but I need some advice."

"I'm going to take your blood pressure and the usual stuff or else I don't get paid - I can't promise you I can really help. Shoot."

"I have spoken to you about this woman before - in the abstract."

She interrupted, "That blood pressure number is not good - your pulse is erratic - let me try again. Be quiet and let me listen to the thumper." She concentrated on the new information,

"Still not good - we'll talk, but I would suggest some more tests. Let's update your history first."

I related all that had transpired in my business of late - the progression of my relationship with Babette, my various bedding partners.

"Tell me about your sleeping experience, exercise regimen, bowel movements - anything different then the last time I saw you?"

"I just don't sleep well - I worry a lot more - you recommended exercise, but I just don't get around to it."

"Do you want some pills?"

"No."

"Good - I need some more information - give me some blood and fluids - I'll get back to you."

"What about Babette?"

"That's out of my purview."

***

I disliked keeping diaries, but in this case, I needed to account for how I used my time. I knew fellow type-A's who had checked out early in life - I could not recall any of their achievements that justified leaving the earth prematurely.

***

I shooed the temp out of my offie an hour earlier than usual and dug into mail and phone messages. My first entry in the soon to be created diary would be how much time I spent in the office - assuming eight to nine hours of sleep per night, I had about six hours to do other stuff. There was exercise - I would join a gym. There was breakfast and dinner - I ate lunch at the office - showering, dressing and undressing would take some time, I liked to read the papers and the latest mystery novels - some of the things could be shifted to weekends - sleep appeared to be the constant need.

***

I quit the office and went home - dinner and the time before going to bed seemed to be too short a stretch.

"How did your day go?"

"Before we go further, do you want your own time slot or do you prefer to be put under miscellaneous?"

"Huh?"

"My doctor told me to limit the stress of work and get plenty of sleep so I figure I only have five or six hours in a day to do other stuff - going to the gym would need to be scheduled but there would be flexibility for things like talking with you - there are some big slots open on weekends - I have started a diary?"

"I like miscellaneous."

"Okay, you're right in there with taking out the trash and laundry."

"Maybe, I'll change my mind later."

69

Two very important looking envelopes were brought to me at my work station. The checks were for amounts far in excess of the outstanding bills for The Hill and the Grand Bazaar. An accompanying letter using essentially the same language referred to "retainer for future efforts."

There was no signature; the check's heading was the same as for previous payments, the payee being a bank in Dubai. I directed Angelica to hurry down to our bank, avoiding the opportunity to exclaim, for all the world to hear, "We're rich,"

***

The team for the Shooting Gallery project had its first meeting in the office to make recommendations to myself and create a design program. We hoped to follow the book as far as the necessary steps to bring the concept to fruition. It was premature to get Benito involved - his presence could be a damper instead of a benefit at this point - it was a matter of personalities - I couldn't afford any intramural animus.

"I think we have the building pinned down, Boss."

"Show me what you have and tell me what we plan to do next."

I looked over the drawings from the archives and as so often they were not entirely up to date - Cynthia and crew had found changes that were probably done piecemeal without benefit of recordation - the latest photographs, scattered over the table, showed desolate uninhabited spaces and serious structural deterioration. "This is just a lot of old construction, in bad shape, that is hardly being used."

Nate and Jeb and Cynthia agreed. "If it wasn't for the bins of dirt, the whole operation could be tucked into the foot-print of a Seven-Eleven."

"So, next?"

"Up to you, Boss."

"See me after lunch."

***

I called Doctor Wang on her personal line, "We need to talk, Doctor - there are some things you should know." I should have been more formal - maybe my voice was not enough introduction - she had seemed quite close up and personal when we last met - I was tempted to hang up and start again - I was angry about all this wasted time.

"I'm glad you called, Architect Boss - I will come to your office immediately." She hung up before I could adjust the time and place of the rendezvous.

I was tempted to spruce up my office with a few sprigs of lotus blossoms from the florist in the arcade - I asked the temp to find some tea apparatus - this whole project was becoming more bizarre at each turn.

I called Babette. "This is business," I gave her a brief summary as to my quandary

"I'll be right over."

The temp brought in a complete four-piece tea service plus cups and saucers, placed all on my desk, and backed out the door, this while the two women eyed each other warily. I made the introductions - Babette was now Advocate Babs - I poured. "I would have gladly come to the Lab, Doctor Wang, but since all our data is here and not fully organized, I am glad to be able to illustrate my predicament here at this office." She smiled. "As you know, the complex belongs to the Feds - I am bound by their rules - my inclination is to tell them to tear it all down - you say you will pay for all the work needed to make the facility whole and to your liking." She smiled again. "Tell me what you see happening?"

"We are a worldwide organization - many scientists want to join us here in our work - their governments contribute to our budget - the Director and I want to make this a prestige place to work."

"Speaking of the director, I haven't seen or heard from him since 'day one' - I understood he was the one who had all the clout with the Feds?"

"Director Beasley is on a sabbatical."

"Uh-huh."

"Please start as soon as possible - submit your bills to me and I will work with the Feds as you call them."

No one had consumed any tea - I personally detested the stuff - the ladies eyed each other again - shook hands - Babette muttered something in Mandarin - Doctor Wang blanched, and whispered a reply in Babette's ear. I scooped the uneaten tea cakes into my IN file and saw to the return of the tea service.

"What was that all about?"

"Just good wishes for the Chinese New Year."

"Uh-huh."

Babette gave a hearty, *"Bonjour mes amis"* to the drafting studio and left.

At lunch, Murphy noted, "I see your friend Babs dropped by to say hello."

Before I could reply, Cynthia cut in, "When are you and Angelica going to, jump the broom, Murph?"

Angelica blushed a very deep red; Murphy choked on his burrito but got out, "Sorry Boss."

We reconvened with Benito on hand. I repeated the concept that I visualized of the Shooting Gallery - the old Paris train station sheds as inspiration - the use of shipping containers in a variety of ways - preserving the existing structure and making it safe, inside and out. "Build study models." I observed all the faces, "Work together - this is an interesting job - there is fun in working on projects with no budget constraints; believe me."

I wrote in my diary waiting at red lights on the drive home. I determined that was not a safe thing to do soon enough and spoke to the Toyota's dashboard instead - I mused about the work on hand at the office and the personnel - perhaps we had grown too fast - so much was on hold.

***

"I have written a memo about the Shooting Gallery job - business for me - put that down as miscellaneous in your diary - what are you doing?"

"Pondering. What was that business with you and Doctor Wang - the Chinese New Year is celebrated at the time of the second full moon after the winter solstice - I looked it up."

"We were both, *pipi sur la bouche d'incendie*."

"Why was that necessary?"

"Did you see that slit skirt she was wearing - take in that perfume?"

"I was too busy trying to remember my tea etiquette."

"You boys are such chumps. *Regardez votre tusch*."

That was the second time in recent memory I had been told to watch my back - albeit for different reasons. My paranoia was being rewarded.

70

The tragedy at the Grand Bazaar became old news very fast - all the various investigating agencies having jurisdiction had come and gone - no disappearances had been reported to Missing Persons - no one seemed to have lost an aircraft.

The Mayor was 'close' to achieving his goal. The insurance companies had joined in on the civil side - the Italian government caved - the Milan-based fabric company paid up without admitting any culpability - future applicants for building permits had been forewarned. I say, 'close' due to the fact that no one was speaking of rebuilding - the mayor wanted growth. The Italian engineers had been fined and placed on probation - all, except one, were on Air France a few hours after the court decision - Allaine spoke up for this one potential emigre whose abilities he admired and somehow was able to offer him a job and opportunity for a green card.

***

Chester knew what he read in the papers. "Not a word to me from the developer," was what he responded, "we could use the work - the back office is sitting around."

***

Susan had arranged for three contractors to come in two hours apart as a prerequisite to obtaining bids for the house for the aerospace engineer and his wife. We were asking contractors to use their uncompensated time so it would have to be honored by me sitting in to make sure they were interested and answer any sort of questions as to procedures. The names were all familiar ones. As a prelude, I helped myself to coffee and fussed over the machine for cleanliness as I knew the husband would be pending time inspecting the apparatus once more. Angelica joined me, "We have been doing a lot of coffee business lately,"

She laughed, "The first two policemen who came here during the summer keep bringing, *companeros.*"

"How about that Latino you sort of liked?"

"He's interesting - he always has some gossip or *misterios* to pass on to impress me.

"For example?"

He says there were four dead people on the plane that hit the helicopter at the Grand Bazaar."

"I hadn't heard that number - really never heard about a suspected pilot."

"He says the police are keeping it secret because they don't want a bunch of *locos* making all sorts of claims - in the meantime no one has been reported missing."

"Interesting."

"The police have DNA but that has not gone anywhere - what's weird is that the four were *cadaveres.*"

"You mean killed - dead? I'm sure they were."

"No - dead for a long time before the accident - *muy extraño - me da escalofríos*," she crossed herself and went to answer the phone.

It was very strange - it gave me the willies as well.

***

The meetings with the contractors went well. I took over my desk to fill out the end of the day.

"How's business?"

Allaine hesitated, "I closed my door, sorry - to answer your question, it could be better."

"Me, too."

"It could be the, 'R' word?"

"The signs are there."

Angelica came back from taking the phone call, "Your doctor wants to see you first thing in the morning."

I stopped for dinner at Costco. The clientele seemed to be in the usual number - people had to eat - architecture was way down at the bottom of the list of necessities.

***

Entering how my day's time was spent in the diary, I realized that this was a useless exercise.

"What are you doing?"

"Pondering once more - I go back to see my doctor tomorrow."

"And?"

"I'm trying to keep my mind off of that - as a diversion, I am working on a mystery."

"You want to tell me about it?"

"Not now - you are the only mystery I want to resolve - sooner rather then later."

"I love you."

"I know you do."

71

I skipped breakfast in anticipation of sacrificing more bodily fluids for further tests - Chico's cooking had been written up as exemplary in the New England Journal of Medicine - not in a good way.

"How do you feel?" The doctor was considering a sheaf of paper as we talked.

"Okay, about the same as last time."

"I'm going to refer you to some specialists, who we in the industry call the wolves - I'll give you some names."

"What are we looking for?"

"I'm not sure - we are going to touch all the bases - the last name is a shrink; I know where you stand on that but think about it."

***

Susan caught me at he door, "All three contractors have asked for additional drawings - it looks like they are all interested - we should get some good bids."

"Good to hear." Actually, this made me additionally anxious for the day - these sort of high-end contractors were notoriously aloof - often stalling, offering an aura of doing you a favor by considering your work thus justifying higher than normal prices or stating they were too busy but reluctantly bidding anyway with the same inflated result - in economic downturns, the shoe was on the other foot.

I studied the latest payroll figures. The temps would go - Genevieve would need maternity leave; she was living with her parents and had little in the way of expenses - Robbie would need to find another intern job. We had deposits for the two big projects but there was no sign they would be starting up again, The Shooting Gallery was billable from two sources. Maybe.

I called the several doctors recommended to me earlier that morning - not the shrink - and made appointments. When asked for specifics, I referred them to my doctor of the day - I had no idea what I was looking for

We had deposits for the two big projects but there was no sign they would be starting up again, The Shooting Gallery was billable from two sources. Maybe.

***

At lunch I guiltily ate and surveyed the sacrificial lambs.

"When's Chuan due back?" Murphy was trying to get some conversation going.

"He's on his honeymoon in Singapore - lots of good jobs there - no problems with security clearances," Cynthia was nursing a grudge based on some questions she was asked by the Feds when she was interviewed last - her student protest activity of years earlier raised a red flag, "Maybe he won't come back. She has all those degrees."

"Let's just wait till Monday," Cynthia could be a pain sometimes, but she had inadvertently added another possibility to my termination list - Chuan's new wife had far better prospects and could work almost anywhere - Chuan would follow.

After lunch, I asked Benito and Cynthia to take me through what they had done thus far on the Shooting Gallery. It was hard not to include Nate and Jeb as study models covered both their work station desks. The five of us circled the display without comment. The existing building was represented in the abstract, the various solutions in more detail and could be moved about to test out different perspectives - all of this in birds eye views. I remembered one of my professors declaiming, "birds eye views are for the birds," but it was appropriate in this case.

"Any favorites?"

"We're still not satisfied," Cynthia was speaking for us all.

"It's a good start - begin weeding." I meant that - it was satisfying to see some decent design coming out of the office.

***

I left the office early to fill out some forms at one of the recommended doctors' offices. I would return later after a specific specialist was assigned. Walking the long way home through the park brought me back by the way of the little used side street providing services such as dry cleaner, sandwich shop and the like. A bright sign caught my eye: "Yoga-30 Day Free Tryout," I had still not joined a gym - maybe yoga was the answer - the fine print for 'free,' was explained in the yoga studio's storefront window along with pictures of happy-happy people stretched out on an uncomfortable looking hardwood floor protected only with a thin mat of rubber.

"Mind and body, Boss, mind and body." The yoga studio entrance door had opened as I squinted at the various placards describing the deals available - the voice was vaguely familiar. I had a few seconds to recollect.

"Hello, Cliff - are you a patron?" He made a more presentable appearance in daylight than when we first met, but was still not wholly without a sinister demeanor. There was no reply and he hastened towards a large black SUV parked at the curb.

***

The young woman at the stand-up desk was perky as could be, snugly outfitted in some sort of stretchy material that exuded energy on its own, and was eager to assist.

"Can we sign you up today?"

"I'd like to try the thirty day free offer."

I was enrolled in less than five minutes including a rundown of the class schedule. "What do I wear," I did not have anything made of that stretch material in my closet.

"A pair of shorts and a tee shirt, no shoes required - the whole idea is to have you relax, get your mind clear and use a few muscles."

Clear my mind - I'll bet she never had a building burn to the ground with four corpses of unknown origin included.

***

"I signed up to take yoga classes today."

"Really?"

"Yes, I was promised that it would clear my mind, help me relax, and maybe, produce a few muscles."

"Was she attractive?"

"If you mean the woman at the membership desk, the answer is yes - she was wearing some sort of stretchable body-suit - do you have something like that in red - I didn't see a similar outfit in your lingerie drawers - I fondled a few items but didn't dig to the bottom, of course?"

"Pierre, we need to have pillow talk."

Babette was kind and understanding - she undoubtedly suffered from the outrageous demands of her profession. If she had ever sought professional help, it was never mentioned. She did not seem to have anything to prove, and was happy in her own skin - 'she looked to the future as the past was now' - it was apparent that she wanted me to be part of that future - I did not want to be a burden.

72

Murphy had successfully negotiated the changes necessary for the Hill building permit to be renewed with essentially all the requirements of the latest codes being met. The office would be busy going through it, page by page, and making sure all of this was coordinated. Very little paper had yet been produced - the computer screen viewing of documents wore thin for me after a few hours - the pending results of the various doctor visits prayed on my mind.

***

"Chester, we are about ready to have the Hill permit up to date - where do you stand?"

"I have become more and more ambivalent about the project - it's got me on edge - the size of it is a real test of our resources."

"What does your sister think?"

"I don't see too much of her anymore."

"What does that mean?"

"Just that - she's in Europe with some of her rich girl-friends - she cashes her check every month and that's about it."

"Uh-huh."

***

Confusion reigned. If Chester had no impetus to move ahead, what was supposed to happen? Doctor Tabershaw said he trusted us to take the project to fruition - there was no plan B. My contract called for me to obtain the building permit - in this particular case to revise as necessary to maintain the permit - monies had been received for that purpose, but if no construction began, by law, the permit would expire in six months.

***

"Good morning, Babette."

"You sound confounded."

I told her of these latest circumstances and confessed my concern for the return of the building industry's periodic recession. "What do you think?" "As your lawyer, I would say finish what you are obligated to do and step back."

"I hear you."

"While I have you on the phone, I want to tell you I will be out of the office - out of the country - for a while - my associates will be available."

I was startled and said so, "What's going on?"

"I'll call you tonight."

***

I went back to my work of reviewing drawings. Babette leaving the country - doctors results - the pending recession - the fate of my practice - it was all, a bridge too far - my concentration was shot. I did not want to share my gloom with the staff and opted for a walk. I wandered through the park, fed the pigeons, listened to a soapbox orator predicting the end of the world - put a buck in the speaker's basket and took a brochure - I read the pamphlet carefully but could not discover a promised date for Armageddon - I was on my own.

***

On my way back to the office, I visited the yoga studio, showed my temporary ID, and sat so I could see a class in progress through the glass wall - it did not look too difficult but I decided to try a few positions out at home before making a fool of myself. As I was preparing to leave, Cliff appeared from somewhere towards the rear and headed to the street, passing right by me without so much as a nod. The same black SUV was waiting at the curb. I nodded goodbye, with raised eyebrows, to the studio receptionist who smiled blissfully.

***

The staff was due to leave when I returned to the office, Cynthia, Benito and the Tuckers were still at it - I purposely did not disturb them. There were forms to sign, phone calls to return

- the IN box was unrelenting - there was no word from my doctor. It was getting darker earlier now and I chose to wait out driving home in the dusk. The Shooting Gallery crew departed on tiptoes.

Judy knocked and entered. We sipped our beers and watched the moon rise.

Talking into the window, I queried, "How about dinner and a sleepover?"

"Really?"

"My apartment is being painted - I need to get away from the fumes."

"Whatever?"

I did not want to be at home to hear from Babette about being out of touch in some foreign country. I suspected it was China - she had Chinese clients - those folks seemed to have plenty of money - China was twelve hours away on the global clock - not conducive to pillow talk - I was a little too old for such a long distance relationship. And, for how long? Time was running out - who knows what the doctors would have to say?

73

Babette and I finally talked before she flew off to China. For her it was the opportunity of a lifetime, professionally and emotionally - she had grown up on the mysterious histories of Genghis Khan and Marco Polo and the Great Wall, and now she could explore this culture on her own - her clients admired her legal skills and were prepared to reward her handsomely. How long she would be away would, "depend."

As it turned out, Babette's legal associates, all women, were fearless replicas of their chief. As to the Hill, I received a memo shortly after Babette left that, summarized, said, "Take the money and run." I did apply for and receive an extension of the Hill permit. Cleve wished me "Lots of luck," and I think he meant it. We never discussed the Grand Bazaar ever again.

***

I informed Chester of the Hill permit status and his attitude was the same as before. I had not a glimmer as to what the repercussions might be if construction did not begin. I decided to drive up to the site out of curiosity taking Murphy with me. 'Murph' brought his hardhat from his previous service at the site and seemed happy to be out of the office. The gate at the highway was gone as was the former temporary access road - we parked and walked - the entire area had been hydroseeded with wild flowers and tall grasses - a slight depression in the greenery gave clue as to where the road had once been and this was the route we followed to the top. Building materials and trailers had been hauled away - demolition rubble was gone - it would take experienced surveyors to find the saved foundations now fully below ground - butterflies and diminutive scurrying wildlife had already found a home in the recent vegetation - perhaps it would stay this way for a long time.

"What happens now, Boss?"

"I wish I knew, Murphy - I wish I knew."

***

If my memory served me, Doctor Tabershaw said to deal with Maria or Lawyer Kline if he needed to be contacted. Maria I viewed as a lightweight - Lawyer Kline on the other hand seemed to crop up on too many occasions related to the Hill, and I knew where to find him. I placed a call to Kline's office expecting to leave a message but he came on the line immediately.

"Boss, how are you?"

"Confused - but maybe you can help?" I gave him an update on the status of the Hill.

"We have been talking about this and think there is a solution." He did not define, 'we.'

"And?"

"I will call you this afternoon."

At least someone else was concerned - another uncertainty maybe heading towards a solution - maybe. For now, I would cancel a staff reduction - the temps would go - Genevieve would be encouraged to take pre-maternity leave - I would hold my breath.

***

At lunch, Murphy described the Hill site - the last visit for us all had been the morning of the planned implosion, "Gone man - nothing but grass - it's creepy."

"Chuan was looking uneasy. Angelica had pulled some of the wedding cake out of the freezer as a welcome back for this latest lunch - Cynthia was paused to make a speech.

"Boss - guys - I appreciate you all coming to the wedding and continuing the celebration today - but - the latest news is I am moving to California." Chuan paused for breath.

"I told you it wouldn't last," this from Cynthia as sat down and returned to her second portion of cake.

"No, it's not that - we both have some very good job offers and this would be the time before settling down."

That made for one more less painless payroll adjustment, "When?"

"End of the month - if that's okay with you?"

"You gotta do what you gotta do." I patted Chuan on the shoulder as I retreated to my office.

If I knew what Lawyer Kline and I were going to discuss later in the day, I would get prepared - absent that effort, I made copies of all the building department correspondence, forms and the like, and the bill for the permit - the permit fee was a whopper and I didn't want it coming out of my account. I waited for the phone to ring.

"Can you come upstairs?"

"Do I need to bring anything?"

"Just yourself - and come in through the door marked, 'Do not Enter,' at the end of the hallway; that way you can avoid our overprotective paralegals."

I took the stairs - that would be my exercise for the day. Lawyer Kline was waiting just inside the prohibited door and escorted me to his office. We shook hands and took time to admire a spectacular cloud formation over the mountains, then retired to the leather couches that made up the more casual area of the sumptuous office.

"Things are moving fast." Kline was looking everywhere except at me. I waited him out.

"Chester will start planning for construction tomorrow." I waited still. "The company has been bought out - his sister signed all the papers in Paris this morning."

"Wow."

"Wow, indeed." Kline appeared quite smug. "My people wish to complete the Trifecta," he moved to his desk and removed some papers, "we wish to purchase your firm as well."

"Wow." I received the paperwork that was crowned with a cashier's check with a lot of zeroes. "Where is this all heading?"

"Let us just say there are folks overseas who want to get a foothold in businesses in this country and would buy viable companies rather then starting from scratch."

"I'm flattered."

"You should be."

"I'll think it over."

"Don't dally."

***

I chose to read the buyout proposal at home. There would be a new company - I would own forty-nine percent - a corporation headed by Lawyer Kline would own fifty-one percent - I was to be the president. My name would be buried under the masthead of the new company indicating I was the one legally practicing architecture. This was high finance - a long way from keeping small change in the cookie jar. I needed to talk to Babette.

74

In the morning, my head snapped back to the word mentioned by Lawyer Kline - 'Trifecta - who or what was number three? I needed to talk to Babette. I left a message at the law office - no one was available to talk to me - I yearned for the days past when I got a prompter response.

***

"Allaine - where are you?"

"Jolly old England chappie."

"First born child problems again?"

"No - I have met someone - a countess or viscountess or something like that - I have an opportunity to become a count or maybe a viscount."

"Are we speaking of marriage - does she come with one of those fox-hunting estates or a castle?"

"No - she's dead broke but a title would be nice."

"Really?"

"It would be good for business - I made a deal with Lawyer Kline by the way."

"Aha - the Trifecta."

***

I made a call to Chester but got his voicemail. There was still no answer from the lawyer's office. I called a friend who had a friend who worked at the State Department.

I obtained Babette's hotel phone number via the American embassy in Beijing - it was required to register with the embassy if you were in China for an indefinite period of time and this practice served my needs perfectly. Twelve hours' time difference would put me outside the etiquette for evening calls but I needed to talk.

"Is this you Pierre - where are you?"

"At my office as usual - I have been trying to talk to your associates about something important."

"I haven't been able to get through either - something's going on.

"Going on - what?"

"I suspect a putsch."

"Really?"

"Those newbies are super ambitious - I have suspected them for some time - the China opportunity overwhelmed me - I didn't know what to do - they are stealing my practice telling all sorts of crazy stories."

"You know this for sure?"

"Yes."

"I'll take care of it."

I told Angelica to call her brothers, round up five or six of their closest friends and meet me at Babette's address - "It's a paying job - cash." Also, call a locksmith and have him meet us there prepared to add locks to an office door. Also, find out the procedures for switching telephones from one office to another." I gathered the Tuckers under my wing and went to help Babette.

***

I walked in with the Tuckers and found a frenzy of copying documents.

Young men were assisting, apparently boyfriends or more recently minted lawyers. "I just spoke to your boss in Beijing - she told me to tell you - you're fired."

"You can't do that."

"Now would be a good time to leave." The menfolks were looking menacing. " My friends here will escort you to the elevator." The Tuckers were eyeing their potential opponents. I opened the office door and brought in the seven Hispanics who were now eyeing the sweet young lady lawyers. I put the locksmith to work. Purses were gathered and retreat made to the elevators, "Put the ladies in a cab and take them to police headquarters - I'll call ahead to explain the theft I found going on here."

That was fun - nothing like clearing up an insurrection before lunch.

I hit the ATM and paid off Angelica's brothers and friends.

***

I looked at the global clock that now hung over my desk - it was past midnight in all of China, but I called anyway to report on the morning's activities.

"I switched your phone lines over to my office - very expensive by the way. I have two temps I was going to release - they will cover for you - they are not lawyers nor yearn to be such."

"Thank you Pierre - I'm truly upset - and sleep deprived - I'll call you back."

Chester returned my call. "You've heard the news, I'm sure? My sister got what she wanted - money - I hope there's enough left over when the time comes to send Saul's kids to college - she's gone and it's not my worry for now - I have an employment contract - actually she won't get all the money - I am, or was, a minority stockholder. I'm good for now."

Saul's kids - I wondered if that included the one that was now incubating?

"Are you gearing up for the Hill?"

"My new boss has to give me the go-ahead."

"Uh-huh."

***

The Tuçkers reported in. "When we got to the sidewalk, the ladies took off their heels and skedaddled - the guys went with them."

"Good work - put this morning down on your time sheet as General Administration."

75

"It's lunchtime here - I begged off from my clients so I could talk to you. How are you?"

"Not sleeping so great - your call is well timed. How are you?"

"Pierre, what happened is awful - I am so embarrassed, I put you in jeopardy - please forgive me and accept my gratitude?"

"Babette, when you get home - no more absentee pillow talk - promise?" "I understand - tell me why you called my office in the first place."

I read most of Kline's contract to her verbatim. "I think its good for me - I will always have my professional skills - the money will be invested - safely."

I agree - cash the check and keep on doing what you're doing - I hope to see you soon - wait till you see the latest lingerie from Hong Kong."

"Red - I hope."

"Of course - I love you."

Sleep still escaped me.

***

I was at the diner at a very early hour. Chico looked at me disapprovingly. "*A partir del día temprano o llegar tarde a casa?*" You don't look so good, Boss."

"I am on my way to the office - it might a well be home. China , *es mi perdición.*"

"China - downfall?"

"It's a long story."

"In China it's supper time - how about the meat loaf special?"

"Coffee, por favor - I'll think about the meat loaf."

The TV news blared on - baseball was over - no other sports interested me - maybe college basketball but I had to be in the mood. The coffee was enough - a takeout order of meat loaf would suffice for lunch, - at midnight, Beijing time.

***

I read the contract over one more time. There could be thousands of words, inscribed on parchment, gold seals and the like but without trust all that was meaningless - I would continue to do my thing - being solvent was a great incentive - maybe I could do some design again.

The manager of the bank opened a special account in my name and forewarned me that even though the check was certified, foreign accounts would be scrutinized for lots of reasons - in other words, let it mellow.

I called Lawyer Kline and left a message that the contract was ready.

The phone people were at work hooking up a link to Babette's law office at Robbie's former desk - there would be an answering machine with a greeting in both English and Chinese - the Chinese by virtue of our talented temp.

Except for the sidetrack to Babette's office the previous day, the process of reworking the ownership of the firm had been a painless one. It was not something I was planning but it was welcome due to the quandary of the economy as well as my health - this reminded me to find out if all the doctors had reported in.

***

"Paper and more paper - I thought computers were supposed to eliminate this," my doctor was shuffling and reshuffling pages of different size and color, "What you need is a summary, right?"

"Okay."

"The wolves and I can't find anything physical that warrants attention - you should stop changing doctors so often - find someone who keeps records - tells you when to have a colonoscopy, a tetanus shot, a PSA test, and to exercise - you know the drill - I still recommend you see a shrink," she was extremely upset, "You're a smart guy - just like my father - he sent me to Med School but he never had chance to see me graduate - he hated doctors - don't ask me why - find someone you can trust. I am giving up my practice here in a few weeks - my life style has attracted the wrong kind of attention - there are other places where I can do some good."

"Wow." I rose to shake hands and ended up giving her a hug - being a fish out of water was something I could understand.

Back in Appalachia, I could understand the aversion to someone different - different meaning 'not like me' - it was not a sophisticated world - many of these same people were one generation away from a country long disappeared and a culture and language tossed in the dustbins of history. Some well known architects had anglicized their names to fit in with 'Mayflower' folks - those wealthy decision makers wanted only to deal with their own kind. A famous New York architect took an opposite approach and only hired people of his same sexual orientation. And, me, what was I really hiding from?

I met briefly with Lawyer Kline - my signature was notarized - a completed copy of the contract handed to me in convenient size to put in my safe deposit box. I would wait for the check to clear and for Babette to read it in toto.

***

Angelica and her two temp helpers were excited. "We talked to Ms. Silver in China - she sounded like she was next door. We told her about the answering machine and the message in Chinese - she was really surprised."

"Any message?"

The three looked at each other and shrugged. "I guess she was trying out her phone to see if it was still working - or something."

"Okay."

76

"Wǒ ài nǐ."

"Huh?"

"That means, 'I love you,' - my Chinese associates have given up seeing me for lunch - they say I'm in love - I am."

"Woe to me, too."

"Close enough - did you see your doctor - what did she say?"

"We're back to square one - she thinks I'm a mental case."

"Things will surely look up now that your business is better financed - and after we're married."

"Hello - bad connection here - I'll get back to you."

I had hang up - why did I think that this nightly flirtation would not be seen by Babette as wooing and having its logical conclusion in marriage - why did I not think of it? And, is that what I wanted?

Neither one of us tried to call the other back this night. I hoped I had not hurt her feelings.

Sleep had not come easily - a new specter appeared every time I dozed off.

***

Chico said nothing - he served me coffee plus a refill and at pay-up time handed me a styrofoam container - barbecued ribs, potato salad and coleslaw was the special of the day.

***

I joined the Shooting Gallery team at work on yet another model. I did not interfere and watched the tweaking turn into a solution that we all liked - it was a satisfactory morning.""Okay, rework the model so it is presentable to the client - we'll need a rendering and a few more drawings - somebody pick a number for a cost estimate - better yet call Chester to come have a look - let's have it ready by two days from now."

***

My lunch was looked at askance by the majority healthy eaters at the lunch table - midway through the meal I placed the remains in the refrigerator - Chester and two of his cohorts had joined us prior to looking at the Shooting Gallery material and their pizzas were more inviting anyway - the conversation was light - Chuan's choice of his new job in California being the main topic.

***

The entire office joined in the afternoon charrette. Cynthia and Benito started from scratch, explaining the needs of the existing facility and its physical condition - they explained that it was a global organization that ran the Shooting Gallery and there were many governments who wanted to participate, each for their own reasons - it was more then just a laboratory. Prestige was involved.

We talked about materials and time constraints and other factors that effect costs. Chester took a scrap of paper and wrote down a figure and showed it to his two associates. There was a lot of shrugging but the three seemed to agree. To me, the number was astronomical.

"You could lowball the estimate and let it skyrocket like that new museum in town - everyone seems to be used to that approach nowadays," Chester was smiling. "Your call - don't mention my name."

"I'll sit on it for the time being."

"Back in my private space, I thought about what sort of presentation I would make to Doctor Wang. I would sit on that as well. I rummaged through the contents of the IN-box and contemplated the dusk-filled sky until the stars were outshining the city lights. I ate my leftover breakfast and some other scraps remaining from lunch and entered a muddled state once more. Babette would call tonight I was sure - midnight seemed to be her witching hour.

***

"I had the hotel check out my phone and they couldn't find anything wrong."

"Same here - the phone company had techies pouring over my apartment."

"Perhaps it was a solar flare?"

"Or, maybe, a rogue satellite?"

"Pierre, when we are married you must promise me not to put your head in the sand like you did last night."

"There it is again - maybe it has to do with time of day?"

"Do not hang up."

"Okay."

"What did you think - that we were going to shack up until we got tired of each other - is that what you had in mind?"

"No - I didn't really think long term - I was enjoying the moments - I never met anyone like you - it's been fun - my sanity is somewhat restored. *Nǐ hěn bǎoguì.*"

"You are precious, too."

77

I invited Doctor Wang to come to the office to see our work product for the Shooting Gallery.

"Angelica, we have to stop calling the Shooting Gallery the Shooting Gallery - what do the Feds call the complex in our contract?"

"Building forty three twenty three."

"Not very appealing - we need something more dignified - something international - I think, 'Earths R Us.' is taken."

"Up to you, Boss."

***

At lunch, I asked the staff to write down proposed names for the project, more than one was okay and we would pick them out of a bowl one by one, have a discussion, and vote for a winner. I had to scrounge for food as I had overslept and missed Chico's offerings of the day. Eating become secondary for all as the novel task was pondered - I put my entries in the naming pool as well.

Lunchtime ran over but every one was having too good a time to cut the debate short.

The winner wound up being an amalgam of several ideas, "And, the winner is - Global Research Institute Terra with the acronym, GRIT." Doctor Wang could change the name to any one she wanted - Shooting Gallery was too difficult to explain to an outsider.

Doctor Wang confirmed for the next day. I put the team on alert to have the model and presentation boards ready. This was not going to be as big a 'show and tell' as the Grand Bazaar - the doctor could be doing this solo - she did not mention staff or advisors - Director Beasley still seemed to be among the missing. I thought about informing the Feds about of the meeting but the last time I met with them, they had all but dismissed participation at any level - I would send a memo.

Technically, this was the first day I was the minority owner of my practice - it did not feel any different - there was no one looking over my shoulder - yet. I decided to skip tea as part of the next day's meeting - I would introduce Doctor Wang to our high-tech coffee machine. I called Allaine's office and asked for one of his associates to come by to look at our concept to be better able to answer questions as to construction feasibility - Allaine would be perfect for this but he was busy in London preparing for his plunge into the royalty scene. I checked in with my banker regarding the check for the business participation, "Nothing negative - it takes time to make sure." I was too impatient as usual. The yoga schedule on the desk indicated there was a class suitable for me and I headed there to finish the day.

***

"I took did some yoga again today - I am particularly good at, 'Dead Dog Rising,' - the instructor had on a new aquamarine stretch suit."

"That's a coincidence - I took my first Kung Fu class this morning - some of the guys are really well-built, quick on their feet; and were very helpful in my learning the, 'Tiger Death Strike.'"

"Continuing on that note, Doctor Wang will be in tomorrow - I have decided to skip a tea service and give her a personal lesson on the workings of our exotic coffee machine."

"Wedding - wedding - wedding."

"Wow, my telephone just became red hot - that's a new problem."

"Don't you dare hangup."

"Okay."

"Tell me how you feel - any problems with your new situation - anything I can do to help?"

"I'm feeling okay - my work on this latest project was enjoyable - after tomorrow I will have a better idea as to how things will move forward - my silent partners remain silent - the bank says the deposit check is still in purgatory. When are you coming home?"

"I'm over committed - I don't know." This time I did hang up.

If I was little younger this sort of exchange could go on indefinitely - we would meet somewhere halfway for the weekend - make plans as to where to live together and start our individual careers - name our first dog - decide on whom of our individual friends could be tolerated by us as a couple - whatever normally stressed people do.

The weekend was coming - would that mean longer phone calls - where was that time utilization list I had once prepared - there were extra leisure hours scheduled as I recall after a typical Friday night"

78

The office was geared up for our GRIT presentation. We were a much more experienced team than the one that presented the Grand Bazaar - Allaine's two associates added even more expertise - there was an unofficial cost estimate in my pocket which I would avoid divulging it if at all possible.

Doctor Wang brought only herself and a video technician. She asked if anybody objected to being photographed - no one demurred - I asked for a copy for our records. All the staff straightened up and positioned for exposure to the camera.

Cynthia and Benito took center stage - I soon realized they had actually rehearsed - the proffering went on uninterrupted - Doctor Wang paid close attention to every word - asking no questions - I stood up to ask her for comments or queries - there were none - she smiled at the staff and thanked them for their good work.

"Architect Boss, please, may we talk," motioning towards my office.

She closed the office door which I usually left partially ajar, "Coffee or something to drink Doctor? I'm going to get coffee for myself?"

She followed me into the kitchen, "Don't you have people to do this?"

"They have more important work to do - if I push this green button - I think - I can draw water for tea if you like."

"That's a very strange looking machine."

"American technology at its finest - a gift from a grateful client - it's one of a kind."

"No tea, thank you, I would like to find out what happens next."

This time she shut the office door with a little more emphasis than last, adjusted the slit in her skirt that Babette had warned me about, "Very simply, you authorize us to proceed to the next stage where we provide more details and some cost estimates."

"Very good, please proceed - send a bill of course." and, as she rose to leave, "there's a Sino-American festival this Saturday - downtown - I'll be there all day into the evening."

I caught Heckle and Jeckle who were conversing with Cynthia, "Take a copy of everything and talk with Allaine and let me know if there are any problems - we need some cost figures."

"The Count is sort of busy right now - we'll take care of it." He said this with a straight face.

"Okay."

The Count - what a joke - I could remember him, 'when' - he would probably bring the bride back home for a show and tell - why didn't I get invited to the wedding? I wonder what sort of nuptials Babette has in mind.

At lunch, we continued talking about the presentation - the opportunity to work on something so complex had produced a great deal of excitement - there was talk of new software that could sort out some of the design problems - I shared in the discussion as part of the team, not just as the Boss.

"That Doctor Wang - she sure doesn't say much - is that good or bad?"

"People of the Asian persuasion tend to be reticent - that's my experience anyway."

"Are we working for her or for the Feds?"

"For the Feds - the government is allowing GRIT to enhance the property at their expense - we are working for both of them - it may get complicated, but not for us."

"It sounds like a 'pig in a poke,'" this from Jubal with all three Tuckers looking dubious.

"You guys are going to be successful architects - getting paid does tell - not every project gets built however - not even ones by the superstars."

***

"Hope you are enjoying a flute as we are here at the Ritz?"

"It's a little early in the day, Count."

"Egads, the cat's out of the bag."

"Heckle and Jeckle let it slip."

"Ah, my associates - they are proud of my new status - best to keep those honorifics you have for them to yourself, chappie."

"The purpose of your call?"

"The countess and I will be coming back to the States in a fortnight - we will be married again to make it all kosher - be my best man like a good fellow."

"Can I bring a date?"

"The more the merrier - ta ta."

***

It took the rest of the afternoon to make notes, get off memos and make sure proper copies of GRIT exhibits were made and distributed. The staff was filing out as I finished my list of tasks. Yoga seemed like a good idea and that's how I completed the day.

I made a mental survey of what was in my refrigerator at home and stopped by the diner for dinner.

***

"You look a little better, Boss, *como mi madre solía decir color en las* mejillas."

I checked my complexion in the reflective glass of the pie display and agreed I did look somewhat healthier "I had a good day Chico - business is good - a friend of mine is getting married."

"Speaking of married, whatever happened to that, *señora exóticos* that was in here one very early Sunday morning?"

"I wish I knew Chico - I wish I knew."

***

The Toyota knew the way home.

***

"Were you asleep - I'm sorry?"

"It's been a busy day - I decided not to fight it - I fell asleep on the couch."

"How are you - I do worry?"

"Allaine called - he married that Countess in England and has immediately taken on his title as Count - it's a lark for him - who knows what she thinks - she has a source for the money she needs - they are planning to marry again here in town - he wants me to be his best man - I asked him if I could bring a date.

"Are you asking me?"

"Of course, we do weddings well."

"Let me know when?"

"What else; let's see - we renamed Doctor Wang's project - it's now called GRIT. The staff did an excellent job on the presentation for our proposal. I took note of that skirt issue you mentioned during my private review with the Doctor - she invited me to a Sino-American festival Saturday night."

This time Babette hung up.

That went well - my conscience was clear - sleep would come easily.

The phone rang once more, "I see your lights are still on - do you have time for a nightcap?"

"Marcie - it's a perfect time for a nightcap."

79

Fridays were always a little different. The weekend beckoned - it was hard to believe that architects' offices used to work half days on Saturdays. An, 'old-timer,' I once worked with told me that this sort of work received no compensation and was mandatory if he wanted to keep his job; and jobs were scarce at the time.

I had skipped Chico's for breakfast to get a head start on the day. All of the work in progress needed to be checked - the time sheets were now on my desktop computer. We had put in a lot of time on GRIT - I felt somewhat guilty as to what the billing would be.

At noon, most of the staff opted to eat out - lunch turned into an early, 'happy hour' on occasion - it was forgivable today - everyone had worked extra hard during the week and it had culminated with the GRIT finale.

Susan's clients, the aerospace engineer and wife with triplets were in the office to sign a contract for the construction of their new home. It was a little chaotic. The kids arrived in a specially designed three-place pram but were soon attracted to all the delights of the drafting studio. Angelica and the two temps were assigned one each to tend.

"Good practice for the future, ladies - Angelica, you should get Murphy up from the pub to give you a hand - it would be good prep for a few years hence," she blushed and the temps tittered.

The husband joined me at the coffee machine as his wife went over last minute details with the contractor. We both seemed to enjoy our brew while standing in front of the apparatus.

"How is it going with the new aircraft design - anything ready to fly just yet?"

"Soon - bigger and better - it's exciting."

"That fellow who commandeered the previous prototype - did they ever find him or the prototype?"

"As far as I know, they never did - it's a company embarrassment. It's funny - he was a nice enough guy - a good engineer - he and his wife were very religious - consummate do-gooders and I mean that in an admiring way - neither of them has been seen since - no one is looking for them as far as I know."

"Uh-huh. That baby buggy your design?"

"Built it myself - I am thinking about a patent - like this coffee machine it's one of a kind and very costly to put together. Triplets are not that common and that point in one's life, the other expenses before considering baby carriages are horrendous."

"Uh-huh."

***

Relative quiet returned to the office by late afternoon. The triplets left with some surplus building samples that would be child safe once properly sanitized. The building contract was initialed and signed and deposit check proffered - a separate contract for Susan to supervise construction was approved.

The staff came back one by one to collect their worldly goods and check phone messages.

Soon, I was by myself. If I listened carefully I could still hear children's screeches of delight. The sun had already set; some showers threatened - I swiveled repeatedly in my desk chair, a familiar rhythm of monotony, contemplating nothingness.

I did not want to go home. The nightly phone calls that began by featuring jocular ripostes turning later to more serious tete-a-tetes and finally to taunting, were not something to look forward to - I was just as guilty as Babette on that score.

***

I reluctantly ran a few errands to gather food and drink and headed home. My lights were on in full blaze and the smell of cooking pervaded over the closed windows mustiness.

"There's a beer there that has your name on it." Marcie was in full, 'let us get it on' regalia if you discounted the skimpy apron.

"I thought food would be a good start for the evening."

"I am not ungrateful for a home cooked meal. Did we arrange to do this last night?"

"You don't remember, do you? You passed out after one drink. You said, 'We'll do it tomorrow night.'"

"This is your interpretation of, do it?"

"The food is an enhancement - the real do it will come later."

And it did. The phone was off the hook.

80

The Sino-American festival had started in the morning, raged through the afternoon and morphed from a family gathering into a more adult affair by mid evening. As with many such celebrations, the food was the biggest attraction. The smell of burning charcoal filled the air mingling with the many spices of the nibble-size offerings being cooked, bought, and rapidly replenished. I had always been a fan of Chinese beer and there was plenty of that as well. The entire culture of China seemed to be summed up in food and drink.

"Enjoying yourself, Architect Boss?" She was extending her hand for a greeting.

"You caught me with both hands full, Doctor Wang."

"A couple of air kisses would do."

The kisses went beyond the gap between lips and cheeks to her satisfaction. "What would you recommend I visit?"

"The men all seem to enjoy the Kung Fu demonstrations."

"That sounds good - I want to learn more about the, Tiger Death Strike."

The curfew for the festival set in - those who didn't go home adjourned to nearby pubs - the city trash trucks took over the streets. Doctor Wang guided me towards a nearby apartment building, "You need to sample our Chinese firewater."

***

"What's it called?" I attempted to catch my breath."

"*Baijiu* - it takes an acquired taste to appreciate its subtleties."

"Back in high school, some of my friends sniffed glue and strained anti-freeze - I did not as I valued my brain too much - this 'Bijou' is more akin to paint thinner - another drink I avoided."

"Do you have any vices?"

"A few - tell me about yours first - I'll keep sampling the, 'Bijou,' in the mean time."

She took a deep sip, "We come from two separate cultures as you know - I was raised by grandparents who had just wanted to stay alive during the time of the Cultural Revolution. I have my education but no moral foundation - I want pleasure - and, to be rich."

"I was sort of thinking about an addiction to Rocky Road or something like that - let's talk about pleasure."

"Your girlfriend-lawyer warned me off."

"Wow - she told me she was wishing you well for the New Year - I checked - the new year is a few months off."

"You don't fall into bed too easily?"

"That is an unfair accusation." My glass was being

generously refilled, "It's a cliche, but I avoid mixing business with pleasure."

We both rose, a mutual mini-stagger brought us into an embrace - we kissed, me with enough passion to show she was missing a good thing - I patted her on her rear end and took my leave.

***

I flagged a cab leaving the Toyota to the wiles of the Traffic Enforcement ladies. The phone was ringing as I managed the front door lock.

"You are drunk."

"A fair accusation I would say, my sweet. That Bijou is sneaky stuff."

"*Baijiu* - where did you get your hands on that - the FDA prohibits it from being imported - you've been seeing that Doctor Wang - you are lucky you're not dead or worse yet, brain damaged."

"The festival was great - I learned several of the defensive moves against the, 'Tiger Death Strike,' and other stuff."

"I'll find out about the other stuff later - clean out your stomach before it's too late."

81

Sunday, had gone on without me. Monday looked almost normal. I got to the Toyota by cab. The stars were in alignment - there were no tickets on the windshield - there was a note in Spanish offering to purchase the car.

The office looked different - everything looked different - maybe Babette was right about the effects of Bijou - I regretted that my doctor had given up her office in the building. Perhaps this was the beginning of the end - coffee could not possibly hurt.

At the coffee machine, Angelica was being chatted up by the two police detectives who had become regulars in the office. They nodded respectfully and made room for me to figure out which controls to utilize to make coffee. Angelica inspected my bloodshot eyes and punched in the appropriate buttons for me. I gave my usual farewell, "Serve and Protect," and headed to my work station.

I realized most of what I needed to do was on the telephone - there was no need to disturb the staff, and went to my office instead.

Chester seemed very happy, "It's in writing - we are to proceed - I ordered trailers for the site - it will take a while to get the subs lined up."

"Go pick up the building permits - bring your check-book." The checkbook was important - the fees would be enormous.

"Keep me informed." Heckle and Jeckle had called - an appointment concerning GRIT was set up for the afternoon. Angelica had handed me this information on a slip of paper along with a fresh cup of coffee.

"Cynthia, go full speed ahead on the Fed part of GRIT."

"You don't look too good, Boss."

"I appreciate your concern."

"Not too good at all." She was shaking her head.

***

"Where am I?" My semi-clothed horizontal positioning and the cold antiseptic scented atmosphere should have answered my own question - the oxygen breathing apparatus at my nose and the IV in my palm indicated I was being tended to - Angelica hovered with Murphy close behind - blood was being drawn - for some reason I was hungry.

"We called your doctor - Doctor Walker happens to be a colleague of mine, we worked together for several years," this from a white-jacketed personage holding an oversized electronic clipboard - "She has agreed to watch over you - your system has been flushed - only liquids for the next twenty-four hours - no prescriptions - certainly, no alcoholic beverages." Things were not entirely in focus - Angelica was writing everything down.

***

I had lost all track of time - Murphy and Angelica had driven me home - I dozed intermittently, in synch with the car's motion - it was very late based on the blinking yellow traffic lights - the whole evening had been surreal.

Murphy let me in with my keys - I could tell they were not impressed by my digs.

Doctor Walker showed up within a few minutes of me being put to bed. "A house call, doctor?"

"Who said the age of miracles is dead?"

"Will I be able to play the piano again?"

"It's almost tomorrow - my former associate said to check in on you - no ancient jokes, please - be quiet, and let me listen to the thumper."

My bedside phone rang, upsetting the doctor, "Yes, who is this please? No, I'm not, 'that bimbo.' No, Boss can't come to the phone - he almost died this afternoon. Yes, I'll give him your message." She hung up and continued her tending - to my raised eyebrows she finally divulged, "Some very angry person - you don't need that."

The house cleared as I fell into a dreamless slumber.

82

My debilitating encounter with the Chinese booze kept me out of the office for a week. In those lost days, I did little but rest - Babette was back to her usual routine of calling at mid-day, her time - there was still no prospect for her return - my banter was limited due to being house-bound. I called the office daily - whoever answered the phone told me everything was under control.

This extra time to contemplate my life was not what I needed - I did that subconsciously on a daily basis anyway - there were some recent circumstances that needed sorting - namely my jump into the big time with accompanying bank account. It would be easy to say I deserved it - hard work will pay off in time and so forth - all those bizarre and unfamiliar people of late seemed to come out of the blue - my fate had become like that interstellar bar scene in Star Wars.

***

Doctor Walker checked in by phone each morning - a health care person came by and took fluids for tests each day - I finally received a reprieve.

"You can go to work in the mornings only until noon - keep on the diet I gave you - stay away from that, 'greasy spoon' I heard about - yoga is okay; admire the instructors from afar. You almost died - we're still analyzing your vital fluids - we'll scan your brain next week."

"About the return of my piano skills?" She had hung up.

***

The staff did not make a big deal about my return. The group as a whole, over time, had hardened to adversity which was good. I went through the IN-box with Angelica and temps hovering. The coffee machine was now only serving herbal tea. My office door was scotched in the open position - shadows drifted by the opening periodically - I was able to read what I needed to read - my signature was a little shaky.

"Chester - bring me up to date."

"We'll be sending you a schedule - we have resurrected the subs that were on board last time around - pricing has held - Jose is back as general superintendent.

"Sounds good - in case I'm not around, work with Murphy here." "Boss - I know the Hill has been a nightmare - are you okay?"

"I'm okay - we will make our mothers proud."

I'm not sure how my mother would have felt - why did I say that?

***

"Cynthia - where are we?"

You look better - not great."

Cynthia was never one to mince words and to her I confessed, "I feel better - the doctor is looking after me - I'm only in to work for a half a day - I appreciate you being frank - making mistakes is not in my nature - look over my shoulder if you will." I knew Cynthia could be brutally blunt as to my input as an architect as well as my health, "Stick to the work part."

"Okay - we have printed a great deal of material for Doctor Wang - she's doing a lot of show-and-tells - in the mean time, we have been concentrating on the existing buildings - Benito is refining the GRIT design."

"Okay."

"Murphy, the Hill will be going full speed ahead as of now - get together with Chester after we receive his schedule - you will be in charge - there will be a lot of shop drawings, change orders, requests for payments, inspections - use who you need from the staff - the Tuckers are a good resource - Angelica and the temps can handle a lot of the paperwork.

"You'll be around, right, Boss?"

"Am not planning to go anywhere," I checked my watch, "except home - it's almost noon."

On cue, Angelica handed me a carryout bag containing lunch - the temps walked me down to the street and hailed a cab.

83

The first day back at work, really four hours, was enough - my catered lunch consisted of rabbit food and flavored water - a nap came easily.

I was sleeping but not dreaming - that was not good - not for me anyway.

**

"I can come by in thirty minutes for a quick checkup," Doctor Walker was to be back with me again, "I'll bring dinner."

The house was in disarray - I cleaned up as best I could leaving me tired once more when the doorbell rang.

"How do you feel - this place is a mess - I'll send my cleaning person first thing tomorrow morning - are you hungry?"

"I'll see how far I get - the carrots and tofu from lunch are still with me - may I get you a drink?"

"A beer would be nice - none for you, of course."

I moved my food around the plate and watched her eat, "Tell me something, please - no doctors I'm aware of provide this sort of attention to patients - what's going on?"

"I am returning a favor to a very good friend - a fellow doctor who was my mentor - more than my mentor - to whom I will always be grateful." In response to my raised eyebrows, "that is all you need to know."

"You need to be paid."

"It's all taken care of - I'll show you my authorization - we will not discuss this again and I will deny I ever told you." She removed a slip of paper from her carry bag, "A woman came up to me on the street and handed me this - she tried to take it back after I read it but I held on - I will hold on to it forever. 'TAKE CARE OF THE BOSS, Tabershaw.' That's all it said - you know the routine - let's see how you're doing."

Doctor Walker said nothing else except, "You can go to work tomorrow - until noon - leave the front door open for the cleaners - remember yoga."

I read from the pile of material next to my bed waiting for the call from Babette.

"You sound a little more upbeat,"

"I went to work today - half a day - I am being tended like a newborn sparrow and eating at the same rate as the bird."

"What does the doctor say?"

"We had dinner together - she is very caring - she says she is being remunerated by a former mentor, someone who I think society has lost track of - someone I am supposed to think is dead. It's very confusing."

"You need your rest - take it easy at work tomorrow - try not to create any fantasies - I love you."

"No fantasies - I love you too."

84

The taxi was waiting at the gate. The designated cleaners walked past me, checking a slip of paper for the proper address - I chose to stay anonymous - I had left monies on the kitchen counter - if they were being paid twice - good for them.

On only my second day out, I broke my discipline and stopped at the diner.

"You are not supposed to be here." Chico was looking into the dining area to check for possible witnesses, "A funny looking guy - maybe it was a woman, threatened me if I served you - his or her Spanish was lousy, but I heard, *las pelotas,* so I got the drift."

My taxi driver had wandered in - he got a free coffee from Chico and we were both shooed out.

***

After only one day, the staff had my routine down pat - I was not quite alone at any time - the herbal tea cup was never empty - the IN-box held only a few documents, those which required my signature - one of the Tuckers always seemed to be in the men's room at the same time I was.

"Angelica, let me see the job list and last weeks time sheets, please?" "All that is on your computer - let me show you how."

***

"I'm back."

"When do I get to meet the bride, Count?"

"There's been a hitch, old chap."

"Uh-huh."

"Passport control at Heathrow - sticky wicket - you know?"

"How so?"

"Face recognition software - shades of Sherlock and all that."

"And?"

"The bobbies took her away - very embarrassing."

"Stiff upper lip - ta ta."

***

I reviewed drawings on the conference room table and signed and sealed where necessary.

"Susan, there are three signed proposals that need to be followed up upon - take Genevieve and visit the people - take lots of pictures - arrange for measurements to be taken - do a code analysis. I know Genevieve is not totally mobile - moving about out of the office can't hurt. See Angelica for the files.

I fiddled with the computer for a while - my preference for paper continued nonetheless - Angelica showed me how to send files to the printer - I had no idea where the printer was located.

I was able to find the yoga studio schedule on the computer and made an appointment for a late morning class.

Jubal 'happened' to be going out to run an errand and walked me around the corner to the studio, carrying my sports bag to the dressing room. My favorite instructor was leading the class, her ensemble was quite outstanding - I couldn't wait to describe it to Babette.

I sat to rest in the waiting area. As once before, Cliff appeared from some recess leading from a door marked, 'private' heading towards the street curb and a waiting SUV.

"How are you feeling, Boss?" I imagined Lucifer on a good day. "Happy to see you up and about," and he was gone.

The temps arrived with my lunch and hailed a taxi.

***

I had snuck out the newly printed computer output in my gym bag. The encounter with Cliff was a reminder to add his name to the chart of new acquaintances in my life over the last year. The lunch was on course for me swearing off food on general principles. It was all too much - a nap was the answer.

I was restless - there had been too much stimulation. I cleared the dining room table and made the space my war room. Making use of various knick-knacks, myself at the center represented by my college beer mug, I set out the various cast of characters - the table cover was washable oil cloth and acceptable to magic marker. Souvenir doodads, coffee cups and wine glasses each represented a person who I suspected - larger objects stood for groups - the building department was denoted by an old espresso maker.

I was interrupted by the door chimes - Chico entered with packages - Doctor Walker close behind. They circled the table eyeing each other and the tableau.

Chico explained, "My Mother-in-law cooks at the hospital - she's also diabetic - she prepared some meals for you."

"I can't stay for dinner - let's take a look at you," she actually smiled at Chico as we adjourned to the bedroom.

"Take care of yourself, Boss." I was soon by myself, having set aside several of my representative surrogates to make room for the microwaved meal - I enjoyed it all".

***

Tell me about your day."

"I took a yoga class - the teacher was wearing an interesting outfit - very clingy and stretchy - I couldn't figure how she got into it."

"Sounds like you are back to doing some critical thinking."

"That, too - Allaine's bride-to-be was detained at Heathrow - he didn't seem too concerned - how would you like to be represented in my tableau by the way?"

"I lost you?"

"I am working on a mystery - like one of those old Agatha Christie movies - gathering everyone together in the drawing room."

"Are you alright - what did the doctor say?"

"They are still doing tests - she and Chico are now in sync, however."

"The Doctor and Chico - who the hell is Chico?"

"Got to go - love you."

***

I rummaged through a boxful of junk until I found an

angel depiction that came one holiday with a gift basket - too well crafted to throw out, it would now represent Babette.

I added a bottle of aspirin to a wine glass - that would be Doctor Walker - I had known Chico for too many years and left him out of the mix.

85

I diverted the mid-day taxi away from home and to Father Gomez's rectory. The church complex was in one of the older parts of the city, close to the Bluffs - we passed the former ball field and the site of the later disaster of the Grand Bazaar - I redirected my attention away from all of this while reading my notes for the meeting.

"Thank you for seeing me, Father."

"It is my pleasure to meet you at last - Angelica and I have conferred from time to time - I know all of her family, of course."

"It is my understanding you have been working on rounding up money for college for Angelica."

"Yes - but my sources are limited."

"I'm here today with a check - it should be doled out anonymously. Where she chooses to go is up to her - surely there are scholarships and the like available once she is enrolled?"

"She will want to stay close to home and family but, again, that's up to her." He folded the check and stuck it in his pocket. We shook hands and I went back to my taxi.

The priest was one of the new breed - casually dressed - only the collar giving away his profession. It was a year round job - congregants of all ages - lots of surprises - emergencies of all sorts - a hierarchy to deal with promoting rigid protocol.

Forget about the rules of celibacy - the job was stress personified. Preparing folks for Heaven - that was okay.

***

I called my accountant from home. "I know it's not Christmas - I want to talk about bonuses - I know all about rainy days - there has been a lot of pressure on everyone and I want them to know the hard work is appreciated - thanks for asking - I'm feeling better each day. It's time for my nap."

Bean-counters - I loved them.

***

I detoured from the bedroom to study the display on the dining room table. I added an old can of Guinness in company with two salt shakers - Allaine was certainly not suspect but Heckle and Jeckle were new on the scene. I circled the table, magic marker in hand, but decided to sleep on any musings.

My mental alarm clock had me up before the doorbell rang. Doctor Walker and Chico entered babbling away in Spanish - they appeared to be on the best of terms. There was dinner for three which we ate in the kitchen. We then circled the dining room table - Chico was miffed that he was not represented, "I know who a lot those people are," he withdrew his keychain and loosened a medallion from a bacon purveyor and set it into his finished glass of Perrier. The doctor surmised which was her marker, picked it up, and replaced it. "Let's take a look at you in private."

The two left after my exam, doing a Spanish version of Alphonse and Gaston at my front door.

"How do you feel?"
"I am on a campaign of spreading cheer."
"You sound upbeat - that's good."
"When are you coming home?"
"Soon - but just not yet.'
"I've got this old fashioned solid brass egg timer - it was

my Mother's - the sand won't come down any more - I've kept it as a memory of happy times - that will be you in my tableau - it will replace your angel."

"Tableau - angel - egg timer - what the hell are you talking about?"

What was I talking about, indeed?

86

"Three guys walk into a bar - an architect, an engineer, and a contractor," it was barely dawn - our booth was far away from the kitchen and the diner's usual early morning customers - Chico served in stead of the waitress to make sure I ate properly.

"Why are we here exactly?"

"I am starting to become uncomfortable with our mutual partners, whoever they really are," Chester was having the Meat-Lovers Special.

"Likewise,"

Allaine had received English muffins in lieu of crumpets with his tea. "I like the money in the bank - I like the steady flow of new work; some of it is actually interesting - why am I apprehensive?"

"Maybe it's because someone did a Lucrezia Borgia on you?"

"We don't know that for sure."

"Okay - what do we know?"

"Let's go back a minute - really to six months ago - what did we learn from the Grand Bazaar - or from the Hill for that matter?"

"Somebody's pulling strings."

"Yes - but for what purpose?"

My mind wandered - I looked out beyond the parked

cars and delivery trucks to watch the sun rise blindingly through the rain stained windows - the hubbub from the multiple TVs had taken over the previously sedate atmosphere - Chico was back cooking at a furious pace. For the future, I had some compatriots to share in my paranoia, "Okay, let's just think about this for the time being."

***

Chester dropped me off at the office. I was alone for an hour before the first of the staff filtered in, coffee cups and lunches in hand. I had spent my time alone wandering around the space thinking back to the time the raw, semi-finished square footage had been shown to me by a self-important agent who opened the entrance door and did little else to encourage my tenancy - the owner of the building had accepted my cut-rate offer to perform tenant work for the entire building - and that was the incentive to move away from my dining room table. I rolled on a sealant to hold down the dust from the concrete floor and set myself up in the middle of the space. From time to time, the janitorial staff told me of abandoned furnishings from businesses that had gone bust and moved out in the middle of the night, and for a few dollars they helped me claim what I agreed to take. I felt badly about failed entrepreneurial ventures being the source of my fittings - I had worked even harder to make sure my assemblage was not passed on to someone else.

***

"Everything okay, Boss?"

"What happened to the bookcase that used to be in that corner?"

"Genevieve saw bugs flying out of it one day - it was infested - the papers inside were disintegrating - we had it hauled away."

"Okay - so much for my least recent past - any other changes I should know about?"

"We rented a place in the basement for some other stuff - ask Angelica?"

Disintegrating - an interesting metaphor.

My IN-box was truly empty - papers requiring my signature were spread neatly over the desk surface with red adhesive tabs attached indicating where to sign - the necessary pen was right there for that purpose - as I scrawled away my sense of usefulness was at an all time low.

Chester was on the phone, "Do you remember when we went to that godforsaken hospital during that typhoon?"

"Yes - with the kid and the swamp buggy - yes, why?"

"There was a person there with the Doctor and his wife - we weren't introduced - did you know who he was?"

"No - the whole evening was already too weird - I just wanted my clothes back and to have dinner."

"I saw him this morning - the stranger - a picture actually - I was with Cynthia at the Fed lab you are working on - she asked me for some advice - the photo was on the wall at the entrance with others of the lab's top personnel - a Director Beasley."

"I met him once - it was a totally unmemorable experience - why are you bringing this up?"

"At dawn today, we all agreed someone or somebody was pulling strings - purpose unknown. The bad booze that could have done you in came from Beasley's co-worker, Doctor Wang - Director Beasley was in the office when you and I met with Doctor Tabershaw and his wife - that would connect Beasley with the Hill - some people think Tabershaw and his wife were in that plane that crashed into the Grand Bazaar." Chester seemed out of breath.

This was just too much gossip and conjecture. "I'm dead tired - come by the house tonight - bring your own dinner."

"Angelica, I'm told we have a dead storage space some-where in the building - is there an inventory of what's in there - how much are we paying - maybe it is time to throw some stuff out - let me know?"

***

The yoga class helped me relax - I participated in the chanting - Babette was my mantra.

The temps showed up to put me in a taxi. I hoped the Toyota was not taking my disuse as an affront.

***

My mental alarm clock had me up and groomed and ready for company at what my stomach determined as dinner time. The front door opened and closed in quick succession creating a full house - Allaine was the only one I had not expected. Dinner was going to be like lunch at the office with a variety of food, very little of which I could enjoy. Doctor Walker and I retreated to the bedroom for the usual routine of taking bodily fluids and the like, "Tomorrow morning we do a brain scan - I'll pick you up here - nothing to worry about - we'll have breakfast afterwards."

We joined the group where they had gathered at the tableau, circling the table without having much to say.

"I understand the espresso maker is City Hall - the pepper shakers I presume are the Brown family and the mayor?" Allaine was immediately into it.

"Let's eat first, then we'll reconnoiter." That didn't work, of course.

We all circled the tableau, food and drink or both in hand - the flow was clock-wise as an off-shoot led to the refrigerator.

"The chopstick person definitely did it."

"Motive?"

"The glass-filled-with-dirt-person was in cahoots."

"Their motive?"

"It's always about money - follow the money."

"True," I said, "but I have no money worth killing for."

"The Dirt guy was jealous - he saw that Chopsticks was coming on to Boss."

"And what was her motive - he's not that appealing?"

"I resent that - but not too strongly."

Chester introduced his hypothesis concerning the mysterious stranger last seen at the hospital meeting we both attended. It was listened to respectfully. The group was willing to accept the director being identified as the stranger and the appropriate inked line was drawn.

More circling and drawing of lines with the magic marker took place in relative silence.

"Think about it," That was my exit line.

***

"Have you solved the case?"

"It was the butler with the parrot in the study."

"That conclusive? How do you feel?"

"I'm okay - the doctor is supervising a brain scan tomorrow."

"Any other news?"

"I chanted today - you were my muse - it was a substitute teacher anyway."

"I'm flattered - I love you."

87

"Your digestive juices are flowing again - the brain scan was inconclusive - no one knows what normal is anyway - there are signs of vertigo - don't walk any tight ropes without a net. Also, you may have some difficulty separating black from white, so stay away from the piano - I made up the part about the piano."

"That's it?

"Find a new doctor - I'll send my report. Watch your diet."

"Would a hug be appropriate?" I did so without giving her a chance to think about it, "I'm keeping your marker in the tableau - just in case."

We never talked about her history with Doctor Tabershaw - it was unlikely that she would speak on the subject - she appeared to venerate the man and that had been to my advantage. I was not joking when I told her she would remain in the mix.

88

"Doctor Walker for you, Boss."

"I am looking for new office space - a building down near the harbor - close to the gay community is in my sights - there is a coffee shop on the ground floor - can you meet me there in an hour and give me your opinion?"

I had the address in hand and flagged down a cab - doing a favor for my doctor was something I was willing to exchange for all the personal care I had received from her of late.

***

The neighborhood was roughly hewn - the two story row houses dated back two hundred years or more - true vertical or horizontal was hard to determine - the streets were of cobble-stone probably brought over as ship ballast from Europe - the mixed scents from the harbor and the persistent dampness from the salt air created a unique gloom. The coffee shop had more likely been a tavern in earlier times. A gradual drizzle was just starting when I left the cab. Doctor Walker was waiting under a huge black umbrella - she signaled me towards the unwelcoming entrance - the gloom followed me inside.

***

"I picked these beans myself, roasted them as well - I left the brewing to the barista - the package on the table is for you to take home."

I sipped the brew, "You are looking well Doctor Tabershaw - how is Natasha?"

"I heard you would soon be married - I should have brought a small token of celebration - Babs is it - I hope you will be happy."

We refilled our coffee cups from a heated flask and listened to the start of rain patter on the metal awning - the earlier chill had brought a storm.

"Doctor Walker said you were curious?

I said nothing.

"Thank you - and thank you to Chester for finishing up the Hill in such fine order."

We had been paid properly and promptly for all our work - my standing on extraordinary compliments was still in place - I added more sugar to my coffee. The sound of hail joined the rain patter.

"Fifty years ago, my father and Maria's grandfather were classmates in medical school in New England. One summer, the two of them undertook a sail around Cuba - the entire island - it was far too ambitious a venture - off the south coast of Cuba, they sheltered in a small bay of an uninhabited island. They discovered a former pirate refuge and explored in an amateurish manner - fresh water was abundant - the wildlife apathetic to strangers - they had food on the boat, but chose to live off the land. This only lasted a few days - the coming semester of school and other commitments beckoned.

Back in the USA, the gospel of Che and Fidel was rabid among the student body - both friends volunteered but my father, as an American, was refused. Maria's grandfather became an ardent communist - a surprise to my father - they never spoke again. Maria grew up hearing about the youthful days in Boston which became more exaggerated over the years - the Red Guard doctrine was firmly in place with her father, native born - an educated doctor as well. For Maria, there were many contradictions. I had never rally completely lost track of this Cuban family - nonetheless it came as a great surprise when Maria contacted me."

The rain had stopped - heat and humidity crept into the shop - water poured down the street as children sailed whatever pieces of debris they could find in the flood down to the harbor. Bottled water replaced the coffee.

"She came with a plan - an audacious one - I laughed her out of my office. Natasha was not so averse. I was very busy with my new hospital and lost track. Before I knew it, I was part of the 'plan' - in fact, without me there would be no plan."

He continued, "Cuba was off limits to Americans but that did not deter the planners - money was the major obstacle - and for the dream, a large amount was needed in a hurry. Natasha drew me in - my hospital was soon catering to the moneyed political misfits of the world who desired to be eternally young. The burgeoning real estate market was attracting [investors - I put together the two major deals you are familiar with - we chose you as the architect because you appeared too inexperienced - it was hoped that the projects would fail leaving us with the investor's money - we hedged by insuring everything we could."

Snacks appeared on the table - we remained the only customers. I dared not disturb the mood with a bathroom break.

"That stupid murder disguised as a construction accident was fortuitous - we had the opportunity to make money three times over. The Grand Bazaar was doomed for economic reasons from the start, but we got greedy. We sabotaged the fabric order. One of Natasha's disciples stole the drone - I provided the four corpses - that was a total fiasco - on the other hand, we still made money. The police are suspicious - no one actually died, except in my operating room. In the meantime, the Hill, the design revised to the latest standards and well marketed was an economic success - it was time to move forward."

I waited for the climax.

"Maria arranged for that uninhabited island of memories long ago to be deeded to use as a site for a clinic. The isolation would allow the same sort of people who previously visited my old hospital to come to the island - I would train Cuban doctors, of which there are an abundance, to do the work - Cubans would be given preference for specialized medicine that was usually sought in Europe - and, I would honor my father's old friend. The hard currency would flow, making the Communist government happy without admitting they were heavy into capitalism."

The sun was shining brightly now, the diffused light reflecting off the wet pavement into the area where we were seated. The odors of cooking from the kitchen were slowly permeating the humid atmosphere. The doctor's face was more readable now - he remained deep in thought and seemed ready to divulge even more.

"Some people would say what I did was stealing despite the collective altruistic motives - what's done is done - not everyone was entirely unselfish and this was hurtful. Doctor Wang want off course early on - she took advantage of Natasha's passion to learn about her heritage and her fixation that the dross from the old cemetery held a clue. They teamed together to expand the research lab - Director Beasley's idea - to attract funds worldwide - it was too easy - Doctor Wang decided to enrich herself - Beasley disappeared - Natasha could not handle the betrayal, leaving me fully in charge. You were collateral damage and I'm not sure whether it was bad booze or something else."

I contemplated the story - the clinic could be real or just another cockamamie fairy tale - it didn't really matter.

"Try the tacos."

The mention of bad booze coupled with the offer of newly minted tacos was too much, "You first."

His lips formed a brief smile. "I know you asked about Natasha earlier on - I ignored you then so I could satisfy your curiosity about yourself. She is in a sanitarium in Switzerland - her mind was overwhelmed and she crashed - I believe she will recover - I talk to her every night and I know she will want to know that we met."

Doctor Walker had disappeared at the start, as soon as I spotted Tabershaw - I never heard from her or saw her again.

As I think back now, the subliminal pull towards the beach and the Cubans had been satisfied - there was no such rainbow enhanced pot of information - the doctor was very logical in his explanation. Wars had been started with less justification.

89

"Did you get caught in the rain yesterday?" Angelica continued to be concerned about my health.

"No - I waited it out - ran into someone I used to know - we caught up on old times - I read the local paper. There was too much coffee as usual - here is a gift sample of some beans."

"Anything I need to do?"

"Not really."

The office looked brighter. Every one appeared to be ultra busy. "Angelica, what did you find in dead storage?"

"It's a mess - the space is absolutely full. I had one of the garage people help me lay it out so you can see it better. Cynthia was the only one who could identify much of it - here's the list."

***

The staff found it amusing to visit the past - the interval was a prelude to lunch for which I would be hanging around, for the first time in weeks - Angelica was right - it was a mess.

Nate started holding up various artifacts, asking the others to identify each in return for some unspecified prize. "Boss isn't included."

I couldn't help myself, "That's a T-square, these are French curves and these are lettering templates - the triangular sticks are scales; architects and engineers - the brushes are to clean away the excess eraser dust. The pencils can't be that foreign. Throw it all out - the boxes of paper and old rolls of tracing paper, too. I'm sure there's no money tucked in any of those manuals. Hold on to that slide rule - it has sentimental value - it was a high school graduation present from my Uncle Al. Someday your computers will be in dead storage replaced by God knows what.

***

I eyed the lunch table trying to remember the caveats from my doctor.

"Are you back full-time, Boss?"

"I am - I missed working - I missed a lot of things - you people took over in a way I never expected - someone has to take the registration exams so you can officially carry on."

There was no eye contact - the thanks were accepted - each had his or her own reasons for not committing to the final step. I was disappointed but made up for it by distributing the envelopes containing the bonus checks.

A bonus for me was having the next job waiting - sometimes I got an, 'attaboy' from a client - sometimes I got fully paid - sometimes I did not get denigrated by a contractor who took a stupid shortcut - the bad booze was another, 'sometime' category.

"Ms. Silver for you on her line, Boss." Babette had never called me on her business phone here at the office before - the temp in charge of the temporary hook-up was wary - the entire staff disappeared as if a fire evacuation had been announced.

***

"It is midnight here - this is important - I have made arrangements for us to be married in Paris. Can you make it?"

The End.

Made in the USA
Middletown, DE
02 June 2017